T0129369

From White Trash to White Coat

The Birth of Catherine's Purpose

Dr. Tabatha Barber-Duell

Archway Publishing books may be ordered through booksellers or by contacting:

Archway Publishing
1663 Liberty Drive
Bloomington, IN 47403
www.archwaypublishing.com
1 (888) 242-5904

ISBN: 978-1-4808-7367-4 (sc)
ISBN: 978-1-4808-7368-1 (hc)
ISBN: 978-1-4808-7366-7 (e)

Library of Congress Control Number: 2019900740

Print information available on the last page.

Archway Publishing rev. date: 01/30/2019

I am so grateful for this life. I cherish my hardships, lessons, relationships, and faith.

To my husband and children, thank you for supporting me during this writing process.

To my patients, thank you for allowing me to fulfill my purpose on this earth.

To my readers, thank you for wanting to read my story.

.

Contents

I'm a Jansen

The little town where I grew up was set up perfectly for a five-year-old like me. My tall red house was right in town, with a small unkempt and overgrown yard. The house had an alley on one side and a yellow house on the other. None of the houses had driveways or garages, so my parents had to park their car on the street.

I lived on Iris Street. All the streets in one direction were named after flowers, like Orchid Street and Lilac Street. In the other direction, they were numbered from First Street on up. I lived between Sixth and Seventh Streets.

All the important places were easy to get to. The main street in and out of town, Lily Street, was in front of my house and up one block. The Frosty Twist was three blocks to the right, on Third Street. The huge, beautiful St. Patrick's Church, which could be seen from across town, was two blocks to the left, on Ninth Street. Rosie's Market was on the highway, two blocks behind my house, at the end of the alley. From those places, I could easily navigate anywhere else I wanted to go. My mom owned a bridal store downtown, a few blocks past the Frosty Twist. Then came the library, the pawn shop, and the drugstore.

I was proud of my mom. She had a big, fancy, pink building downtown, on the end of Main Street. There was a big white rose on the sign that read "Juliana's Bridal & Accessories." My dad and I got to help her move in. They made the sign out of Styrofoam, using fancy, cursive letters. My mom drew a huge rose on the Styrofoam, and my dad cut it out with a long electric saw. We painted the rose white, and my dad went high up on some scaffolding and glued the sign to the building.

Inside, my mom hung all the dresses for sale along the walls. There were jewelry cases back by the dressing rooms, and displayed all over were satin shoes that could be dyed any color to perfectly match a bridesmaid dress. She had four fancy dressing rooms with big mirrors. Inside one there was a huge gold door that led into an actual vault.

I found the vault the day we moved in.

"Why do you have a real vault in here, Mom? Are we rich? Do we need to lock up all these fancy headpieces and jewelry sets?" I yelled to her as she organized the mannequins in the window.

She came over, carrying a poufy, pale-blue gown shoved up over her arms like she was about to drape it over some mannequin's bosom.

"This used to be a bank a long time ago. That is a real vault, but we're not really rich with money—just with God's love," Mom said as she walked into the dressing room.

My mom was always saying corny stuff about God and Jesus and love being enough.

"We can put the extra jewelry stock in here if you want. See all those little white boxes on the counter? Bring them in here and organize them," she directed.

"No. I want to decorate the window mannequins with you." And off I ran to the window.

I loved helping my mom with all of her inventory, and I loved playing in her store like it was my own private playhouse. The building had a basement where my mom did all the ripping apart of poorly made gowns, sewing, ironing, beading, shoe dyeing, and such. There were so many cool backroom areas that my friend Brandy and I set up our own pretend store under the stairs.

Soon we ventured into the scary room way, way back under the sidewalk. There, we created a fancy pretend beauty salon. We also played banker in the back stairwell, along with whatever other creative thing came to our minds. I wasted endless amounts of blank billing and invoice papers, buttons, beads, little storage boxes, and shoe-dye kits. I also ruined mannequin wigs, fancy boxes, and extra fabric.

One day, Brandy said, "Isn't your mom gonna kill us for using all the glue?"

Funny, my mom never really yelled at me for wasting or ruining her stuff. "Nah, she's so busy she doesn't care," I surmised.

"Yeah, and she won't do anything about it; she knows you won't listen anyway!" Brandy said as she laughed.

Later, I wondered if my friend was right. *Do I always ignore my mom's rules? Has she given up on trying to control me? Oh well.*

My parents also never got upset when I ruined something nice at home. When Brandy scratched her parents' car, her mom screamed at her, calling her a careless idiot and grounding her for a week. When I spilled grape juice on the living-room carpet and it left a big purple stain, I didn't get punished. My parents never made me feel that material stuff was more important than people.

My parents were always so industrious and creative. They made stuff out of seemingly nothing. My mom had taught herself how to sew when she was young, and now she could make wedding gowns from scratch. Everyone in town knew her for her talent. She could take an ugly, ill-fitting dress and make it fit like a glove. She could make anyone look beautiful. She was truly talented and such a hard worker. She was ashamed to admit it, but she had never graduated from high school. She had gotten pregnant with my older brother and hadn't finished.

"People didn't need a diploma back then. Your dad made enough at the drive-in to pay our bills, and I stayed at home with Steve," she would say in her own defense whenever I asked her about not graduating.

She was right. She didn't really need a diploma or college education, because she was brilliant. If I called a dress pink, she would correct me, saying, "That is salmon, which is paler than peach and definitely not as bright as coral."

When I was younger, like three and four, she made us matching dresses. I was proud of my mom for her talents, but that didn't mean I was comfortable wearing a dress—whether she or JCPenney made it. She pointed out to me and anyone who would listen that I was often a difficult child.

Once, she told a customer, Miss Connie, with me standing right there, that she had worked so hard to make us matching dresses and then I refused to wear them. "Cathy is such a tomboy. She won't wear a dress to save my life."

"That's awful!" Miss Connie replied. "She should realize how lucky she is to have a mom as talented as you."

Yeah, my mom's right, I thought. *I am a tomboy.*

I liked fancy, beautiful stuff, but not *on* me! I left that to my friend Brandy. She had long, beautiful, shiny chestnut hair and was always brushing it, curling it, or spraying it with something. Her clothes were always clean, ironed, and matching. In contrast, my curly dishwater-blonde hair was rarely brushed, and my clothes were never ironed. Most days, they probably weren't even clean.

In fact, one Saturday, I spent the morning watching Brandy dust her oversized oak bed, straighten out her dresser doilies, and vacuum her plush pink carpet. *Who is this girl, perfection in the making?* I thought to myself.

"Can we go play yet? My mom just got new tiaras to make veils, and I want to organize them in the display case," I finally said in a rushed tone.

"Well, yeah, let me just have my mom check my room. Then we can go," Brandy said in a surprised, excited voice.

I spent endless days at my mom's store that summer, and going back to school didn't stop me. I started kindergarten, and my brother was in sixth grade at the same school. He and his friends spent most of their recess time torturing me and my friends on the playground.

"Come on, Steve, be nice and push us on the merry-go-round," we said, begging my brother and his friends to spin us.

"All right. Let's go, girls," Steve said. "You're gonna regret asking us!"

He and his friends spun us so fast that, all at once, we were laughing and crying for them to stop.

"No way! You wanted us to push you," Steve yelled, laughing.

His friends all laughed and pushed the merry-go-round faster until my friend Alicia flew off into the dirt. Alicia was what we called "a big-boned girl." She lay there in the dirt, muffin top hanging out of her T-shirt, crying like she was dying. The boys took off running as the recess lady came to check on Alicia.

I decided I wasn't going back to class. "I hate my brother," I mumbled to myself.

I wanted to hang out with my mom, where I could be happy. I walked all the way to her store, grumbling about my stupid brother and his friends. As I walked, I looked for my old nearby preschool. *Now I just need to get to Lily Street by Gena's house, go downtown, and turn by the drugstore.*

I was already at Mom's store by the time the school called her and told her I was missing. Apparently, I had no fear. I would cross the street in the middle of traffic, feeling confident that I could time the cars passing by and not get hit. I don't think I used a crosswalk correctly until I was a grown-up. No one ever scolded me for such things. As I got older, my mom bragged about how I ran the town from age three on.

The years drifted by slowly, with endless days of playing with Brandy, Alicia, and others, running around town, and hanging out at the bridal store. By the time I was seven, I knew every store on Main Street, and I had been in every house, backyard, alley, and church in a ten-block radius, either by way of friends, selling Girl Scout cookies for my friends, or just being snoopy. I had no fear. I went anywhere without a worry, knowing my town like the back of my hand. I felt a sense of ownership, of belonging, because my family had such a long history there.

My grandfather Robbins had owned a furniture factory, which my grandma and aunts inherited and continued to run. I felt proud when I went to those factory buildings with my grandma Robbins. My mom would always brag about her father's accomplishments, their big house on Ninth and Magnolia that she grew up in, and their boat trips as a family. By the age of five, I had a strong sense of who my family was, and that was how I defined who I was.

One afternoon lunch with my mom stands out in my memory. As we sat at the lunch counter inside Ben Franklin's eating fries, I asked, "Mom, why does everyone know who I am when I walk downtown?"

"Because you are a Robbins like me, and you are a Jansen like your dad," she replied.

Somehow, I understood what she meant, and I smiled with pride.

She then told me about my dad's family and boasted about what great entrepreneurs they were. "Your great-grandpa opened the first theater here and the marina boat shop. ..." And on and on she went. "The Jansens are always doing business somewhere. Someday, you'll probably want to own a restaurant like your dad."

"That would be cool," I replied without any hesitation. "I think we should just own all the stores downtown, so I can have all the clothes, toys, candy, and ice cream I want."

My mom got huffy and said, "You'll never be satisfied, will you?"

What did I do? I wondered. *What's wrong with wanting it all? What's wrong with dreaming big?*

I was confused by the idea that I was supposed to be ambitious and make something out of nothing, while being content with what I had. That didn't make sense.

My mom would always say, "You're just an ungrateful kid. You don't understand."

My dad, Don, was one of eight kids, so there were plenty of Jansens in town. People would say, "Wow, they're not Catholic?" I guess because they had a lot of kids, and that usually meant you were Catholic. His older brother, Jack, owned three bars. My dad was in the middle of opening a restaurant. He also had a little summer business going with Uncle Jack. My dad sold flavored popcorn that Jack made at one of his bars. He also sold fireworks out of my mom's store, through the scary basement entrance under the sidewalk. I helped him with that, and he paid me in fireworks.

Summer was so much fun in our little beach town. We had a festival during the Fourth of July week, every year. My dad made me and my cousin, Jessica, pull wagons at the Fourth of July parade, selling the flavored popcorn. It was a huge hit! The flavors were blueberry, sour apple, watermelon, grape, and strawberry.

"This is the future, kids!" my dad exclaimed.

He was proud to be on the cutting edge of the popcorn business. He was generally a quiet man of few words, but this kind of stuff brought him to life.

The kids' parade was great that year. Jessica and I had to fend for ourselves, as usual, when we decided that morning that we were going to be in the kids' parade. We needed to come up with costumes to wear, and we frantically ran around the house, looking for ideas, because the parade started in a half hour.

Jessica pulled a big button-down shirt out of my dad's closet. "Let's go as Siamese twins. Come on! We can both fit in here."

We buttoned ourselves into the shirt and pretended to be connected at the torso. We ran all the way downtown to the parade's starting point, almost tripping each other about ten times. It was a miracle we didn't fall and break our necks.

"I guess we should've waited until we got here to put the shirt on," I said.

"Then they would know we aren't real Siamese twins! Duh!" Jessica said.

We actually won second place! I think they recognized us from selling my dad's popcorn two days earlier.

"How's your dad's restaurant coming?" some guy asked.

"I don't know," I replied and walked away.

"That was kinda rude," Jessica said.

"I'm wasn't being rude," I snapped. "I really don't know. No one tells me anything."

My dad's younger brother, Kent, owned a hair salon. As summer continued on, I was so excited because Jessica and I got to spend the week at our grandma and grandpa Jansen's farmhouse. They had a big vegetable garden on one side, and our Uncle Kent lived with his boyfriend across the street. They had an in-ground pool out back.

Papa Jansen picked us up one afternoon. We stopped for ice cream on the way, and Papa Jansen started to tease us. "You're going to get fat like your aunts," he said as he squeezed our sides.

"I don't care; I love ice cream!" I snapped.

"I'm not fat, am I, Papa?" Jessica said seriously.

"Not yet, Beautiful," he said with a smirk.

After ample begging and whining, he took us to our uncle's

hair salon to get our ears pierced. It was exciting, painful, and kind of awkward. Papa always gave Uncle Kent attitude. That day, we realized it was because he liked "girlie" things, like doing hair and making jewelry, and he had a boyfriend. Jessica and I didn't care what that was about; we thought he was the best uncle ever.

We spent the week picking veggies out of the garden with Grandma Jansen, watching *The Young and the Restless with Papa*, and swimming in Uncle Kent's pool. We also hung out at Uncle Kent's because he had cable, and we watched it while he was at work. We watched *The Texas Chainsaw Massacre*, *Valley Girl*, and other inappropriate movies with violence, nudity, and sex.

We went snooping around his bathroom and found a tube labeled "lubricant" in the drawer. When our brothers and cousins came that weekend for a pool party we showed them what we had found.

Our cousin Mike chimed in, "That's for when Kent and Leo have gay sex in the butt, so it doesn't hurt."

The boys were all grossed out, but Jessica and I didn't think much of it. Kent and Leo had always lived together, so we figured they loved each other and that was a normal thing to do.

What's the big deal? I thought to myself. *Grandma knows, and she still loves him, so it must be okay.*

Jessica and I thought it was cool that they lived how they wanted to and did what they wanted. They weren't hurting anyone, and they were fun to be around.

"Besides, he pierced our ears, he perms our hair, and he has a swimming pool. He's the best uncle ever!" we exclaimed with pride.

My Grandma Jansen was loving and accepting to a fault. Nothing ever fazed her, and if it did, she definitely didn't let it be known. The concept of unconditional love that the nuns were always trying to drill into my head, at Sunday school, was evident in my Grandma Jansen, even though she wasn't Catholic. She wasn't anything religious. The Jansens didn't belong to a church, but my mom said that was okay because they were good people. In fact, my Grandma Jansen was a prime example of compassion, empathy, strength, and unconditional love. She was my idol. I wanted to be strong and loving the way she was with everyone. Jessica and I loved her to pieces.

Jessica was a great cousin to have, but her mom moved them around a lot. She never moved too far, usually just across town. Their last move was different, though. My aunt married a guy from Las Vegas, so Jessica and her sister Jennifer moved far away.

I cried to my mom, "I'm so jealous! I want to go live with Aunt Cindy! Please! Please! Please!"

I felt abandoned and lonely and wronged. The little voice inside me said that I was destined to be someone famous and do something amazing.

"Las Vegas is where I belong," I insisted aloud.

"I don't think you were invited," my mom said slyly.

As we got older, Jessica wrote me letters bragging about all the celebrities she met and how *rad* everything was Vegas. She took weekend trips to California and told me how much I would love it there. I felt like everyone else was getting to go do amazing, adventurous things, while I had to sit there in my house on Iris Street, in my rinky-dink little town.

"I'm so sick of living here. I want to move. Why can't we move?!"

I whined to my mom at least once a day. I felt trapped and stifled.

"I've lived in this same boring house for an entire decade, and Jessica has lived in like ten different places. It's not fair!" I screamed.

"The Jansens get antsy," my mom explained. "They don't stay in the same spot too long. I'm sure you'll run off as soon as you're old enough."

She was right about the Jansens. Grandma and Papa Jansen used to live across the street from us, and then they moved to Florida. When they left Florida, they lived in the farmhouse that Jessica and I loved. Later, they lived by the high school, then they lived in the apartment above my dad's pizza shop, and then they moved to senior housing.

Somehow, I got the impression that they didn't necessarily always want to move; it was more that they had to move. My mom would say things about them running away from bills they couldn't pay. She would talk about how Papa gambled and drank away all their money, and Grandma somehow salvaged the situation and made it all better.

My mom met my dad when they were young. She told me that he only owned one pair of jeans and one pair of shoes that had holes in the soles.

She always spoke highly of her mother-in-law, though. "Your grandma Jansen is a saint, and it's amazing that she stayed with your papa and kept that family clothed and fed. She's the strongest, smartest woman I know."

All I knew was that I wanted change in my life; moving to other places sounded like a welcome change. "Can I at least paint my bedroom a different color?" I asked.

"I guess," my mom replied.

I would rearrange my bedroom furniture every few weeks, so that wasn't super exciting or different.

"I want a huge rainbow and cloud on my wall, like Punky Brewster has! Come on, Mom, let's go get some paint!" I insisted.

"Okay," she conceded.

My aunt Cindy, opened a bar in Las Vegas, so the Jansen blood was strong in her too. I think they liked the idea of having something tangible to see from all their hard work, something to call their own. So many times, growing up, they had nothing, or they had to leave behind what they had when they moved and then start anew. In addition to their strong desire to create, build, and own something, what I quickly learned was that the Jansens were survivors. They were also opportunists with huge hearts, and they enjoyed a good time. They continually moved on to the next idea, career, or party, and even to the next relationship.

I am definitely a Jansen, I would tell myself, to justify the burning desires in my heart and in my head.

Then there was my mom's family. There were many differences, but I eventually came to understand that there were similarities as well. My mom had nine or ten sisters and one brother. I don't know off the top of my head exactly how many sisters she had because I just remember her saying, "There's ten of us" or "I'm one of eleven." Did that mean how many sisters she had, or did it mean all of them, brother included? I never stopped to think it through. They were Catholic; hence there were a lot of them. Some of my aunts had children older than my other aunts, their sisters. It was all very confusing. They were all talented, creative, and humble people.

My mom's sisters were all so different, but they all enjoyed each other's company. Some of them were so much older than my mom that it felt like they should be my grandmas, and some were young enough to be my sisters. It was confusing, and I would get embarrassed trying to keep them all straight.

As I said earlier, my grandpa Robbins owned a furniture factory. He died when I was little. Some of my aunts ran the business and were involved in the church. I knew which one was Aunt Gertie because when I went to church on Sundays, I watched her do the readings. She always started out with something like "This is from the Gospel according to Luke" or "This is a letter from Paul to the Corinthians." A few other aunts usually sat in the pews across from us. I knew their names but couldn't remember which one was Agatha and which one was Pearl.

The Robbinses were a little eccentric and sometimes down-right embarrassing, but I eventually came to appreciate my mom's family. When I was young, I had mixed feelings about going to Grandma Robbins's house. I learned how to play bumper pool there, upholstered chairs, collected sea glass, avoided dead fish heads while looking for driftwood, and pretended to play the organ to eight-track tapes—all with many cousins whose names I couldn't keep straight and only saw once or twice a year.

We went for Thanksgiving one year. My dad and brother slowly made their way to the car, grumbling that they would miss the Lions' first quarter. When we got there, I felt lost in a sea of people I recognized but didn't know all that well—let alone remember whose name was whose.

"Oh yeah, you're Cathy, Juliana and Don's daughter." That was how people referred to me, and that was all I knew.

My aunts were loud and boisterous, and they seemed to really get a kick out of each other. They laughed at everything.

My cousins and I were playing bumper pool in the huge dining room overlooking Lake Michigan when we were startled by roars of laughter and table slapping coming from the women in the kitchen.

An older cousin shot me a look like she was embarrassed for all of us just for being associated with them.

Crap! Is that Valerie or Vanessa? I thought to myself. I couldn't keep them straight.

Then, we all laughed, eerily like little versions of our mothers.

My older brother, Steve, sat in the corner with the adult men watching the Lions game, trying to ignore those loud women in the kitchen.

What's so wrong with being wild and having fun? I thought to myself. *Grown men don't like loud, crazy women? Oh well. The women don't seem to care.*

Much later in life, I came to appreciate my mom and aunts for their ability to show their emotions, let loose without fear of judgment, and just enjoy the moment. I had a few aunts who stood out, mostly because they treated me like I was important.

My aunt Lucy had five boys, all around my age. We played together at family functions. She and my dad ran races together and drink beer afterward. I have a lot of fond memories of being with her and her family. She seemed like the "normal" sister of the bunch, minus the purple hair and crazy yoga poses she'd configure herself into. She had a beautiful garden and greenhouse, and she taught me to enjoy the beauty in small, everyday things. She was my godmother and gave me special gifts at Christmas and my birthday, things no one else got.

When I was ten, she forgot, and I felt heartbroken. She came by the house with a present for my baby sister but no present for me. I felt invisible and no longer special to her. I brushed it off and made an excuse for her, telling myself, *She's just busy. She didn't really forget that she's your godmother.*

Looking back, I can't really blame her. I wasn't an outwardly grateful child, and I had no manners, so I probably didn't thank her properly or let her know how much it meant to me.

Why am I so quiet around grown-ups? Why can't I talk to them like my friend Brandy does? She sounds like a grown-up and always says please and thank you. I thought.

I would tell myself to do so, but I couldn't muster the confidence. *That's the problem; I don't have confidence like Brandy. How come she is so confident?* I pondered this many times over the years.

My aunt Jillian was my mom's twin, but they were nothing alike. She never married or had kids, but she always had a quiet, live-in boyfriend. She was obsessed with her cats and had little patience for kids. Even at an early age, I felt her annoyance around kids, but she seemed to treat me and my siblings a little more special, probably because of the twin thing.

My aunt Annie was a lot younger than my mom, and she would come in and out of our lives. I think she lived in Colorado for a while, as a grower. Once, she stopped by with a painting she had made. It was for me. She painted a picture of me sitting in a field with my pink teddy bear. *Why would she do such a nice thing?* I thought to myself.

Of course, I didn't say thank you to her, but I should have, because it was really special. I guess I was too embarrassed that someone would do that for me without my asking, but I never remember my parents making me thank people verbally or otherwise. It wasn't until high school that I realized the importance of saying thank you to people or writing them a note.

Then, there was my uncle Gerald. He was the only boy. He was very quiet and awkward. He had no social skills and didn't care about his appearance. He always looked a little scary with his long, thinning, scraggly mullet and ragged old clothes. He lived with my grandma Robbins until she died. My mom and her sisters would always speak so highly of Gerald. "He's so sweet and thoughtful. He's so brilliant and talented with his car rebuilds."

They would sing his praises, and I would wonder why they felt that way about him. Being only seven or eight years old, I didn't appreciate the fact that they had an entire lifetime together that I knew nothing about.

Oh, and I can't forget about my crazy aunt Franny. Sometimes she was fun and sometimes she was frightening, which I enjoyed, but it caused my mom and her family a lot of stress. Eventually, I came to understand that she was schizophrenic. She lived with my grandma Robbins on and off for much of her adult life, but my grandma was in no position to take care of Franny, and Franny was often in no position to take care of my grandma.

My grandma suffered for two decades from Alzheimer's disease. I have almost no memories of her without a confused look on her face, a shuffling walk, and a repetitive speech pattern. I would tell myself, *Having all those kids must have made her crazy!* Things weren't really explained to us kids, and it was scary at times.

As time went on, I started to worry about my own mental health, and I thought for sure I would become afflicted with some genetic mental illness, even one that hadn't yet been discovered. I finally came to realize that my grandma was put on all kinds of experimental medications that had horrible side effects, such as paranoia, anxiety, body shaking, and confusion. the same thing had happened to my aunt Franny.

My mom would say, "Your aunt Fran is off her meds, so she's hearing voices again."

Those diseases were still being researched then, and doctors didn't know how to manage them or slow their progression. It seemed as if they were part of medical experiments gone bad, so medicine and doctors became a scary thing to me.

Early on, I wondered, *How could a family so well known in the community be so weird and different?* I didn't understand their loud conversations, cackling laughs, weird dress, and blatant disregard for normalcy. My mom didn't seem to quite fit in, which gave me some solace. She looked put-together, had a current hairstyle, was very healthy, and had a "normal" life with a husband, kids, and a business.

But, over time this idea of mental illness haunted me. I was sure I would develop schizophrenia, bipolar disorder, multiple personality disorder, or, at the very least, Alzheimer's disease. The idea of going crazy or becoming suicidal and ending up in a psych ward or a solarium against my will, at some point, became my biggest fear in life. Those thoughts and fears later sparked a deep interest in psychology and psychoses.

I tried to understand the Robbinses. I wondered and imagined how their lives must have been growing up. How could they have such rose-colored glasses on when that was not what the rest of us were seeing? I wanted to understand the dynamics of their dysfunction. What was it that taught them acceptance, contentment, understanding, forgiveness, and true peace within themselves, enabling them to act without fear of judgment?

From the stories my mom told me, they had to fend for themselves as kids and take care of each other because my grandparents were too busy running a business and having babies.

How could my mom paint her father out to be such a great man, when, in reality, he worked his life away, drank, and smoked too much? How could she only see the good in her brother, who never amounted to much by society's standards? How could she have such patience and compassion for her sisters' erratic behavior? How could my mom's heart be so big and forgiving and understanding?

It was her faith.

It took me many years to become comfortable around my mom's family, but once I finally truly understood their free spirits and their faith, I was comfortable around them.

My mom and dad were busy with work and owning businesses in the same way as their parents had been; this left me to fend for myself most of the time. I didn't have rules—at least nothing I was held to. I didn't have to check in during the day or ask permission to go somewhere. I just did what I wanted to do.

When I was young, my dad cooked dinner every night, and we ate as a family, so I usually showed up around then. But, when he opened his pizza shop, that all changed.

Unlike his siblings, my dad was quiet and reserved, especially at home. Oftentimes he would zone out in front of the TV, drinking his beer. The other Jansens were fun and cool and liked to party. They played card games and hung out on the weekends, but my dad was never really into that. Was it because my mom didn't act that way?

I have many fond memories of spending quality time with my dad when I was young, like going to get blueberry doughnuts, cooking in the kitchen, working on my grandma's seawall on Lake Michigan, and taking trips down to Chicago.

He wasn't overly affectionate or energetic, but he was reliable and present. He seemed very content with having minimal possessions, he wasn't motivated to change his position in life, and he seemed to love his family in his own quiet, passive way. He always had a little baggie of leaves on the dryer, along with a tiny box of papers labeled "Zig-Zag." Sometimes I would pull out all the papers because they looked like an accordion. It wasn't until junior high that I realized what they were. *So, that's how he puts up with us.* I thought to myself.

My parents and brother were so quiet and reserved at home that I felt uncomfortable laughing out loud or telling a story. We didn't seem to express much emotion in my house; we kept to ourselves. Later, I came to realize not only that my mom acted more alive when she was around her sisters, but also that my dad was more outgoing at work.

My brother obviously understood this as the norm. He was so quiet at home and family functions that people thought he didn't talk. But, one day, I looked through his yearbook and saw that he had been named class clown and most popular. *My brother is nice and fun to be around?* I wondered to myself in disbelief.

No wonder I'm so wild and always getting in trouble at school. I hold all my feelings and emotions in and worry about being judged at home, then I go to school and let it all out. The rest of the world gets to deal with the real me. My family and I just act differently around different people.

That gave me pause.

It was an eye-opening moment for me. People are not always as they seem. I thought family should be the closest people in your life and know you better than anyone else. In reality, mine didn't know me at all, and I didn't know them. Granted, I was only like six years old at the time, but I had already learned how to suppress my personality to fit in with the people I loved.

Subconsciously, I knew I could be myself around strangers; or, maybe, it was because I didn't care what they thought. *Be yourself. See who likes you and who doesn't, then hang out with the ones who like you. You don't get to choose your family, so you better make sure they like you. Just keep your feelings to yourself.*

I tried to follow in my brother's footsteps, acting one way at home and being myself with my friends. I struggled to keep the real me on a tight leash and tamed when I felt I needed to. This got me into a lot of trouble for a lot of years. I struggled to keep my mouth shut in school and to do what I was told at home. But I couldn't help but say what was on my mind or do what I wanted to do; I had no regard for others or authority.

My childhood definitely helped shape me into a strong-willed, independent tomboy. Or, maybe, that was just my personality, and my childhood became what it did *because* I was a strong-willed, independent tomboy.

I'm Cathy, the Sinner

My mom had an unbreakable faith in God. She went to St. Patrick's every Sunday, without fail. She made Steve and me go when we were little. My dad wasn't raised Catholic, so he stayed home. By the time Steve finished confirmation, he quit going, so it was just my mom and me after that. I would reluctantly go to Sunday school, then mass; it made for long Sunday mornings. Somehow, I made it through my first communion and, later, my confirmation.

Don't get me wrong. I loved Jesus, but there was a lot of information relayed to us by strict nuns who didn't seem to appreciate my energy or my inquisitive mind. I often got in trouble for asking too many questions and doubting the stories in the Bible as they were presented. I was told that I needed to have faith, which I took to mean "blind obedience," without reason or explanation. That didn't sit well with me.

"Jesus loves you; He died for your sins!" Sister Ann yelled at me.

I asked, "Why? I'm always in trouble; why do I deserve that?"

"Stop sinning, and you won't have to worry about it," she said, without clearing anything up.

Thinking back now, I can't believe a grown woman would tell a five-year-old to stop sinning. I didn't even know what that really meant. I was trying to understand the point of Jesus.

I wondered, *Why would God send His only son to earth to die for us?*

The nuns painted God out to be this dictator-type Father who had many demands and rules. He also seemed to want to punish women. I did not appreciate all the stories of suppressed women in the Old Testament. I tried not to pay much attention to that.

"I really only like the New Testament," I would say during Sunday school.

I struggled with this idea of Jesus coming to save people, and yet being beaten and killed in order to accomplish it. It wasn't until years later that I came to understand sacrifice and unconditional love. It took me many years to understand and fully grasp those concepts.

I realize now that the nuns were trying to make it easy for us by getting us to think in black-and-white terms: if you are a sinner, you got to hell; but, if you believe Jesus is your Savior, then you can repent, be forgiven, and go to heaven.

Even my five-year-old little brain knew that it was impossible *not* to sin, so I wanted more than anything to believe. Grown-ups said I was too inquisitive and skeptical. I never took things at face value. I challenged everything I was taught. I may only have been four years old, but I wanted more details and specifics; I guess I wanted to understand the fine print. What hidden exclusions did I not know about that would get me kicked out of heaven?

Even though it was confusing and sometimes terrifying to think about God, being inside our church felt good. It felt comforting like my Grandma Jansen's big hugs. I loved listening to the bells and organ music. I sang all the hymns and studied the stained-glass windows. Each window depicted a different story, and I would find myself thinking about those stories and not listening to all that grown-up talk. The altar was massive and beautiful, with fancy gold trim. Above it hung the crucified Jesus.

I thought He was so beautiful, with His long hair and crown of thorns. I spent many Sundays staring at His forsaken face and feeling sorrow. I didn't understand what I was feeling, really; I just knew that I loved that man and wished He wasn't in pain.

It took many years for me to understand that His suffering was for me and that I was worthy of His gift because of the mere fact that I was a child of God.

But I digress.

Okay, where was I? Oh yeah, thinking about my childhood.

I'm Fearless Cathy

Early on, I often played with a girl named Kendra; she lived one block down, on Hyacinth Street, between Fifth and Sixth. Her house was a hideous dark green, with most of the paint chipped off. Granted, my house had chipping paint, and the grass needed to be cut, but the houses and yards on her street were in much worse shape than mine. Her cement porch steps were broken, and the handrail fell over if you touched it. She had big dogs that I always smelled when I went inside. I wondered why they lived that way, with everything so dirty. There were two holes in the dining-room floor, the table was always covered in garbage, with empty beer bottles and old cigarette butts everywhere. There were usually a few piles of dog poop in the kitchen.

I tried not to care about the fact that I was so uncomfortable inside her house. Who was I to judge? Usually, we played outside or at my house.

I had many adventures around the neighborhood with Kendra, but a few scary ones top the list.

One day, I went over to play and found her eating from an open can of cold SpaghettiOs. She offered me some.

"Ah no. I'm not hungry," I replied in disgust at the thought of cold SpaghettiOs.

"K. Let's go play. I hope we don't run into Damian. He was being a total jerk yesterday," Kendra warned.

We rode our bikes past Damian's house, just to know where he was. Suddenly, he ambushed us around the next corner. He grabbed Kendra off her bike and threw her on the ground. Right next to him was a pile of something shiny, stinky, and slimy. He pulled Kendra's shirt up, grabbed some of that nasty-looking stuff, and rubbed it all over her back. She screamed and kicked and cried to get free, until I picked up my bike and threw it at him. I screamed and warned him that Kendra's brother was coming. He threw the stuff into the street and took off. I helped Kendra up. She reeked of dead fish, and I took her back to her house.

We didn't get to see her brother beat up Damian, but he definitely did it; we saw his face the next day. Her dad thought it would help for her to soak in tomato juice, so he sent her sister to Rosie's Market to buy some.

I sat on the toilet lid, trying not to care about the pee on the floor around the bowl or the mildew on the tub wall where Kendra was lying in tomato juice, crying.

"Let's try to wash the scales off with the shower hose," I suggested.

I gently pulled each sticky scale off her skin and cleaned her up. I took care of Kendra the best I could, mostly because I felt bad for my friend, but also because no one else was going to do it.

"Damian better hope we never see his ugly face, because I will ride over him with my bike!" I declared.

Kendra laughed and agreed.

The other time we were scared was the day she came over and brought her dad's cigarettes. "Well, should we try one?" she asked.

"Do you have a lighter? You need a lighter," I replied, hoping she would say no.

"I'm sure your dad has one. Go get it," Kendra insisted.

I went downstairs, and there was his lighter, next to his big brown recliner. He was in the bathroom. *Darn, I have no excuse,* I thought.

I grabbed the lighter and ran back upstairs, and we slid my really long bookshelf in front of the door. We lit the cigarette and tried taking a puff. I started coughing so hard my eyes were watering.

Next thing I noticed, my door was being pushed open and my bookshelf was sliding across the floor.

I quickly ran to the door, trying to close it. "What do you want? We're rearranging my room."

I felt a huge knot in my stomach.

My dad pushed the door harder and moved the bookshelf, grabbed my arm, and calmly asked what I was holding behind my back.

I showed him the cigarette.

"Kendra, go home," he said quietly, and then continued, "You are seven years old. You are too young to smoke cigarettes. Why would you even want to do that? They're disgusting and make you smell bad." After a long pause, he added, "Now go out and play."

Later, I thought to myself, *Why does my dad want to smoke? Why do my friends' moms and dads?*

My mom didn't smoke, and she never drank alcohol. My dad, on the other hand, drank beer every night after dinner and smoked cigarettes all day long.

I can't wait to be a grown-up so I can do what I want.

I had experienced fear and came out on the other side—unscathed. I started feeling like a really tough kid, like I could handle anything.

I'm Charlie's BFF

Walking home in second grade, I met my best friend, Charlotte. I called her Charlie. Her little brother, Jason, hated that. We were pretty much inseparable that year. I became another child in their family; Charlie and I didn't really give anyone much say otherwise. We built *Star Wars* forts in her basement, Ewok treehouses in her yard with Lincoln logs, and got our first albums together. We became obsessed with the Michael Jackson *Thriller* album, Cyndi Lauper, and Phil Collins's *No Jacket Required.*

In addition to being a tough kid, I was very competitive. I think it came from my stubbornness and desire to be special. Once, Charlie and I were playing in the alley behind her house, and I challenged her to prove her love for Michael Jackson.

"Whoever walks the alley the longest in their bare feet loves Michael Jackson the most!" I dared her.

"You're on!" she shouted, without hesitation.

We ran to the top of the alley, took our sandals off, and started walking the alley. She jumped off right away, but there was no way I was going out like that. I would prove my love and prove my fierceness. I walked all the painful long way down to her garage. It was at least three houses down. I was so proud of myself. I felt fearless.

"Charlie, I love you more than I love Michael!" I said as I tackled her to the ground, laughing, my feet throbbing.

"I love you too, Crazy Cathy!" she replied, laughing and out of breath.

That summer, Charlie went away to camp for a week. When she came back, she taught me her camp songs, and we sang on the porch swing for hours. We would sing and sing, until her brother came by. He would annoy us until we stopped. I wanted to beat Jason up probably a hundred times that year; and he, me.

"Hey, now that my dad opened his pizza shop, your mom is going to babysit me for the rest of the summer!" I exclaimed to Charlie as she walked out her front door one day.

Her mom, Lauren, was a stay-at-home mom. Actually, all my friends' moms stayed at home. I noticed that they all liked to work on their tans, drink Tab diet pop, and talk on the phone. My mom wasn't like any of the other moms I knew. That made her special to me.

"Yeah! You can come to Manhole with us every day, and we never have to be apart!" Charlie declared.

Jason came walking out behind her, grumbling about how miserable the rest of the summer was going to be. "I'm getting Ethan. I'm not going to the beach with you two!" he insisted as he went storming next door to find his friend.

Manhole was a little lake that was made next to big, cold Lake Michigan. Manhole was over the sand dunes. It was warm and fun. It had black sand under the regular tan sand, so it was cool to draw in. There was a really steep drop-off as soon as you walked into the water, so we needed to learn how to swim. Lauren took us to the city pool and made us take swimming lessons so she could relax at the beach, reading her romance novel, drinking her Tab, and not watching us. That was really smart of her.

We spent half the summer working on moving a huge drifting log from the other side of the lake, down to the best drop-off point by Lauren, to make a diving board.

The day leading up to our victory stood out. I thought we had secured it, for sure, but it floated away once Ethan jumped off it. "You're too big!" I yelled.

"No, it's too slippery!" he snapped back.

The yelling got louder as the log drifted farther away.

Charlie and I insisted that Jason and Ethan swim out to get it for once.

I must confess—it was kind of creepy swimming in Manhole. If you swam out a little bit, it got really dark and deep and even a little cold.

People said there were big bulldozers at the bottom that had fallen in when they were plowing it out to make the lake. Somebody told us there was even a car down there. When I swam too far out, I started to feel panicky because I thought my legs were going to get trapped in one of those machines, like in a horror movie, and get ripped off.

As we packed ourselves into Lauren's Subaru that morning, I thought, *Today, we are going to make that log stay, and it's going to be an amazing day! I'm going to jump off that log right into the dark, deep water and swim out as far as I can; definitely farther than Jason and Ethan. No fear! No fear!* I chanted to myself as we walked along the hot black and tan sand to the water.

"Yes, the log is still there. Let's do this, boys!" I said to Charlie, Jason, and Ethan, even though Charlie was technically a girl.

She liked to act like a boy and didn't mind if people mistook her for one. Maybe that was why she liked to be called Charlie. Her hair was very dark and short, like her mom's. Some would say it was shaved like a boy's, but her mom made it look pretty. Either way, Charlotte was definitely different from my other friends, like Brandy and Alicia. They were girlie girls, but Charlie was even more of a tomboy than I was. I didn't know that was possible until I met her.

What an amazing day it turned out to be. We got the log to

stick deep into the sand, with help from some older boys, and we all took turns diving off it. I swam out farther than I ever had and still had my legs.

"I wish summer would last forever," I declared as we brushed the black sand off our feet and piled back into the Subaru.

The day Charlie told me they were moving away broke my heart. I felt lost and empty. I didn't want to play with anyone else. I loved my surrogate family.

A few days later, I walked over to Ninth Street, down past Ethan's house, and stood in front of Charlie's empty house. It was a nice white house with a big swing on the porch that we had spent many hours swinging and singing camp songs on, but no more. I looked in the windows, and all their furniture was gone. Charlie's bike wasn't parked outside the garage. There was no rake lying in the yard, and no dog wagging his tail in the window. It was the saddest house I'd ever seen.

I walked back up the street to St. Patrick's and sat inside for a while, thinking about my friend. We had taken guitar lessons from one of the nuns there, but that was a disaster. Remembering how much we despised the nun made me laugh through my tears. I looked up and saw the crucified Jesus looking at me with tears on His face and realized that He must know what it felt like to lose your friend. I was comforted by the familiarity of my huge, beautiful church, and I felt the warmth of God's love hug me.

I believe that Charlie's family changed the course of my life. Every experience shapes the direction of your ever-evolving path in life, and having them in my life for a short time no doubt influenced that. It didn't directly lead me down a path of success or goodness, but it helped me realize that when you make a mistake, you can go in reverse and change directions. They made me realize that I was special and people would be willing to help me along my path, if I just let them join me.

They did this, probably unknowingly, by showing me they cared about me. Me—an overzealous, energetic, smart-mouthed little girl who marched to the beat of her own drum.

They took the time to correct me and guide me. They made me use manners and proper etiquette, just like Charlie and Jason had to. They held me accountable for my actions and made me suffer consequences for my actions. This was new to me, and, believe me, I protested, but Lauren and her husband, Dan, weren't having it. If I wanted to play with Charlie and go places with them, then I had to behave properly.

They were active, purposeful parents, but, in addition, they were awesome people. They knew how to make the most of life, and they taught me how to enjoy life. They taught me how to be brave but smart at the same time. I had so many firsts with them. They took me camping, tubing, canoeing, skiing, and waterskiing; they taught me how to shoot a bow and arrow, how to swim, and how to do countless other fun things. In addition, they made me rake the yard and do spring cleaning with them. They didn't let me say no or slack off. They always included me and treated me like one of their own.

I developed confidence and felt more secure than ever to be my wild, adventurous self because I knew that Lauren and Dan accepted me, for better or worse. I knew that they would still love me and not forsake me.

It wasn't until long after they were gone from my life that I came to understand and appreciate what they had done for me.

At the time, I felt like my real family didn't seem to care if I was around or not. My mom lived at her store, my dad worked there and at a restaurant downtown. Steve was six years older than I was, so he wanted nothing to do with me if it didn't involve torture or teasing. I was lost and lonely. Charlie and I became pen pals, and that helped for a while.

I'm Chatty Cathy

Overall, my elementary-school years were full of crazy memories with friends, doing mischievous things. I came and went as I pleased. If I wanted to build a fort and use old furniture in the basement, I would. If I wanted to paint the sidewalk, I would use my brother's spray paint and do that. If I wanted to sleep at Alicia's house, I just would. I rarely got in trouble.

Sometimes I would be told to not do something, but I rarely got in trouble for wasting, destroying, abusing, or neglecting my belongings—or anyone else's. I was rarely held accountable for my actions. I received some empty threats but no actual follow-through. I think my parents just took care of the mess and assumed I was just a kid being a kid.

This became a huge problem. Because I didn't respect other people's things, I had no boundaries on what I could do or take or use or say. Where was the guidance I so desperately needed? Why did my surrogate family have to move away? Looking back now, I realize that I wanted to be a good kid, but I needed structure in my life.

By the first week of third grade, I already hated my teacher, Mr. Wacker. He drew a ladder on the chalkboard and explained that it represented our levels of success in the class. He wrote everyone's name on different ladder rungs and put my name on the very bottom one.

"Really? I'm the worst kid in this class?" I snapped out loud.

"This is a bunch of crap!" I yelled the last part, hoping my class-mates would agree and chime in.

Instead, Mr. Wacker replied, "Take your desk, and go sit in the hall."

I have never been more embarrassed in my life. All day long, kids walked by and asked why I was out there. The only conclusion I could come to was that Mr. Wacker was the worst teacher in the whole world. I responded with snarky remarks like "Mr. Wacker can't handle a girl who sticks up for herself" and "Apparently, I know everything, so they're letting me skip class until they find me a spot in fourth grade."

If he thinks this is going to shut me up, he's sorely mistaken. It's gonna be a long year, I thought to myself.

I guess one word to describe me would be *stubborn.* I do not appreciate being labeled or told where I belong on some success ladder. I will be the one to make that decision for myself, not some stupid old guy.

He doesn't even know me. What did he even use to make that decision? I know it isn't from Mrs. Singer, my second-grade teacher, because she loves me, I pondered.

I might have gotten in trouble for bugging Joey Mitchell all the time, but I was a good kid in second grade. And I wasn't dumb!

Thinking back, I reasoned, *I couldn't really help it with the whole Joey Mitchell thing; he was blonde and shy, and I loved him.*

Mrs. Singer understood, but Joey didn't. He was always telling on me for bothering him. "Please, Mrs. Singer. Tell her to leave me alone."

"He should be so lucky," I would say to her in my own defense.

I just wanted Joey's attention. I wanted him to love me as much as I loved him.

Maybe Mr. Wacker is jealous that I don't love him, I thought. *Gross!* I then replied to myself.

I'm Crabby Cathy, the Black Sheep

That year, my mom became pregnant. I was so excited! I couldn't wait to have a baby brother or sister to play with. I almost felt like an only child because Steve wasn't around much. I loved the idea of having someone always around to play with.

Steve and I woke one morning, and there was a note on the table, next to a box of raisin bran. In her fancy cursive, Mom had written, "We are at the hospital having the baby. Make sure you get to school on time. Dad will be home later."

The next day, Alicia and I sat on the front porch giggling in excitement. My mom and dad pulled up in their little white Pontiac with royal-blue suede seats and carried a baby seat past us and into the house.

I ran in and looked. "She's so cute and chubby!" I smiled.

"Oh my gosh, she's just so cute!" Alicia agreed.

"Her name is Isabel. Isabel Juli Jansen," My mom said with pride. (She thought it was neat because my middle name was also Juli, and her name was Juli-ana. Get it?)

"Can I hold her? Please? Please? Please?" I begged.

I had a sister. I was in love.

Well, that got old quick.

Every night, she woke me up with her crying. Every day, she got to go to the bridal store with my mom. *What about me?* I thought.

It seemed like if we weren't doing something for the baby, then we were going to Steve's football game or watching whatever TV show he wanted to watch.

I did get to watch *Jeopardy* at least. I loved *Jeopardy*. For some reason, it made me feel smart, and I thought Alex Trebek was cute. I have some vague recollection of an episode that went something like this:

"Nicknames for 200, Alex," one contestant ordered.

"It's what we call the middle child who doesn't fit into the family."

"What is a black sheep?" some really smart guy asked in response.

"Me! I'm definitely a black sheep! That's me!" I answered out loud to the TV.

I was surprised to learn there was a name for my situation. I realized there were others who felt out of place in their families. I wasn't the only one.

So, instead of worrying about not having any attention from my family, I started concentrating on having fun with Alicia. We wrote songs. We sang along to my Amy Grant album and her Madonna album. Funny enough, at the time, we were too naive to realize the dichotomy between those two women and what their songs were about. One minute, we'd be singing the Christian song "In My Father's Eyes"; the next, we were slinking around the floor, performing "Like a Virgin."

We had big dreams of being famous singers, which later evolved into rock stars. We rode our bikes back and forth from my house to her house multiple times per day. We rode all over town. We went to boys' houses and bugged them. Sometimes, when we were trying to be cool, we walked.

One day, we noticed that there were always cigarette butts lying on the sides of the road. By that time, we were smoking socially and had a lighter with us. One of us found a cigarette that was barely burned and thought it would be fine to smoke the leftover butt.

Honestly, we were excited because it wasn't always easy getting cigarettes; we thought we were geniuses. Once we smoked that one, we continued looking for butts worthy of lighting.

Thinking back now, I'm disgusted. At the time, though, it was me just finding a way around the rules.

Alicia was also Catholic, and even went to the Catholic school for a few years, until they doubled the tuition. Her mom decided that Alicia and her older sister had gained enough godly fear to handle public school. We shared the fear of God, the memories of torturous catechism classes, and evil nun stories. We relied on confession to help us live with our sins.

Not soon after my sister Isabel started walking and babbling, Alicia told me that her mom was going to have a baby. "I'm so excited because it can be best friends with your mom's new baby."

"Isabel will be two years older. I doubt they'll play together," I responded.

"No, I mean the baby your mom is going to have in March. She's due the same time my mom is. It will be so cool," Alicia explained.

I was livid. Why didn't I know that my mom was going to have another baby? Why did I find out from Alicia?

When I got home, I asked my mom, and she said, "Yes, we're going to have another baby. I was afraid to tell you because I knew you'd be mad."

I thought, *Why would she think I would be mad? Well, now I'm mad, but it's because no one tells me anything and I look stupid, not because she's going to have another baby. Why do I even care? Maybe because I already don't get any attention?*

"I don't care what you guys do. I'll be in junior high soon, so I won't be home anyway," I said as I huffed up the stairs to my bedroom.

My middle-child syndrome intensified.

I very much assimilated to the black-sheep role. I felt ignored and not good enough. My brother was super popular, he was a great football player, the homecoming king, and, according to his friends, fun. My parents were always bragging about him to people, and my mom often made comments about what an easy kid he was until I came along.

I was proud to be Steve's little sister, but, at the same time, I felt like I could never live up to that, so I didn't bother trying. I embraced my wild side and got attention for being bad. I made it so Steve wasn't proud to be my brother.

During those years, I felt free but, at the same time, lost. Who was I? I used to be Cathy, Juliana and Don's daughter, then I was Charlie's best friend; then my mom came up with Crabby Cathy because I acted miserable, bored, and unhappy so often. That was definitely *not* who I wanted to be.

At times, that loneliness and lack of identity and purpose in my life pulled me into a scary place inside myself. I dealt with severe depression that I didn't share with anyone. At the time, I didn't know what was wrong with me. It wasn't until later, in high school, that I realized I had suffered major depressive episodes with suicidal ideations.

I lay on my bed, wanting to be dead. I thought of ways to kill myself, while keeping it clean and not gruesome. I contemplated overdosing on pills, drowning, or suffocating myself. I didn't like the idea of shooting myself. I didn't want people to have to clean me up like some mess.

I went and took all the pills I could find, but I just became nauseated and threw them up. Turns out my family didn't have anything stronger than Tylenol, Bayer aspirin, and cold medicines. I lay back down, still feeling miserable, but then my head was pounding and feeling like it was as big as a hot-air balloon. I couldn't stop crying, which made my head feel bigger and bigger. I must have developed a migraine from my crying and retching.

Just then, I heard my church bells ringing from up the street, and a little voice inside me said, "You are not alone."

"Please, God, I hate feeling this way! Why can't I stop it?" I cried aloud.

I reasoned with myself, and the little voice inside me said, "You can't die, silly! You are too special. You are going to do amazing things, so cut it out."

I prayed some more. I thanked God for watching over me and begged Him to take away those ugly, horrible thoughts and feelings.

I had tried to kill myself and failed. No one even knew that I had those feelings, and no one knew what had just happened.

I thought, *How could I even begin to tell anyone? Where would I start?* There was just too much to even explain, so I stuffed it away.

I figured the mental illness I dreaded was coming to get me. Then, my stubbornness kicked in, and I insisted that I could control my thoughts and feelings. I vowed to myself that I would not let that happen again.

Around this time, a TV network made a series of short movies, thinking they would help kids to deal with things like suicide, bulimia, rape, drinking, and drugs. Alicia, Brandy, and I watched these after-school specials on TV that dealt with difficult subject matters. I don't know if it helped other kids, but it had the opposite effect on us.

We got ideas on how to do those things, not ideas on how to *not* do those things. We dabbled in bulimia and anorexia and even thought it would be cool to have a drinking problem. We joked that we were tough enough to handle that crap and not let it ruin us. We hated the idea of being a victim. We thought those kids struggling with problems were weak.

Thinking about it now, our way of thinking was really fucked up. How did I get like that? Was it the mere fact that I was almost a teenager and so I thought I was invincible? Was I so lost that I just went along with whatever my friends thought? Or, was I truly desperate for attention and an identity?

I really didn't know who I was or where I fit in with the world. I felt like an outsider with my family and my friends. All my free will and lack of accountability soon gave me a bad reputation.

For a while, Alicia and I were inseparable. Everyone in our family thought she was a really good girl and that I was the bad seed making her do bad things and corrupting her.

I'll never forget the day my uncle Jack was surprised that I wasn't at the party that got busted for minors drinking. "It was Alicia and not you? And I always thought you were the bad one," he said to me with a surprised tone as he jokingly spanked my butt.

That pissed me off.

Alicia was so much worse than I could ever be. She never hesitated to take it to the next level. When we partied, I would drink beer, and she would smoke pot. When I made out with a guy, she would be in the other room giving a blow job. But she was smart. She acted so prim and proper, and she was an amazing liar. She acted the way she knew adults wanted her to act and said what they wanted to hear, and she was able to look her mom in the eye while telling her a bold-faced lie. It was impressive. I admired Alicia for that ability, until it eventually got her into real trouble.

As far as school was concerned, nothing much had changed. I continued to talk in class, interrupt the teacher, and not do my homework. I went to a conference with my mom once. The teacher was telling her how I couldn't keep my mouth shut and didn't pay attention.

My mom politely said, "It's too bad you don't have something more creative or worthwhile for Cathy to do. If you did, maybe she would excel. Maybe you should take advantage of her talking skills and have her teach the class. I think she's just bored."

Hearing that surprised me, and the little voice deep inside me said, "See? You are smart and special. Your mom just admitted it."

I wished that little voice spoke to me more often. Maybe it tried to, but I was too busy or too stubborn to listen. Maybe all I could hear was the echo of my mom and brother calling me Crabby Cathy.

I'm Cat, with Nine Lives

The summer after sixth grade, a new girl moved into the house behind me. Her name was Crystal, and she was three years older than I was. I thought Alicia and I were wild, but Crystal took it to a new level. She was so different, which attracted me to her immediately. Very quickly, Crystal and I became "partners in crime." We got into every bad thing you could think of.

One night, we were walking down to Rack-Em-Up (a dirty pool hall across from my mom's store), when Crystal asked, "Does your mom keep cash in her store?"

"Yeah, my dad keeps it in a bank bag in the desk in the basement. Why?" I replied.

"Do you think they would notice if some of it was gone?" she wondered aloud.

I became interested and asked, "How are we supposed to get it?"

"I don't know; it was just a thought," she muttered as we walked in to play pool and pick up guys.

Crystal was a great wingman to have because she had big boobs (for a soon-to-be tenth-grader) and long legs. She always wore really short miniskirts. I was pretty cute and looked much older than twelve—at least that was what guys would say when they met me.

A few days later, I noticed my dad put his keys on the shelf above our coats when he got home. That night, I said I was going to hang out with Crystal, and I very quietly took his keys as I went out the door. *They'll never notice; they're too busy with those kids*, I thought.

I met up with Crystal in the middle of the dark street, and we walked down to the bridal store. We found the key to open the side door under the sidewalk, the scary door that led into the basement. It was dark and musty, and I wasn't sure if they had any alarms or floodlights, but we were about to find out.

They didn't.

We stumbled our way into the main part of the basement, went right to the desk, and opened the bank bag. The cash was all in order, but there were a lot of the same bills, so we took a few of each, reasoning that they wouldn't notice if the same amount of fives, tens, and twenties was missing. I know it's dumb, but it made sense at the time.

"You sure they won't notice?" I asked Crystal, obviously looking for a reason to put it back. I was feeling really yucky, like I had a bad stomachache.

"They definitely won't notice, and, besides, you would've asked them for money tomorrow, and they would have given it to you, right? So, what's the difference?" she reasoned.

That made sense. So, we carefully sneaked back out the way we had come, without turning on any lights or disturbing anything. We locked the door and ran over to Rack-Em-Up.

We paid for everyone's games that night, smoked cigarettes, and got walked home by the two guys we'd met a few nights prior. I clearly remember that walk home because he held my hand and swirled his finger into my palm over and over again. How could something so little feel so exciting?

We got to my house, and he started kissing me.

"Time to come in, Cathy," I heard my dad say sternly from the porch.

He started smoking outside once my mom had more kids, so he spent a fair amount of time on the porch.

Oh shit, he must know I took his keys! Oh my God! Oh, God, please don't let me get in trouble! I begged inside my head as I looked toward St. Patrick's brightly lit steeple at the end of my street.

"'Bye!" I yelled to the cute guy as I ran up to my house.

Noticing that my dad wasn't right behind me, I threw the keys on the shelf, took a deep breath, and went back to praying. *Oh, Lord, I am not worthy to receive You, but only say the word, and I shall be healed.*

I continued to chant that in my head as I quickly walked upstairs to my room and went to bed.

The next day, I told Crystal what happened and said that he never asked about the keys, so we laid low for a few days. My parents didn't ask about the money, so I knew we were in the clear.

Crystal and I usually hung out at her house, listening to the Cure, Billy Idol, the Beastie Boys, and some of her parents' old records, like Elvis Presley and the Moody Blues. We talked about ridiculously inappropriate things, like how we would fuck Billy Idol if we ever met him, or Kirk Cameron from *Growing Pains* or young Elvis from *Blue Hawaii*.

One day, she got antsy and insisted we walk to the drugstore. I figured we were going shopping for more hair dye or eyeliner or something.

"I'm gonna show you how to get a five-finger discount. I've done it plenty of times; it's easy. I promise you won't get caught," she explained on the way.

It turned out that I was really good at it. That quickly became a common thing for us to do. We were usually bored and looking for a thrill. No one was around to question us when we came home with bags full of hair products, fake nails, makeup, douches—you name it; we got it. Her dad was usually passed out in his living-room chair, and her mom was at work.

The thrill and desire for a challenge led us to my mom's store again. Too many times to count, I'm afraid. My parents never said anything, so I never worried about it. I figured they weren't missing it, until one day when I overheard my mom accusing my dad of spending the money on pot and lying to her. I realized he was being blamed for what Crystal and I were doing.

That gave me pause.

I realized that my careless actions were actually affecting people. It wasn't just money that I was taking; it was people's respect and trust. I felt so full of sin that I was sick to my stomach and had episodes of diarrhea.

I told Crystal we were done doing that; I said that we needed to go to confession. See, she was Catholic too, but she said she didn't believe in God or Jesus.

"I only go because my parents make me. I'm an atheist," she said.

I think she just said it to be different.

She was always going against the establishment, testing the rules, and criticizing the popular, "normal" kids.

I wanted to tell my mom that I took the money so that she would leave my dad alone, but I just couldn't. I could never bring myself to tell my parents it was me. I couldn't bear the thought of that shame. *I pray that God will forgive me, but I don't think my parents can.*

Crystal and I refocused our efforts and sought new challenges—boys. We were obsessed with boys. I had a huge crush on Jake Flint, who was sixteen. I was only thirteen at that point, mind you, but I didn't care. I started wanting to go to church every Sunday because I could guarantee he would be slumped over the edge of the pew, looking uninterested or asleep, but also very cute. I would stare at him the entire fifty minutes and thank God for his existence. It turned out he had a girlfriend, but I stalked him anyway, until he gave in.

Crystal liked his friend Jimmy, so we had them come over to

her house one evening. Crystal and Jimmy went into her bedroom, and Jake and I went into her parents' bedroom. He laid me on top of the slippery, polyester floral print bedspread and pulled his pants down. He pulled my pants down far enough to penetrate my thighs. He thought he was fucking me, but, somehow, I knew he was doing it wrong. I didn't dare say anything or move because I didn't want to embarrass him or make it last any longer, so I just went with it.

You asked for this. I told myself.

Telling myself that didn't make it feel any better. I don't remember kissing or even looking at each other in the eye, really. It was very awkward and anticlimactic; not at all exciting or loving like I dreamed it would be.

Secretly, I was happy that he didn't take my virginity, but I pretended like he did, for his sake. I lost interest in him after that night.

A short time later, I heard that his girlfriend was pregnant. I was so relieved but somewhat surprised that he had figured out how to do it right. *Dear Lord, thank You for saving me from that disaster,* I thought.

So, for now, I was still a virgin, but I definitely wasn't a good girl. Crystal and I partied wherever and whenever we could that summer, with whatever older boys we could find. She would always go to the limit, and I would often enjoy by proxy; after all, I was three years younger than Crystal and everyone else we hung out with. I was afraid of fully giving myself away and being let down again.

I wanted to have fun, but I always heard the little voice inside me reminding me, "You're too good for this. Be careful, or you'll ruin your life."

I really didn't know where that voice was coming from. No one was directly telling me not to do things; I just knew I deserved better. I had to watch out for myself. I had to guide myself. My only moral compass was my love for Jesus and not wanting to let Him down.

I just felt my little voice to be the truth.

Some nights, I lay in bed and thought about all the wild and dangerous things we did. I felt ashamed and wished I could go back in time and stop my first best friend, Charlie, from moving away. I wished I would find different friends. *Dear God, why am I so bad? Why do You let me make such bad decisions? Why don't I get caught and punished?*

I realized that not getting caught or punished helped me to justify my actions and continue them. *If I could only hold myself accountable and punish myself.* Maybe that was why I struggled with depression and suicidal thoughts. Was I trying to punish myself?

I tried to make sense of it all, but I just couldn't.

Crystal and I had total disregard for authority and the holy sacrament. Once, we actually went into the back door of the church and played with the holy bread wafers, the goblets, and the bells that the altar boys ring. I don't know how we didn't get caught or what possessed us to even want to do that.

Later, I thought, *Oh, Lord, I'm going to hell. What is wrong with me?*

One time, we hitchhiked to the next town over to hang out at some festival that was going on, and we made out with some guys we met. We got drunk and ran into my brother and his girlfriend.

"Look, Steve, it's your little sister!" his girlfriend shouted from across the street.

Steve came over to me. "Why are you such white trash? Go home!" he commanded as he shoved me and walked away.

That was only one of many times I showed up where my brother was and pissed him off. No wonder he couldn't stand me.

A few times we TP'ed (toilet papered) the popular kids' houses and wrote nasty things on their parents' cars with shaving cream.

We not only destroyed other people's property, we also tried to destroy ourselves.

We dyed our hair every other week. We pierced each other's ear cartilage and belly buttons. One regretful time, I let Crystal cut my hair. That was the worst decision ever! She cut all the hair on the top of my head so that it was spiked, leaving the back long. She insisted it was cute and that I could pull it off. I still can't believe I went to the dance that night and talked to Jake Flint; she had given me a mullet!

We went to every party we could and hung out with dirtbags three to four years older than we were. We even shared the same guy one night. We were at a house party, lying in bed with him, and we took turns making out with him and each other.

The first week of seventh grade, Crystal helped me dye my hair jet-black. Unfortunately, it shimmered like a horrible witch's green potion instead of being a sleek Joan Jett black, and I had to go to school like that. I'd never been so humiliated. The popular kids teased me hard core. That night, I begged my mom, the shoe-dye wizard, to fix it. Turns out that knowing how to perfectly dye shoes doesn't give you the ability to dye hair. Thankfully, my uncle Kent came over and stripped my hair with some nasty chemicals. Then, it was just an ugly brown.

"You need to quit hanging out with Crystal; she keeps talking you into ruining your hair, and God only knows what else she's talked you into doing," my mom said in an annoyed tone.

She was right; my hair couldn't take any more stolen hair-box dye jobs, and I couldn't take much more ridicule at school. I was already getting called "white trash" and "slut," and now I was getting called "ugly witch" and "dumb bitch."

I got away from Crystal a little bit, and that helped me realize how self-destructive she was—and how I was on her slippery slope. Not too long after, I heard she was caught doing coke in the school bathroom and got sent away to boarding school out East.

Unfortunately, I hung around her long enough to get a very bad reputation. I didn't blame her; those were my decisions. I just knew that I couldn't easily make different decisions if I continued to hang out with her. So, I had to deal with being thought of as a slut, white trash, and a loser by most of the popular kids.

I was trying to hang out with people my age again, so, one night, Brandy and I went sledding at the high-school hill with my cousin Mike and a bunch of kids. We jumped on the inner tubes and flew down the hill, catching air with every bump, squealing with pure delight. It felt so good to have fun without feeling guilty or worried that I was going to get in trouble. We smiled and laughed until our frozen little faces hurt.

When I left to walk home, I walked down the lot between the football field and the buses. It was dark and cold, so I was focused on getting to the street, where there were lights overhead.

All of a sudden, my cousin's friend, Darren, came running up behind me and put his arm around me. "I can make you warm," he said.

"Oh hey," I replied. "You walkin' home too?"

"Yeah, but first come over here and let me warm you up," he said as he forced me between two of the buses and pinned me up against the side of one. "I hear you're a really good kisser. I wanna see for myself."

And, without letting me respond, he mashed his face into mine and stuck his tongue in my mouth.

"Get off me," I said, trying to push him away, but he was much stronger than I was; he held me against the bus, so I was trapped.

Again, he started kissing me and reached up under my coat, grabbing my boobs. I clenched my mouth shut as tight as I could and kneed him in the balls.

"Ahh! You're such a cunt! You have no problem making out with older guys, so what's your problem?" he snapped as he bent over, grabbing himself in pain.

He pushed me back against the bus with one hand as he tried to get up, but I took off.

As I ran, I screamed, "I'm not a cunt, you piece of shit!"

I ran until I could see St. Patrick's steeple lit up ahead. My little voice whispered, "You didn't deserve that. You are not what they say you are."

All the rage and disgust I felt melted away. "Thank You, God, for giving me the strength to get away."

I prayed as I walked the rest of the way home, my lungs burning from the cold. "Please keep me on the right path and give me a second chance, dear God. Please help people to see the real me."

Most boys in my class wouldn't even give me the time of day in public because they thought I was trouble. Their mothers warned them to stay away from me. I tried to stick up for myself. I told them I hadn't even had sex yet, but no one believed me. *Why should they?* I thought. *They're right. I'm out doing everything else I shouldn't be doing. Oh well.*

At that point, I was truly lost, and I had no one to confide in.

I tried hanging out at a party where the popular kids were, but, once again, they made me feel worthless. Sam was there; he was actually the first boy I kissed, back in fifth grade, on the playground. We were joking around and having fun at the party when he mentioned that he needed to leave soon.

I teased him for having a curfew. "You're just a mama's boy, I guess."

"Well, at least my parents care about me and want to keep me safe!" he snapped.

"Jeez, I was just kidding. My parents trust me because I'm smart," I snapped back, then walked away.

He was right: his parents cared about him, and that was why he had a curfew. Did that mean my parents didn't care about me? That question cut me deeply and actually made me angry. *I'm sure they love me; they are just busy and know I can take care of myself,* I reasoned in my head.

But the reality was that I couldn't take care of myself. I was failing. I felt like I was back in third grade, stuck at the bottom of Mr. Wacker's goddamned ladder.

"You don't belong at the bottom! You're not a loser!" the little voice inside me shouted, but I completely ignored it.

I was having an even tougher time at school. I was taking very easy, basic classes and barely passing. I got in trouble for talking in class so many times that I would get sent to principal's office. It got to the point that I had to sit through Saturday school many weekends, just to stay in school.

I was in there with the really bad kids: the one who was suspended for bringing a knife to school, the one who called the teacher a cunt, and the ones who did drugs.

I did a lot of self-reflection during those many hours of sitting there with nothing to do. We were only allowed to have one piece of paper and a pencil. Some kids couldn't behave for four hours to save their lives. They would get kicked out within the first hour. Some made it closer to lunch, but they really pushed Mr. Lynch's buttons.

Mr. Lynch was the gym teacher. He was a dirty old man. Once, I wore white shorts in gym class, and he told me that hot I looked in my shorts. I wanted to vomit.

I did not like being in Saturday school, and I came to the conclusion that I didn't belong there. I worked hard to keep my mouth shut in class from then on, and I tried to change my ways.

I may have issues and talk a lot, but I'm not white trash. I'm a Jansen, I thought to myself.

Pussy Cat Takes Control

Then, I met Sophie. When we first became friends, Sophie insisted I go on a Bible retreat with her. I finally agreed. We showed up at her church and loaded into the bus. It was a tight fit, and we are all talking and goofing around. I saw this hot, older guy sitting behind me and immediately started talking to him.

"Hi, I'm Cathy."

"Well, then, can I call you Cat?" he said in this flirty, cute way as he touched my hair.

"Sure, you can call me Cat. Pussy Cat," I said provocatively, then giggled out loud.

There was instant attraction, and I spent the entire two-day retreat trying to hang out with him.

Sophie realized and pulled me away, saying, "He has a girlfriend, my neighbor Sara, and she is here! You need to stop talking to him."

"What a douche," I said. "Okay."

I definitely didn't want Sara to feel bad, so I asked him about it, and then he broke up with her later that day.

On the bus-ride back home, he gave me a ring and asked me out. I couldn't imagine where he'd even found the ring, but I was no longer interested because I saw Sara looking at us with a very sad expression.

"I don't want to take the ring because we don't even live in the same town. If it's meant to be, I'll see you again," I said, letting him down easily.

I never saw him again and honestly can't even remember his name.

This seemed to be a recurring theme in my life. I guess I legitimately just like people. It was easy to find something about a guy that I found attractive, like his shy smile, sexy walk, goofy jokes, headbanging abilities, or confident arrogance, and I then focused on that and just enjoyed his company for the time being. It usually ended as quickly as it began.

If that's what it took to be a slut, then I guess I was a slut. I just think that I lived in love, in the optimism of hope and love. I saw the good in people and wanted to be a part of that. But, I definitely didn't want to hurt any girls along the way. That would not be cool. I'd rather hurt a guy than a girl.

We girls needed to stick together and have each other's backs, I told myself.

I continued to occasionally steal from stores. When I became friends with Sophie, I taught her how to do the same. Unfortunately, she didn't have the confidence or lack of regard that I did, so she got caught on her first try. She got taken away by the cops and had to go in front of a judge. She was put on probation, and she was mad at me for a while. That event actually scared me straight—mostly. I quit stealing and found my thrills in other ways.

More importantly, Sophie showed me what it meant to be a true friend. To my surprise, she didn't rat me out or blame me. Her parents were very apprehensive of me at first, but she assured them that I was harmless. She took responsibility for my influence over her. Secretly, I think she got a taste of the thrill and wanted more.

When she met me, she explained that being Baptist meant that she wasn't allowed to dance or party, or let loose and have a good time. I spent all my energy trying to "save" Sophie from what I thought to be catastrophic thinking.

"Your religion has it all wrong, Soph. There is nothing wrong with enjoying life. God made us capable of dancing and having fun for a reason. As long as you mean well and ask for forgiveness of your sins, God will forgive you. That's what Jesus is for." I explained this to her too many times to count.

I made it my life's mission to show that girl how to live. In my mind, she had been sheltered and repressed. I thought it was my duty to set her straight and teach her how to enjoy life.

Surprisingly, her parents came to love and accept me. Probably because they didn't know half the things we did. Sophie always tried to make me look wholesome and innocent, and, by that time, I had become a really good liar. I could get away with almost anything. We were a good duo for a while.

Sophie and I hung out at Rack-Em-Up on a regular basis. On the weekends, we often went to the roller rink. They had teen night on Fridays. We smoked and drank and hung out with boys we didn't know. That was where I first met Noah. He was an awesome skater and he had the softest brown curls in his hair. He was two grades ahead of me, and we had mutual friends. He was my new prey.

Once again, I was in love and obsessed. We had so much fun, and he was a great kisser. We messed around a lot, but we never "did it." I enjoyed talking to him on the phone for many hours every night, and we hung out like friends, swimming, riding his moped, fishing, hunting, and going to school dances. He was an only child with rich parents and got to do whatever he wanted. They bought him whatever he wanted. Between the two of us having almost no active parenting, we did whatever we wanted.

By this time, I was babysitting my younger siblings on the weekends and sometimes on weekdays too. I left them unsupervised many times while Noah and I went down to the basement to make out.

My desire for him got me into real trouble with my parents. Somehow, I had read part of a trashy romance novel and got the brilliant idea to write something sexy to Noah. It was about one page long, and it said stuff like "I want you to slide your manhood into my hot, wetness until we both explode." Granted, I hadn't yet experienced anything like that in life, but I found it easy to imagine and express in words on paper.

Unfortunately, Noah's dad found the note and called my dad. I'd never seen anger like that from my dad before. He went up to my room and pulled the cords of the phone and stereo out of my wall, ripped all my posters down, and told me I was grounded. "You will never see Noah again! Understood?"

"Okay! God! You didn't need to ruin my room and break my phone! I hate you! I hate you!!" I screamed as I slammed my door.

My mom told me I needed to go to church more and stay away from boys. Because they weren't good at following through on punishments, I got my stuff back a few days later.

I made it very difficult for them to punish me because, in my mind, it wasn't fair. They had let me be independent for as long as I could remember. I learned by making mistakes and suffering the natural consequences of my actions. I knew how to redirect myself and make different choices when necessary. I couldn't accept the idea that now, all of a sudden, they knew better than I did and were going to tell me what to do and how to live.

I felt like a cat who had lived in the wild for fourteen years and then got caught and put in a cage, never to run free again. I was not about to just stay still and lie down. I fought it and terrorized them until they let me loose, so to speak.

I didn't stop seeing Noah; I just became more careful about

hiding what I was doing. His parents hated me after that, so it was harder to talk on the phone, and it changed our relationship.

Shortly after that, I went to a party in the woods. Noah's friend Alex was there, without him. I realized Alex liked me when I lay down next to him in the bed of his pickup truck and he started kissing me. He was a bad kisser, but he really liked me, and I was drunk, so I went along with it to make him happy.

I need to teach this poor boy how to be a better kisser, I thought to myself.

The crazy thing was, I really loved Noah and cared about him (as much as a fourteen-year-old can). Later, I couldn't understand why I had done that to him.

My cousin Mike pulled me off the truck and said, "What the hell are you doing?"

"Oh my God! Don't tell Noah! Why did I do that? What am I gonna do now?"

Mike laughed and said, "You're just like your dad."

"What the hell are you talking about?"

"You know, how your dad just cheated on your mom and got caught!" he explained.

I had no idea what he was talking about, and I got pissed.

"How do you think your dad broke his arm? Your mom showed up at some chick's apartment, and he jumped out the window to not get caught," Mike said flippantly.

My heart broke for my mom. I wanted to believe that Mike was lying and just being an ass, but my dad *did* have a broken arm.

From then on, I paid close attention to my parents' relationship, looking for clues. If my mom knew, she hid it well. She acted the same when I was around, strong and exhausted. I never saw them fight about anything major.

My mom went to church every Sunday without fail. Her faith was strong enough for my whole family. Looking back now, I realize that was how she kept our family together: through faith, prayers, forgiveness, and grace. She always credited my Grandma Jansen for keeping my dad's family together, and I realized my mother did the exact same thing.

Damn, I come from strong women! I thought.

So, back to my debacle. The next night, at a school dance, Noah found out what happened. Alex insisted he would beat up Noah if he tried to stop him from being with me. Noah was smaller than Alex, and pretty much smaller than all of our friends, so he got scared and told Alex he could have me. I think I broke his heart. He never really forgave me.

Then, I was Alex's girlfriend.

Forgiveness and Humility

Unfortunately, it wasn't that easy to be Alex's girlfriend. It turned out that his ex-girlfriend, Becky, was obsessed with him and hadn't accepted their breakup. She was a tall, scrawny bitch who wore tube tops and jean shorts that rode up her crack. She started relentlessly prank calling my house, threatening me through friends, and harassing me to the point that my mom called the cops. They went to Becky's house and warned her to leave me alone.

The next day, she found me in the hallway at school and punched me in the face. My friends rushed me into the principal's office to tell on her, and she was suspended from school. But that was only the beginning.

When I told my dad what had happened, he gave me very clear, sound advice. "Try to stay away from her. If she corners you, and you have no choice, then you hit her first, and hit her hard. And don't stop hitting her until she's down for good."

Very soon afterward, that advice proved to be great. It was Friday night, and I was with Alex, Sophie, Brandy, and a few others, walking to Greg's house. Becky and her best friend, Jan, who used to bully me in elementary school, were with some guys and saw us walking down the hill. Becky ran toward me, cornering me between a building and the hill below Greg's house. She started egging me on, threatening to kick my ass and finish what she had started at school. Alex tried to shut her up, but the guys with her insisted he let us fight it out.

Remembering what my dad had said, I thoughtfully switched Alex's big class ring from my left hand to my right. *No fear!* I told myself.

"Go for it, bitch!" I yelled.

As she ran up to attack me, I lunged forward, punching her in the face. I kept pounding her until she was lying on the ground, crying. One of her shoes was off, on the ground some ten feet away. A clump of her overbleached hair covered my hand, sticking out of Alex's class ring.

Jan ran to help Becky up.

"Don't ever fucking mess with me again!" I warned Becky as I walked away with Alex and my friends.

I was so pumped up; my whole body was shaking with rage and excitement. It felt amazing to be able to defend myself. I was so proud that people were there to witness it. I thought I was a badass.

Deep inside, I also felt bad for embarrassing and humiliating her. Really, I didn't like to hurt people, but there was no way I was going to let her continue to bully me and get away with punching me at school. If I hadn't beaten her up that night, she would have beaten me up, and then she would have continued to bully me. She gave me no other choice. She came to respect me after that night, and we even partied together after that.

I never hold grudges. I've always been quick to forgive and move on. Partly, because that is what I would hope for in return; but, even more so, it's for me. I hated feeling that anger and hatred toward others. It ate me up inside. I felt like I was being poisoned when I was mad at someone. They were poisoning me, and the only way to stop it was to stop feeling that way toward them, despite their inability to apologize or treat me right.

I learned about Jesus's ability to forgive. He always had the power of forgiveness, and it seemed so impossible. I wanted to be like that.

From an early age, I studied the adults in my life. I paid attention to how they reacted to situations, what their body language was saying that they weren't, and if they were happy or miserable (and, by *miserable*, I just mean that they complained a lot and frequently had issues with friends or family members). I quickly realized that the miserable ones were always angry at something that someone had done to them that they couldn't forgive; they held grudges. They would talk about it until the other people around them were sick of hearing about it, and then they would find something new to be pissed about.

Some of my friends' moms lived in that negativity all the time. They would sit on the phone for hours complaining about how miserable they were and how it was all the fault of everyone else: their husbands, their friends, or their kids.

The happy people didn't gossip, complain, or go on rants about what people did or did not do to them. My mom was one of those people. She never sat on the phone gossiping or bitching about anyone. I knew people had hurt her and disregarded her feelings at times, but she would try to understand and let it go. She didn't dwell on it or live in the negativity. When my mom would hear women bitching about petty stuff like that, she would say things like "Those women have too much time on their hands and not enough Jesus in their hearts."

I came to understand that not forgiving, not letting go of negative feelings, really hurts that person much more than it does the person they are mad at. It poisons your heart and leaves no room for happiness or joy. As I became aware of this, I tried to make conscience decisions to not live in negativity. I realized that when I felt miserable and hopeless, it was because I was blaming others and letting their issues become mine. I tried to understand where they were coming from and why they were the way they were. I would forgive (despite not getting an apology) and move on. I tried not to live in negativity.

I wasn't trying to excuse their behavior; take Becky, for example. I knew she had no dad in the picture and her mom partied all the time. Becky had no guidance and thought she could do whatever she wanted. She was heartbroken and didn't know what to do with her anger, so she directed it at me. I tried to ignore her, but she made it my business. I understood why she punched me and bullied me. I taught her a lesson, but then I let it go. I knew that holding a grudge against her would only ruin my peace of mind and my happiness.

Sex

Anyway, I grew to love Alex. How could I not when we spent every waking moment together? We did silly things, like frosting each other's hair; we played pool, and we liked the same music. We spent many hours playing Nintendo, listening to "hair" bands like Ratt and Mötley Crüe. Alex had a drum set, and his brother had an electric guitar. They tried to play Metallica and Megadeth and would playing the same riff over and over—for hours, it seemed.

I dreamed of being a drummer like Tommy Lee and Lars Ulrich. I never actually owned drums or tried to make it a reality; I just enjoyed the dream. Alex accepted me as I was and made me feel so comfortable with myself. He let me mess around with his drums and encouraged me to go for my dreams—whatever crazy thing my dream happened to be any particular week. We often talked about our future together.

Naturally, our relationship advanced physically. One fateful evening, his parents were outside drinking with the neighbors, so we were making out on his bed. He unbuttoned my pants, and, instead of his finger, I felt the weight of him as he slid into me. I was in shock. It only lasted a minute, but that was it. He was my first. He was obsessed with sex after that. It was a daily event; sometimes multiple times per day, for the next half a year.

I never physically enjoyed the sex; actually, it was usually pain-ful, but I loved feeling desired, and I loved knowing that I was making him happy. It was a thrill to get naked in the middle of the day in a wide-open field and have sex at fourteen years old; or to do it on the pool table in Alex's basement, with his parents upstairs. It gave me the rush that I longed for. It made me feel wanted and needed and special.

Alex and I often babysat for his cousin's baby. One evening, they wanted to stay out late, so we told them we would spend the night. I made the mistake of telling my mom where I was staying. At midnight, my dad showed up at the door to take me home. I was sleeping on the pullout couch with Alex, in my underwear. I quickly got dressed and answered the door.

"Let's go, Cathy," my dad said.

Reluctantly, I left with him. I insisted that I had done nothing wrong and was just babysitting, but he said it wasn't appropriate for a girl my age to have sleepovers with her boyfriend.

I quit telling my parents the truth after that.

While I was busy hanging out with Alex, Alicia was busy hanging out with guys too. Unfortunately, it wasn't just one guy. When she ended up pregnant at fifteen years old and didn't know who the father was, it turned into a big mess.

"Brandy's older sister has a friend who is going to take me to a clinic somewhere to get this taken care of," Alicia explained.

I was afraid to ask her any details. I wouldn't even know where to start. I knew she was going to get an abortion, but I really didn't understand how any of that worked. I don't think she had any idea either. I wanted to hug her and tell her it was going to be all right, but I really didn't know how she was going to handle it. I was afraid that going through that would make her want to drink and smoke more, to numb the pain.

"You sure about this? I can help you tell your mom if you want," I offered.

"Hell no! She will kill me! Do you think I'm jokin'? She thinks

I'm going to the fucking waterpark for the weekend with Brandy. Don't you dare tell anyone!" Alicia insisted.

Alicia seemed to avoid me after that. I don't know if she was ashamed or just didn't want to be reminded of it or if she didn't trust me to keep a secret, but I didn't say a word—not out loud at least. I prayed for her to be okay. I prayed for her to find forgiveness within herself. I prayed that she wouldn't have to make such difficult decisions ever again. I prayed she would find her truth and make smarter choices from then on.

My praying didn't seem to work, at least not immediately, so I became discouraged. *Maybe life just happens, and you're supposed to just make the most of it, as they say, and party like it's your last day.* I tried to let all those deep thoughts go away, telling myself, *Alicia is a strong girl; she'll be fine.*

The next few years consisted of me being obsessed with "hair" bands, boys, drinking, and smoking. I wanted my entire life to be a party. I idolized rock stars who partied constantly and did whatever they wanted. Brandy and I had dreamed of becoming groupies so that I could marry Tommy Lee and she could marry Bret Michaels.

The song and video "Girls, Girls, Girls" tattooed onto my brain the idea that a woman's body was her biggest asset. I learned to use my body and my sexuality to get what I wanted. I thought of becoming a stripper, but, luckily, my lack of self-esteem prevented me from ever pursuing that.

Later, I was thankful that there were not any strip clubs or tattoo parlors in my town. I'm afraid if I'd had access, I might have made some very regrettable decisions. I'm grateful now to not be covered in overly sexualized tattoos like Bon Jovi's "Slippery When Wet," Poison's "Slide It In" tongue, or the Guns N' Roses album cover of a huge-breasted chick holding a machine gun.

In seventh grade, I had to do a book report on an autobiography.

I chose *Elvis and Me* by Priscilla Presley. It helped solidify the thoughts I had, subconsciously anyway, that sexuality was a tool, a powerful tool. I learned to control my boyfriends with sex, and I was never single. From sixth grade on, I was never more than a few days without a boyfriend, and, eventually, a husband. My friends were always commenting on how my boys adored me and how my boyfriends' friends always wanted me. Unfortunately, that always complicated things. That turned out to be a recurring theme in my reckless, selfish days.

Why could I never be content with what I had? Why did I always long for more? Why wasn't my situation ever good enough? Why couldn't the man who would die for me be enough to keep me interested?

Meanwhile, school was the last thing on my mind. Doing my schoolwork was a rare thing. My parents didn't ask about homework or check to see what assignments I had. I only did the work when it interested me. Like always, I thought of school as social hour. It was a time to hang out with friends and have fun. I didn't struggle with learning; I just didn't care enough to pay attention. This finally came back to bite me in a memorable way in ninth grade.

My counselor explained that the only way I could start high school was to repeat eighth-grade math. This meant I had to shamefully walk over to the junior high every day and redo math with the eighth-graders. There was no hiding it either, because the two buildings were connected, and people in my class saw me walk over there. I got teased hard core.

"Wow, you're so dumb you have to repeat basic math!" one popular kid said really loud as I walked down the hall.

I laughed it off and acted like it didn't bother me.

Ya know what? I'm not dumb, and it doesn't matter what they think. I know what I'm capable of, I thought as I stomped my way up the stairs to the eighth-grade hall.

That gave me pause.

From that day forward, I paid attention and rocked the class. I helped a few cute boys who were struggling in the class, and I used myself as an example of what not to do. I said, "Pay attention! You don't want to be walking up here next year like some white-trash loser who has to repeat the class, do you?"

They thought I was hilarious, and they were so bummed when I passed and went on to ninth-grade math.

That lesson in humility was a hard pill to swallow, but it was good for me. I realized that sometimes I needed to conform and do what was necessary. There were things that I was required to do, so I could either be a loser, or I could be amazing. The outcome was all up to me. If I put in some effort, I could do whatever I set my mind to.

I started to believe the little voice inside me that said I was special and that I was destined to be something amazing, but it took a long time to go from hearing that, to believing that, to actually doing something about it. I had to figure out how to work the system to my advantage.

I had always thought of school as stifling and unnecessary, and following the rules as giving in to authority, but that experience of repeating eighth-grade math helped me to see it in a different light. I started to see it as an opportunity and something within my control. I was still obsessed with boys and having fun, so that idea didn't stay at the forefront for long. But I did make sure I did well enough to not embarrass myself anymore, and I knew that someday I'd be somebody.

Humility

Early in ninth grade, I was no longer into Alex, and he must have felt the same way because he cheated on me. How did I find out? Well, I got crabs!

Yeah, he tried to tell me he got them from work, but I knew better. After he gave me a big bottle of medicine for it, I told him to fuck off. As I coated my body from neck to toes with that sticky crap, I cursed him and told myself I would never let a guy do this to me again!

Then, I moved on. I was interested in seniors—the very cute, popular seniors. Somehow, they wanted me too. In the span of one week, I found myself being hit on by four different guys who were totally hot. It was kind of overwhelming because these were jocks; they were popular guys I had dreamed of being with. To complicate matters, they were friends with my cousins and brother! I thought I was moving into a totally different world.

One of the popular girls in my class burst my bubble, saying, "They just want to sleep with you; they don't actually like you. You're never gonna get a decent boyfriend; you're too much of a slut."

Then, I met Luke. He was a senior, and, somehow, we had home economics together. Before class one day, he and another guy were looking at the *Sports Illustrated Swimsuit Edition.* I distinctly remember Elle Macpherson on her knees, legs spread, wearing a tiny triangle bikini, looking straight into the camera, eyes saying, "I want to be fucked."

I slid in between the two guys as Luke said, "She is the hottest chick ever."

"I'd do her," I said in an attempt to get his attention and interest redirected to me. I knew that guys always liked the idea of two hot chicks getting together, so his response would tell me a lot.

"I'd like to see that," the other guy said.

I wanted more than anything for Luke to have said it. I wanted him to say that I was just as hot as Elle Macpherson, but he just laughed shyly.

That desire to be admired like her made me do something I would soon regret. I wanted to do a photo shoot of myself, so I could see how I compared to those *Sports Illustrated* swimsuit models. I recruited Sophie to be my photographer, but she didn't have a camera, and neither did I.

Here's the dumb part: I borrowed one from Alex, even though we had broken up.

I had Sophie take provocative pictures of me in a few different bathing suits and ripped-up jean shorts. I did the spread-knee pose like Elle, and a few on my bed, squeezing my breasts together like I had seen in *Playboy*. Then, I did a few without a top on, using my sheer, lacy white curtain to cover myself. I thought I was being sexy.

The next day, I was going to take the film to get it developed, but I couldn't find the camera. "Where is that camera?" I huffed.

"Alex stopped by and picked it up. He said that his mom needed her camera back," explained my dad.

I was mortified. I immediately called Alex and begged him to get me the film so that I could get it developed.

"Sorry. My mom already took it in. What are you so worried about?" he asked.

"Nothing. Just tell her not to look at my pictures. I will pay her for mine. Ask her if I can I pick them up for her."

"Yeah, okay," Alex replied flippantly.

I didn't hear from him. A few days later, I was at the gas station during lunch, and a few dirtbags came up to me and told me how hot I was.

One said, "I saw your pictures. You are fucking hot! Can I see the real thing?"

Okay, *now* I was mortified! Alex's mom obviously saw my pictures and gave them to him! He showed my pictures to all his friends (and every other piece of white trash who wanted to see them). I was so pissed, but there was no way in hell I was going to give him or any other dirtbag the satisfaction of knowing it upset and embarrassed me.

"Enjoy, assholes! You wish you could have me!" I said, laughing it off like I couldn't care less.

I told myself to be proud, not ashamed. If they saw me ashamed, it would just give them the power.

I never did get to see my pictures. To this day, I wonder how bad they really looked. In perfect Cathy (Pussy Cat) fashion, I learned my lesson the hard way.

Cathy, the Good Girl

Luckily, Luke didn't hang out with anyone who saw those pictures, so he never heard about it. In fact, he didn't know about me or my past at all. It turned out that he had moved to town a few years earlier, and he wasn't that close to my cousins. I still had a chance to make him mine.

Luke was beautiful, smart, and athletic; he seemed untouchable. He was so far beyond my league that when he asked me out, I almost died. He wanted to go on a date; he didn't act like he just wanted to hook up. I fell head over heels in love. I worshipped him. I thought he was perfection. We spent every minute together until he went to college. Everything I did was to make him happy and keep him loving me. I didn't feel worthy of being his girlfriend, but I was going to pull it off somehow.

I quit partying and stopped hanging out with Brandy and all my white-trash friends. My world revolved around him. I tried to do well in school, only because he wanted me to. I tried my hardest to be the girl I thought he wanted and deserved.

In one sense, this made me a better person; but, in another sense, I was denying who I was. I stifled the real Cathy. I wasn't being who I really was, but maybe that was okay because who I was wasn't working out so great for me.

So, in ninth grade, I went with Luke to his senior prom. I found a gorgeous, form-fitting, white lace dress with spaghetti straps and an asymmetrical hemline in a magazine, and I gave the photo to my mom. I was worried that she would try to tell me I couldn't go to senior prom, but she said nothing about the fact that I was only a freshman. She seemed excited to make me a dress. Somehow, with her amazing talent, she whipped me up that exact dress, but it looked even better. Meanwhile, all the girls in town brought her their cheap mall-store dresses, and she had to alter them to make them fit half as well. I felt so fortunate to have her to make me look so good!

Luke picked me up and brought me to his house, and his parents took pictures of us. He looked great. I couldn't believe I was going to senior prom with Luke, my boyfriend. He took me to a fancy restaurant. I tried a fancy spinach salad for the first time in my life, and I ate the most amazing chocolate mousse for dessert.

The entire experience made me feel so grown up. We went to the dance long enough to make an appearance and dance to our song, "When I See You Smile," by Bad English. Then, he took me to his parents' cabin. He made me stay in the car for a minute, then he came back out and got me. He had placed rose petals all over the bed, lit candles all around the one-room cabin, and had a bottle of champagne with two glasses on the table. Was this real? I felt so special and so loved. I felt like I was in one of those cheap romance novels that had gotten me in so much trouble with Noah.

The next morning, he dropped me off at home. I was worried my parents would be mad, but my mom just asked if I had a good time.

"Yes. He's amazing," I said and went to bed.

After that night, we felt the need to be together as much as possible.

He had made a copy of his parents' cabin keys so that we could go there again. Luke and I spent many weekends at that cabin, just the two of us. I told my mom I was going camping with friends or staying at a friend's house. We usually stopped at the little country mart out there and bought snacks, firewood, and soda to go with the rum he took from his parents' stash. We had long lovemaking fests on a regular basis. We taught each other about romance and intimacy. During those times, I didn't have a care in the world.

Making him feel happy made me feel special and important. It made me feel irreplaceable, and that was what I needed. I think subconsciously I felt like my parents had replaced me with my younger siblings, and that broke my heart. Did I mention my mom just had another baby? Now there were five of us!

I wanted someone to love me so deeply that they couldn't bear to live without me. I had finally achieved that.

We drove down random dirt roads and took walks in the woods, just enjoying nature and our special time together. We carved our initials in a tree and solidified our promise to each other.

A few times, we took a blanket down to the beach by his house and made love under the open sky. Once, his neighbor's dog ran up and caught us in the act. Luckily, by the time his neighbor could see us, I had covered myself up. The dog saved us from too much embarrassment.

We even had sex in the middle of the day on the end of the pier, with boats going by. I loved the thrill and excitement. He sat down on the ledge, and I sat on his lap, facing away from him, and rode him until he finished. We both laughed and quickly put ourselves back together as a fisherman came walking toward us.

Cat in a Cage

When Luke went off to college, we wrote and sent letters every single day, sometimes more than once a day. I quickly had a shoebox filled with letters. Despite our desire to be together, it wasn't feasible. He was playing college hockey, with dreams of being drafted into the NHL. He was going to have to spend all his free time practicing and being on travel teams. I wanted to support him, even though, selfishly, I wanted him to come home and visit me instead.

The longer he was away at college, the more I started partying again with old friends during the week. It quickly got me into trouble because he didn't like that. He didn't want me partying, drinking, smoking, and dancing on cars in the woods.

"How would you ever think that is okay?" he demanded. "You have no business partying, and you sure as hell shouldn't be flaunting yourself around every guy who wants to fuck you!"

That made me feel like I was his property and only he could decide what I could do.

That gave me pause.

I realized I had done something that I wanted to do, and he didn't accept it; to me, that meant he didn't accept me—the real me. He always criticized what I wore and how I behaved. He would say things like, "That shirt makes you look like a slut. Take it off."

I told myself it was for my benefit, so I went along with it. However, it was becoming more difficult because he was at college having cool experiences but expected me to be home and alone, waiting for his call.

A large part of the problem was that I was a very social person, and I enjoyed hanging out with people and having fun. I enjoyed being with him as well, but he was gone now. I was an extrovert, and he was an introvert. He couldn't understand my need to be social, so he wouldn't accept it. I came to resent him and saw him more as a father figure than a boyfriend. I never liked being told what to do—and definitely not by my boyfriend.

So, when the opportunity arose to go swimming with my girl Sophie, her brother, and his friends, I went. To my surprise, my old boyfriend, Noah, who I'd never really gotten over, came with them.

Remember, we never had sex because I cheated on him with Alex before that ever happened. I imagined having sex with Noah would have been a magical connection—maybe because he had been my first real boyfriend, or because I was used to Luke, who was very romantic, slow, and loving, and I figured it could be like that with Noah. So, I made a very poor decision and let Noah drive me home that night; he wanted to show off his new truck.

When he drove me home that night and kissed me in front of my house, I gave in. Oh, how I missed kissing him; it made me forget about everyone else. I wanted what I had screwed myself out of before (yes, pun intended). I encouraged him to drive away and find a place to take me. He drove for a while and pulled over on the side of a dark rode.

He parked his truck and pulled down his pants, then mine. He smashed my legs against my face and the truck window, and, with my pants locking my legs together in front of my face, he fucked me for about two minutes, then was done. He brought my legs down, kissed me, smiled, and put himself back together. Then, he drove me home.

It was the most humiliating, degrading thing that ever

happened to me. He acted all cool and happy. He dropped me off back at home, kissed me, and that was that.

I never cried as hard as I did that night.

Remember, I had Mr. Perfect at college, who was trying to call me, and I wasn't home because I was throwing my relationship away on a promise from my past. Noah used me and threw me away like trash, which I knew that I deserved.

For the longest time that broke my heart because I thought Noah loved me and wanted to love me, not just fuck me like a dog to add to his list.

More importantly, it broke my heart that I ruined my relationship with Luke. I was so conflicted that Luke didn't accept me for me, but now I had just given him good reason to not trust me. It was like I'd dug my own grave and deserved to be thrown into it. I knew I deserved everything that was to come. I felt worthless, and I knew that I didn't deserve Luke; but, damn it, I couldn't lose him. *He is the only part of me that is worth anything, and I cannot lose that, or I will be nothing.*

After I lied through my teeth for weeks and begged and begged, Luke took me back. During that time, he had been asked by a girl named Nicole to go to her prom. He had said yes. He insisted he wasn't going to back out and screw her over like that. The entire ordeal almost killed me.

She was super smart, pretty, and athletic. I had looked up to her for years and now she was getting Luke. He made me suffer over all of that. He told me he would call me after he got home from prom, but I couldn't get a hold of him until the next day. He made me think that he slept with her, just to make me feel how painful that would be. Eventually, it all calmed down.

I knew I wasn't good enough for him, but I desperately tried to be.

I quit partying and vowed to myself never to cheat on him

again. I thought I should be smart like Nicole, because that was obviously what he wanted, so I started trying to do well in school. I tried to behave in all the good and proper ways he wanted me to. I started reading books because she did. I suppressed my rebel free spirit for the next year and kept him mostly happy with my behavior. I was the best girlfriend I could be.

Reading led me to the poet Sylvia Plath, and I became obsessed with her. One day during library time, I picked up this little red hardcover book entitled *The Bell Jar.* The back paragraph told of the author's tormented life and her struggle dealing with depression. It said she committed suicide on February 11, which is my birthday. I slipped *The Bell Jar* into my bag, and that was the last thing I ever stole.

Sylvia described in haunting detail the struggles of her mental illness. Many times while reading it, I thought to myself, *I could end up just like her.* She lived out the same fears I had about my depression escalating to psychoses and being treated unfairly and even against my will. She was locked up and treated with electroshock therapy, against her will. Her story seemed all too possible.

Sylvia Plath spoke to me: to the deepest, darkest part of my soul—my fear. I read her poems and tried to understand how she ended up the way she did, mostly so I could hopefully avoid the same demise. My heart ached for her. She was a strong, independent young lady who wanted to conquer the world, but depression conquered her first. I promised her that I wouldn't let her death be in vain; I vowed to not let my mind succumb to itself in that way.

In my mind, I thanked her many times for writing her story and showing me that I wasn't alone. I kept that book with me wherever I went, like a security blanket. Having Sylvia with me gave me strength.

I took a psychology class during that time. I learned about Pavlov's dogs, Erikson's child-development theories, and Freud's psychoanalysis of dreams and sexuality. We watched *A Clockwork Orange* and talked a lot about mental disorders. I found it fascinating but, at the same time, terrifying.

I had days when I struggled to function. Sometimes I felt so physically sick that I made my dad call the school and let me stay in bed all day. I was just starting to understand that I had depression, that it was an actual illness that I didn't have control over. I feared that it would progress into something uncontrollable, like my aunt Franny's illness had. The more I learned how common depression was, the more I worried.

Once that class was over, I tried to not think about psychology anymore because I didn't like the feeling of living in fear. I wanted to focus on being the best that I could be. I wanted my life to play out differently than the lives of the people I read about. I fought against those feelings of wanting to be alone and not be seen. A few months passed. I emerged from my "funk" and felt ready to conquer the world again.

I made a bet with one of my friends at the beginning of eleventh grade that I could get all A's that semester. It was partly to impress my English teacher, Mr. Cage, whom every girl in school had a crush on. He was the track coach. He had the most beautiful runner body with sun-kissed skin, spiky blonde hair, and a gorgeous smile. Girls joined the track team just to watch him run in his shorts. I wanted to, but I hated the thought of running.

Another reason for making the bet was to show my friends that I could do it; but, more than anything else, I wanted to prove it to myself. I told Mr. Cage my grandiose plan, and he encouraged me all the way.

He gave me the book *The Fall*, by Albert Camus, and made me come in early in the mornings and discuss it with him. At first, I did it to sit and stare at him, but my purpose soon became deeper than that. He challenged me to use my brain and was interested in my potential, not my short skirt. We had discussions like grown-ups, and he treated me like a person whose opinion mattered.

Speaking of short skirts, one day, I wore a short white skirt to school. After class, he said to me in a very nice, respectful way, "Cat, that skirt is not appropriate for school. I know you want to look cute, but you are distracting to others. You are too smart to use your body for attention. Use your mind instead."

If anyone else had said that to me, I would have been pissed and shown up with an even shorter skirt the next day, but, because it was someone I idolized, I took in what he said and was able to see his point of view. What he thought of me mattered, and he was telling me I was smart and had potential. That brought out my little inner voice, who agreed and screamed over and over in my head, "You are smart! You are smart!"

I started to realize that there was more to me than being cute, having fun, and being good in bed.

A Grand Obstacle

Luke came home for Thanksgiving break my junior year, and I was taking antibiotics for strep throat. I was taking birth-control pills, but I found out later that antibiotics sometimes make them less efficacious; that is, they don't work as well. I found that out during Christmas break, when I didn't get a period. Luke and I bought a home pregnancy test, and it was positive.

"Holy shit! We're gonna have a baby? How are we gonna have a baby?" he asked nervously.

We were in shock and scared to death.

I went to the health department, and the nurse confirmed that I was pregnant. She gave me a bunch of information and told me to call the welfare office to apply for Medicaid.

That day changed the course of my future in a big way.

When I got home that night, I was terrified about what to do.

I waited until I was alone with my mom, and then I handed her the Medicaid application form. "Do we qualify for this? Because I'm going to need it."

"Oh, Cathy," she said in the most defeated, disappointed tone. "Your dad is gonna kill you. Yes, I'm sure you'll need to get that." She handed the form back to me, with tears in her eyes.

"You'd better tell him for me," I insisted.

I avoided my dad for days, hoping to let things calm down.

In the meantime, Luke made me go with him to tell his parents.

We sat them down and told them we were going to have a baby. His mom didn't say a word. She stood up and walked straight into her bedroom.

Luke tried to remind his dad that they'd had him at a young age, and everything turned out fine. He explained, "We're going to make sure we do everything we need to do to make it work. I'm going to make it into the NHL, and then we'll be fine, just like you and mom were fine."

His dad turned bright red and yelled, "You think this is fine? You think I wanted to get married that young and work my life away? I never saw your mom. I worked ten hours every day, got home at 2:30 p.m., and she left for work at 3:00 p.m. I took care of you and your sister every night. Our lives are miserable. I don't want that life for you!"

Luke insisted that he was going to take care of everything and figure it all out. The arguing went nowhere, so we left. They didn't speak to us for three months.

I spent the next few months feeling exhausted and nauseated all day long. I ran out of English class almost every morning to throw up. Mr. Cage kept me after class one day and asked me about it. He told me that his wife just had a baby and she was really sick like that. I admitted that I was pregnant. He was understanding and supportive and told me I would get through it.

Finally, I thought. *Someone believes in us.*

Shortly after that, the school counselor met with me to talk about my classes for my senior year. "I heard a rumor that you are pregnant. Is that true?" she asked in a judgmental tone.

"Yes," I answered bluntly.

She became short with me and said, "Well, in that case, I don't think it's a good idea for you to continue with school. You'll start to show soon, and we don't want other girls seeing you and thinking it's okay to be pregnant."

I took a minute and thought to myself. *I have never done what authority told me to do, why the hell would I start now?*

So, I asked, "Are you kicking me out?"

"No."

"Well, then, I'm not going anywhere. I will show you and all the girls in this school that it is okay if you get pregnant. This is not ruining my life, and you certainly aren't going to tell me what to do about it," I said as politely as I could with major attitude, and left.

At that point, I became very focused. I was tired of people not believing in me and not supporting me. Getting pregnant was a surprise, but, by far, it was not the end of the world. I had dreamed of marrying Luke from the day I met him, because he was so beautiful and perfect, so having his baby was an exciting thought.

A few weeks later, he came home again, so we could brainstorm on how to keep him playing hockey, stay together, and raise our child. I suggested we get married, saying, "We are going to get married eventually, so why not now?"

Luke hesitated, then he tried to act all excited about what he was about to say. "Cat, I've been offered to play for a minor league in Canada. It will be really good exposure for me. It will be good for us."

"Wow! You're gonna move away when we're having a baby? Who's gonna help me?"

"I will be here for you, and, eventually, you can come be with me. I promise."

"Okay, I guess. I'm happy for you, Luke."

What else could I say? I just took in the idea and tried to stay positive and believe in us.

By this time, my mom had accepted the fact that I was pregnant and that my baby would only be two years older than my newest little brother.

Remembering her own mother's situation, she joked, "Thank

God your father got snipped. It wouldn't be good if I had a baby after you. I'd turn into your grandma Robbins."

I told her about my desire to get married, and she got excited and told me that she would make me a wedding dress. "Something like a white satin tea-length skirt and a fancy blouse with a peplum to go over your bump. I made my wedding dress when I married your dad, and it was short. It was adorable."

"Stop, Mom! He doesn't want to get married. He's gonna move to Canada and play in the minors. I'm supposed to be excited for him—and us!" I yelled at her, then started crying.

She just hugged me.

I felt something bump my belly. "What the heck?" I said, looking at her.

"That's your baby, Cathy. I guess he wanted to be in on the hug," my mom replied, laughing.

It was amazing. I could feel this life growing inside me. I realized that I loved the baby growing inside me more than I could possibly express.

I started writing letters to the baby and seeking God, asking Him to come back into my life:

What's in My Heart

I feel so much unconditional love for a child that I haven't even met. God, You have put this totally dependent little body inside me, with a soul all its own; a child that is half me and half the man that I love. Soon, this child will have to leave its safe, predictable, nurturing world to bless everyone with his or her softness and innocence. Our helpless little child will come into this world—an unsafe, unpredictable world—frightened and cold, yearning for the warm, comforting feeling of my womb and the continuous beating of my heart. Luke and I will take one look at this perfect gift and wonder what we ever did to deserve such a miracle. All the undying love I feel for Luke will shine all over my face, and to my love will be added this instant love for our new baby and our brand-new family. I couldn't be more excited to share with Luke this little baby that has brought out the love in me that I so strongly feel for him. I realize more and more every day how wonderful Luke is and how much I have grown to love him, cherish him, respect him, and trust him. It shouldn't take a gift from God for me to realize the extent of my love for this man, but it did. And now that I'm aware of how powerful these feelings are, I will never for one minute forget. I hope Luke will be as happy with his new little family as I am now just thinking about it. I will do my very best to make sure our baby is always happy and feels loved by both of us. I will never let anything ruin what Luke and I have together, and I will try to remember that love has no room for jealousy and accusations.

Dear God, please guide me through this life and help me make all the right decisions that are good for me and, most importantly, my family. If I do one thing right in this lifetime, that will be loving Luke and our child (or children) unconditionally! All I pray for now is that Luke and I have a totally healthy baby boy or girl real soon.

Patiently waiting,

Catherine Jansen

I wanted to thank God and ask for His protection and strength to help me do this. I felt His presence in my life, and that gave me the confidence to do what I needed to do despite my lack of preparation.

I finished out my junior year of high school proudly showing off my growing belly and kicking ass in my classes, not that they were all that difficult. The only science class I took was a basic biology class. Inside the classroom, Mr. Richards had a little office at the end of a long desk that we weren't allowed to go behind. Rumor was that his coffee cup had whiskey in it and that he was always drunk, because he sat in his office the entire hour. The class was a free-for-all. That was when I usually wrote notes to Luke.

Anyway, I did my homework each night as I lay in bed, feeling my baby kick and move inside of me. I talked to my baby and made promises that I intended to keep: "I will do everything I need to do to make sure you have better opportunities than I did. You will always be my priority. I already love you unconditionally and will make you proud!"

Once spring came, Luke had to move to Canada to start training with his new team. He made enough money to live on and send me small amounts now and then. I was working at my dad's pizza shop, with the hopes of saving enough money to move out. I also got food stamps and food from WIC.

I was on Medicaid for insurance coverage during my pregnancy. It was the first time I ever had insurance. Because my parents were self-employed, we never had insurance. I was assigned to an old, male family-practice doctor who was on the verge of retirement, but he delivered babies, so he became my doctor. When I went to my appointments, he and his office staff made me feel so ashamed. They made it clear that taking care of me was an inconvenience because they got paid pennies on the dollar for Medicaid patients.

They also made it clear that they didn't approve of my situation, and they talked down to me like I was white trash.

I held my head high and killed them with kindness. I was trying to find my voice, and I vowed to prove to everyone that I was worthy. I vowed to be grateful to the people who helped me, whether they wanted to or not.

The Birth of Mother Catherine

I tried to be the best pregnant patient I could. I ate as healthy as I could and took prenatal vitamins every day. I went to every appointment and did everything the doctor recommended. I lay on my left side, did my Kegels, and walked every day for exercise. I took Lamaze classes and planned to breast-feed. I read every book about pregnancy that I could get my hands on.

Most importantly, I started going to church again. (I had quit going in junior high. Luke's family also went to St. Patrick's, but they usually only went on Christmas and Easter.)

By the time summer was over, and I had survived the August heat with my huge belly, I was ready to have that baby. I completely believed that I was having a boy. We didn't get to find out the sex, and, for some reason, I assumed it was a boy. I never even thought of any girls' names.

My due date came and went. I saw Dr. Griffin at forty-one weeks, and he said I could be induced the following Monday.

That Saturday morning, two days before I was supposed to go in, I felt a gush of fluid while lying in bed. I looked at the sheets, which were white with tiny yellow flowers all over, and saw a big green circle. "Mom, my water broke! And it's green! I think the baby has that meconium stuff."

I called Luke. "Guess what? We're having a baby! Please figure out a way to get here, like soon!"

"I'll do my best. Do you think he's coming today? I might not be able to get there until tomorrow," he said.

"I don't know; just make it happen. I love you, daddy-to-be!" I grinned with excitement.

"I will. I love you too," he assured me.

I was all smiles when I got to the hospital that afternoon. I had an ultrasound done to see if the baby had any fluid left and make sure he was head down. I had a lot of blood drawn and sat in bed hooked to monitors all day, doing nothing.

By the next morning, my cervix still hadn't dilated, so they gave me Pitocin in my IV. I finally started having contractions. By that afternoon, I was crying in pain. My entire body was shaking uncontrollably, but I tried to sit through receiving an epidural. I didn't feel any relief; instead, I became nauseated and vomited many times. I insisted that it didn't work, and I cried with every contraction.

My mom had left to take care of my siblings, but she finally came back. She wiped my forehead with a wet rag and helped me calm down. "You need to hold off having this baby until tomorrow because that would have been your great-grandma Holliday's nine-tieth birthday," my mom said, not really joking.

My great-grandma Holliday had just passed away two months before, so she knew I was pregnant and was very happy for me.

"Do you hate me? I don't want to keep doing this till tomorrow! This baby needs to come out already!" I insisted.

Then, I started asking for a new epidural, so the nurse game me some IV medication, which made me groggy. Sometime early Monday morning, the medicine wore off, and my contractions be-came unbearable.

I had the sweetest nurse named Maria. She checked me and said, "You're finally dilated to ten centimeters. You can push the baby out now."

She taught me how to push. She draped my legs over some stirrup holders and gave me handles attached to the bed to hold on to. I got to the point where I couldn't even think straight because the pain was so horrendous.

I spent the next three hours pushing with every contraction. I would push for a count of ten three times with each contraction, and this went on every two minutes for what felt like eternity. I was so exhausted that by the third hour I was literally falling asleep after each contraction, only to be woken up by the urge to push. I pushed out so much poop that they put the garbage can under my butt.

"How can he not be coming out? I'm pushing so hard!" I cried desperately.

All of a sudden, the nurse urged me to get up on my hands and knees because my baby was not doing well.

I was crying and begging for a C-section. "Please, please just cut me! I want my baby to be okay! It hurts so much, and he's not coming out!"

I didn't realize until years later that Dr. Griffin couldn't perform C-sections because he wasn't an obstetrician, so that wasn't really an option.

Dr. Griffin finally came in and made me turn back over. He said sternly, "Now listen, I need you to be quiet and do what I say, okay?"

"Why?" I replied, feeling very scared.

He didn't answer.

I felt very cold metal being pushed into my vagina, then the most excruciating burning pain imaginable ripped from my vagina through to my ass.

Clang! Clang! went the metal forceps as they hit the cold tile floor at 4:19 a.m.

That noise sent shivers up and down my spine, and still haunts me to this day.

And just like that, my baby was whisked to the warmer and dried off. I heard a faint whimper, then a pathetic attempt at a cry. It was the most beautiful, relieving sound ever. My mom was audiotaping the last few minutes for Luke, and it recorded me begging for the pain to stop, then me professing my love to my new baby, and, finally, crying tears of joy.

I watched the nurse take care of my baby while I endured more torture.

"It's a girl!" my mom called to me in complete surprise. "And she's perfect!"

"A girl? What?" I asked, exhausted and confused.

"Yes!" Nurse Maria exclaimed. "And she's a stinker. She came out stargazing; that's why she wouldn't fit. Watch out, 'cuz she's gonna be a dreamer!"

Then, without warning, I felt a horrible stinging pain shoot into my vulva. "Oh my God! What was that?" I cried.

"I'm numbing you up; sit still," warned Dr. Griffin.

Fuck! I screamed in my head.

He repeated that five or six more times. I couldn't decide which was more painful: the birth or the repair. I had a fourth-degree tear, meaning that I tore completely through my vagina and perineum into my anus. He struggled to sew me back up, and it seemed to take forever.

I couldn't sit upright for days. I had to take stool softeners so my ass wouldn't tear back open. I couldn't wipe; I had to squirt the area with a water bottle, then gently pat dry. I had to stick witch hazel pads in my butt and wear huge Peri-Pads for the next six weeks. I bled and bled and bled. I passed such huge clots that they slid off right past the pad, without being absorbed. I was a mess. Never mind me, though; I had a baby to take care of.

Luke finally arrived, and he was in love. He loved his little daughter the way a father should. He just stared at her in awe. He apologized profusely to me for missing her birth, but when I saw how he felt about her, I realized that there was nothing to forgive. I felt like a family. This man had made me a mother. I was no longer Crabby Cathy or Pussy Cat. I was Mother Catherine, the most important title in the world.

For two days, our beautiful baby girl had no name. We couldn't leave the hospital until we came up with something. Well, it turned out that my mom got her way. She was born on my great-grandmother Holliday's birthday, so I wanted to use her name somehow. My favorite cousin, Jessica, had the middle name of Holliday, and my mom suggested I do the same. Luke's Grandma Delilah had passed away many years ago, but he loved her dearly and asked if we could name our baby after her.

We finally came up with Delilah Holliday, daughter to her seventeen-year-old mom and twenty-year-old dad. What a blessing.

So, let me just tell you—breast-feeding proved to be more difficult than I imagined. Some people told me, "It will be the best thing for both of you" and "It's natural, so it's much easier than bottle-feeding." They were full of shit!

Then, I had to deal with Luke's mother and grandmother. They did not support the idea at all. They whined, "How are *we* supposed to feed the baby and bond with her if you always breast-feed her?"

That made me all the more determined to do it.

Well, my first attempt was mortifying. I tried to put my baby to my nipple and get her to open her mouth, but, instead, she screamed and cried and thrashed around in my arms.

The day-shift nurse finally came in to help. She was a crotchety, gray-haired old lady who didn't even talk to me. She grabbed my boob, grabbed the baby's head, and smashed them together. She yanked on my nipple so hard, I started crying. She told me sternly, "That's how you have to do it, so you'd better figure it out."

Well, I couldn't figure it out, so I called my mom. She was my savior. She showed me how to get the baby to latch on, without humiliating me or hurting me like that crotchety, old nurse had. The baby finally latched and quit crying. I felt a strong pulling sensation from my nipple up to my clavicle. I prayed she wouldn't stop, for fear I would have to go through that hell again with the nurse. Well, she did stop, and I burped her. Two hours later, we went through the same misery again.

More than anything, I wanted to be a great mom. I knew that breast-feeding was the healthiest thing for her and that it was good for her development to have all that bonding time and physical interaction.

The next day, my favorite nurse, Maria, was back, and we had a great day. She taught Luke how to change a diaper and swaddle the baby, and she made sure I had breast-feeding figured out.

I then felt confident that we could go home and be parents.

My Voice

I was off work for the next six weeks, and Luke had eight weeks off before he had to go back to prepare for hockey season. I tried not to worry about how I would handle Delilah on my own; I just enjoyed every day that the three of us had together. I wrote in her baby book every day and documented her every move. Luke kind of seemed like he wanted to be involved, but, more than anything, he was preoccupied with working out and getting back to Canada for season preparation. I felt us not connecting, but I was so exhausted and preoccupied with Delilah that I didn't give it much thought at the time.

Dr. Griffin was now Delilah's doctor as well. When I took her in for her checkup, he said she was doing great, but he told me that we needed to get me birth control and make sure I didn't get pregnant again.

I agreed.

We didn't have any sort of discussion about birth-control options. He did a speculum exam and said to the nurse, "She needs a seventy millimeter," as he walked out.

"I need a what? Am I okay?" I asked the nurse.

"Yep, honey. You just need a diaphragm so we don't have another teenage pregnancy on our hands," she explained as she pulled one out of the drawer.

She showed me how to use it, clean it, and check it for holes.

I figured I could use it, but, man, that seemed like a lot of effort. And, it turned out, it was. Having sex was a huge ordeal for a while; using the diaphragm was cumbersome, and I didn't have time for that—but, you'd better believe I made time.

Meanwhile, I was struggling with body-image issues. My body had changed so much from being pregnant and nursing, and I was mortified. I started out at 104 pounds, with perfect skin, nice boobs, and a cute butt that everyone liked. I gained fifty pounds during my pregnancy, despite doing everything right.

I lay in bed one morning and took my bra flap down to nurse Delilah; all I could see were bright-purple stretch marks all over my boobs. My butt was even worse. I broke down crying to Luke, devastated that my body was ruined. I felt guilty for being vain, but I kept thinking, *I'm only seventeen years old, and my body looks worse than my grandma's! I can't live like this. I never want Luke to see my body again.*

That struggle worsened because of the shows he watched: *Baywatch, Jerry Springer,* and *Married with Children.* Pamela Anderson, with her huge fake boobs and long blonde hair, was the most desired woman in America. Her unrealistic, over-the-top look was what I thought I had to look like to be beautiful.

Those shows always had beautiful, sexy women with barely any clothes on. I internalized that to mean Luke wanted me to look like them. The more he watched, the more I became obsessed. I made it clear that it upset me, but he insisted he wasn't watching it because of the slutty girls and that he wasn't interested in them.

I wasn't hearing that. I didn't believe him, mostly because I thought I looked hideous. How could he not see what I saw? I insisted he was lying to appease me. Even though I exercised daily and breast-fed and got back down to 105 pounds, all I saw were ugly scars, cellulite, and imperfections. I only see him watching gorgeous women while I sat there physically destroyed. Just as I was feeling my lowest, Luke had to leave. The loneliness was unbearable. I needed to get out of my body, out of my mind, out of that house. I was mentally torturing myself.

Soon after, my old friend Alicia called. "I want to come see your baby. I miss you, Cat."

"I would love to hang out. We haven't seen each other in forever," I said, feeling somewhat alive again.

I was excited by the idea of having a friend again. I was such a social person, but, somehow, I now found myself completely isolated and alone.

It turned out that Alicia wanted to show me her new boobs. She had gotten implants, which was a big deal because this was 1990, and we lived in a small town. I was already struggling with my ruined body, tormenting myself about Luke watching *Married with Children* and *Baywatch* and then leaving for five months, and comparing myself to Pamela Anderson, whom I saw as the epitome of beauty.

"I'm kind of nervous about what people are gonna say, but I look hot, don't I?" Alicia asked.

"Yes, you look great. If people say something, they are just jealous. Tell them to screw off!" I joked.

She stayed for a bit and filled me in on the latest gossip at school, but she never asked to hold Delilah. When I offered, she became uncomfortable and said she had to get going. I realized that she was probably thinking about the baby she ended up not having and didn't want to deal with those thoughts. I couldn't blame her, so I didn't force the issue. I was glad that she was trying to be happy, but, man, was I jealous. What an ugly feeling to have toward someone you care about. It's quite screwed up when you really think about it.

So, instead of obsessing over Alicia's new boobs, I tried to focus on Delilah and told myself that having her was worth ruining my body, worth losing my sex appeal, worth having to push on my vagina for the poop to come out right, worth never being able to wear a bathing suit again, and worth the shame of never wanting to share my body with Luke again.

I felt alone. I had no one to talk to. I told myself that I couldn't talk to Alicia because she couldn't possibly understand. My other friends were busy getting their senior pictures done, being asked to prom, applying to colleges, and having fun. Any way I thought about it, I felt alone. The only one I had to talk to was God. I sought out comfort and acceptance within myself through reading the Bible, and I felt strongly that Delilah needed to be baptized. I wanted her to have forgiveness of her sins and the strength of Jesus to guide her as she grew.

Because we belonged to the Catholic church, we had a lot of hoops to get through to make that happen. Luckily, Luke and I both had made confirmation, but our monsignor told us that we needed to get married in the church in order for Delilah to be eligible for baptism. Somehow, I talked Luke into getting married after hockey season ended. I think he liked the idea of having something to come home to. I think he was homesick. Because he was such an introvert, he didn't love going out to the bars after the games, and I gave him so much grief because of my insecurities that he said it wasn't even worth going.

In order to get married in our church, we had to endure many evening hours of relationship classes taught by the nuns, of all people. All the other couples in the class were much older, and everyone was amazed by our maturity and willingness to do the right thing. Overall, I think it strengthened us because we took the time to focus on our relationship and creating a family.

The day came when Monsignor performed a simple ceremony at St. Patrick's to bind us in holy matrimony. I wore my white lace prom dress from almost three years before, and my mom made Delilah a beautiful baptism dress. I called my old friend, Charlie, and she came to the wedding. She was so excited for me that she insisted on being my witness and signing our marriage license. That was pretty special. Despite Luke's parents' lack of church involvement, they insisted on being Delilah's godparents. I knew my mom would have been a more appropriate choice to give my child spiritual guidance, but it wasn't about that. It was about appeasing my new mother-in-law. It was about appearances and titles. I knew my mother wouldn't be offended, so I went with it. I wasn't about to sweat the small stuff. I learned to pick my battles and give others what they needed, even if I did not necessarily agree with it. It was okay, because I felt blessed and happy that day. God was giving me a big hug of forgiveness and acceptance.

Shortly after that, my mom had to sell her building and move her business home. She couldn't afford it anymore, and she couldn't handle the hassle of it all while taking care of young kids, so I had to move out of the house. Luke had to leave for Canada again soon, but his parents were nice enough to let Delilah and me stay in his old bedroom. It was very generous of them, but they only agreed if I used my food stamps to buy their groceries. I thought that was a fair trade, and I planned to only be there a very short time.

Luke's mother acted very loving, but she definitely had a hard time letting me be the mother. She constantly questioned my breast-feeding and insinuated that Delilah was still hungry or not getting enough. (She was growing perfectly and was as happy as could be). Living there taught me so much about compromising, keeping my mouth shut, and learning to be patient, understanding, and grateful. His parents drank way too much, and they had a very dysfunctional relationship. I often got pulled into the middle of it, but they loved Delilah more than anything, so I put up with it. I tried to always do the dishes, do the laundry, and clean the house, but they still acted very put out.

I hated doing the grocery shopping. Once, I went shopping and got the WIC food—cereal, milk, and peanut butter—then used food stamps for the rest.

One of my old classmates was the cashier. "Wow, it looks like you're doing really well for yourself, Cathy," she said in a sarcastic, snotty voice.

"Thanks for being so supportive," I snapped.

"Are you ever gonna come back to school? I would hate for you to be a dropout and not graduate," she jabbed.

"I'm sure you really give a shit. Actually, don't worry about me; I'm gonna be just fine," I said, using the best badass tone I could muster.

I walked out to my car, with Delilah and groceries in hand, feeling ashamed.

That day, I vowed aloud to myself and to Delilah, "Someday I will make so much money and pay so much in taxes that I'll pay back what I used in food stamps twenty times over!"

When I got home, I told my father-in-law what my former classmate had said.

He told me to never feel bad about getting help from the government. "We've paid taxes for twenty years, so if my kids need help for a bit, then they should get it! Don't even worry about it. You know it's temporary. Luke is gonna get into the NHL, and you guys will be fine."

I realized then that I needed to figure out a future for myself and my child. The thought of relying on Luke and the remote possibility of him getting drafted into the NHL in order for me to have a future was scary. I have always been independent and never relied on anyone. I needed to figure out how to take care of myself and Delilah. *What if Luke doesn't make it? Where will we be? I'll be a high-school dropout with no future.*

I needed to go back and do twelfth grade. I called my old high school, but they told me it was too late and that I needed to get a

GED. After some searching, I found out that I had to take some classes through winter and spring, then pass some tests.

So, I drove to a nearby town three evenings a week in the snow and blizzards and sat through classes with a lot of different people. Some were much older than I was, with kids my age. Most of them would take smoke breaks and complain about how hard the tests were going to be. I listened to their stories about how they had ended up in their situations, and I realized that I was going to be okay if I just kept working at it. Many of them had lost a lot of years to partying, alcohol, or just surviving and raising their kids.

I vowed I was going to get my GED while I was still young enough to do something with my life.

The people in my GED class had hard lives, but they showed me empathy and encouraged me to do what they had waited too long to do. I really appreciated getting to know them.

I passed the tests and finally got my GED. *Now what? I guess I have to go to college*, I thought.

It turned out that I needed to take the ACT, which was not that easy. I took a practice ACT test and couldn't even finish it. I had no idea what some of the questions were even about. Here are two examples: What are tangent, sine, and cosine? How are pressure and volume affected by changes in temperature?

Luckily, by that point, I had learned how to graciously ask people for help. I realized I was going to need help if I wanted to take the ACT and do well, so I went and talked to my high-school teacher, Mrs. Diebold. She spent many after-school hours teaching me college-prep math—the math that I should have learned in high school, when I was too busy talking in class to pay attention.

That gave me pause.

What a gift Mrs. Diebold gave me, and she didn't have to. Actually, I didn't deserve her time at all, but she gave it to me without hesitation. She gave me a second chance and believed in me. She said, "I know what you're capable of. Now you're ready to do it, so of course I will help you."

I am forever grateful to all my teachers.

I did great on the ACT and applied to all the surrounding universities because I had no idea where I was going to end up needing to go. Luke was being scouted, and there was a good chance he was going to get to play in the states, closer to home. The day I got my first response from one of the universities, I opened it in front of my mother-in-law.

It read, "Congratulations! You have been accepted on a trial basis for the incoming fall semester."

I was so proud that I cried.

Her response felt like a knife stabbing my heart. "You guys can't take Delilah that far away from us."

She didn't say "congrats" or "good job" or "I'm proud of you; that's amazing." She was only concerned about herself.

I didn't let that break my spirit.

I thought, *I'm going to college, and I'm going to make something of myself. And no one is going to stop me, especially not my in-laws.*

I wasn't content with the idea that Luke was going to make something of himself and then just take care of us. I didn't like the idea of relying on another person for my entire life.

My little voice inside reminded me that I was smart and special and worthy. "You are going to make something of yourself. You are going to take care of people instead of them taking care of you."

Lost and Lonely

While Luke was in Canada, I stayed home with Delilah during the day, cooking, cleaning, and being the best mom I could be. In the evenings, I worked at the pizza shop. That was a difficult year for me because I worked with young people around my age whose circumstances were nothing like mine. They were taking college classes and partying on the weekends. They were dating and enjoying their freedom, whereas I was eighteen, married, raising a child, and running a household. I was cutting coupons and planning meals for the week on a tight budget. In contrast, they were going out to eat and worrying about what outfit to wear to a party or what subwoofers to buy for their car.

When I first started talking to people at work, they would say, "No way! How do you have a one-year old kid and a husband? I can't even imagine! I can't even take care of myself!" and "I don't envy you!" and "How are you ever going to get through college? I can barely pass my classes, and I don't have a kid to take care of."

Those conversations scared me into thinking I wasn't going to be able to make something of myself—that I would support Luke and help him be successful, but then I would end up with nothing. I felt powerless, alone, and cheated. I felt robbed of my youth, my freedom, my beauty, and my future.

I wanted so desperately to feel young and beautiful again that I sought out attention from guys. I was attracted to a guy named

Marcus, and I found myself seeking not only his attention but also the thrill of getting away with something, just like I had when I was younger. That led to me cheating on Luke and stealing money from him, my own husband, to buy Marcus stuff.

I lied and said I was going to the library, when, instead, I met Marcus to have sex in his car in broad daylight. I went to a party at his house one weekend, and we had sex in his bedroom. Everyone there knew I was married, but I didn't let that stop me. I should have been too ashamed to show my face, but I was focused on the excitement of getting away with something and enjoying the attention from Marcus.

I never took off my padded bra because I was too ashamed of my saggy, scarred, deflated breasts. I dreamed of getting implants and exercised every day to at least make my stomach, legs, and ass as sexy as possible in clothes. I bought a bathing suit, with the crazy idea that I would go into Marcus's hot tub, but my stretch marks continued past my chest and butt. I was too disgusted with myself to ever wear it and decided that there was no way I would ever go into that hot tub. I threw the suit away and avoided wearing a swimsuit altogether for the next five years.

It was such a painful time because Luke knew I was up to something. He was living in Canada and busy trying to get drafted into the NHL; plus, I don't think he wanted to face the painful truth, so he chose to believe my lies. What I was doing to him was unforgivable, but when he came home for a two-week break, I turned it all around on him. I was cleaning the bathroom and under the cabinet drawer I found a *Playboy* magazine. On the cover, huge boobs spilled out of Anna Nicole's dress. I completely lost it and went wild with anger. I tore the magazine into a thousand little pieces and wrote all over the bathroom mirror with red marker, "Go to hell, you piece of shit!" and "Die, you lying motherfucker!"

I told myself over and over, *Luke lied to me, just like I insisted all those times. He is obsessed with those sluts with the big fake boobs and perfect asses, everything hanging out of their low-cut tops and short skirts. He wants their bodies, not mine. He isn't attracted to me, the one who gave up everything to have his child!*

I resented him for getting to have all the wonderful aspects of having a baby, while I was stuck with all the scars and work and pain. I told myself that his life wasn't negatively affected in anyway. He was still playing hockey and living out his dreams; he still had a perfect body and didn't have to live in shame. He still felt like a twenty-year-old, while I felt like a fifty-year-old.

The rage I felt that day was dangerous. I wanted to hurt Luke the way I thought he was hurting me. Unfairly, I blamed him for my pain. I blamed him for making me seek out attention and love elsewhere.

Once again, Luke reassured me that I was wrong and forgave my behavior.

The irony was that I was cheating on him and ultimately hurting him, myself, and our family more than any magazine or TV show ever could, but that wasn't how I saw it. It took a long time for me to realize that he didn't rob me of anything. I robbed myself by caring about superficial things and focusing on what I didn't have instead of what I did have.

I was so alone and broken, and there I was, trying to raise my baby girl and give her everything I didn't have. I hated myself more and more every day. I prayed to God and begged Him to fix me. I prayed for the days to go by quickly so that I could go to college and start over. "Dear Lord, I don't want to hurt Luke. Please give me another chance to do it right. Give me the strength to be the wife and mother I need to be and to not care about such superficial crap. Take away my desire for freedom and the thrills of sin. Why can't I be happy, Dear Lord? Why can't I just accept the fact that my body is ruined? Please, please help me to stop caring about that. Please help me find happiness and contentment."

I cried and prayed often, but I just couldn't stop myself.

The Price of Chance

I then decided that the time had come for to go to college. I wanted to impress people with my brain instead of my body. I wanted to start fresh and be a good wife and mother. I ended it with Marcus. I was so relieved that I no longer had to go on living a lie, but I felt so alone. Luke got drafted to another minor league team. This one was close to the university, so we decided we could make it work. The move distracted me, and I refocused my feelings back to Luke. We were a team, and I needed to be faithful and trust him to take care of us while I started my new adventure.

Quietly, I kept pondering my issues: *Why do I have such a deep need for approval and attention from other people, often strangers? Why can't I accept myself for who I am and what I look like? Why am I not good enough? Why can't I ever just be satisfied with who I am and what I have?*

I heard my mother's voice in my head, saying all that to me so many years ago. It was fifteen years later, and I was no better than I'd been then. I felt ashamed of my failures and my inability to get my shit together and act like a grown woman.

When moving day came, Luke's parents were very upset, but they helped us pack up a U-Haul and drive to our new place. We got a family-housing apartment on campus. It was on the fifteenth floor, at the end of a narrow hallway. The smell of curry overpowered the senses as soon as you walked in from the street. We needed keys to open the entrance, to ride the elevator, and to get into our apartment. (It was a little scary, since my parents never even locked the house when I was growing up.) Moving in was a huge feat, especially because of Luke's heavy workout weights and equipment.

His dad pointed out, "There ain't any white people livin' in the building. All I see are Arabs and black people."

I was thoroughly embarrassed, but I ignored him. I was actually excited about the diversity. I wanted to meet new people and experience new cultures. I was more than ready to be away from our sheltered, all-white little town.

His parents were beside themselves when they left us there. "How can we possibly let you two raise Delilah in this place? There's nowhere for her to run around and play. This is no way for her to live!" his mom cried.

"She is a baby. We will make sure she's happy and has everything she needs. This is the best thing for her," I replied.

The next day, I went to orientation and all the kids were fresh out of high school, talking about partying and their newfound freedom. There I was, married and a mom with a one-year-old.

They all responded to me with disbelief. "No way!" or "You had a baby?" or "I can't even imagine having a boyfriend, let alone a husband. How are possibly doing this?"

These reactions were totally different from the ones I got at the pizza shop. This time, I was seen as impressive, someone to look up to; they knew college was going to be tough for them, so it would be even more so for me. This time, when I met people who talked about partying and their newfound freedom, I didn't feel like I was missing out; I had focus and purpose in my life, and it felt good.

I was really looking forward to starting my classes, but then something horrible happened. I expected Luke home around midnight, after his game, so when 12:30 rolled around, I got worried. We didn't have a phone yet, so I couldn't call anyone. As I sat there in our unfamiliar new apartment, watching our baby sleep soundly, my mind started racing. I went from horrible thoughts of him getting hurt, to him out partying and making out with some slut. It was almost too much to bear. Finally, around 2:00 a.m., one of his teammates came to our apartment, buzzing for me to let him in.

He explained that Luke had been carjacked. Luke's friend was going to take me to the hospital to be with Luke. Luke's friend calmed me down and took care of everything, saying, "We can take Delilah to my house. My mom is great with kids, and she can stay there while we go to the hospital."

We got to a huge hospital about an hour later, and poor Luke was still in the waiting room, blood spattered over his shirt, his hand wrapped up in a bloody rag.

He told me that, after the game, he had walked down to a nearby parking lot, and when he went to get into his car, a guy attacked him. "All of a sudden, I felt a knife pushing into my back, and some guy told me not to move or he'd kill me. All I could think of was you and Delilah. My whole life flashed before my eyes. I swung around and tried to fight the guy. He slashed at my hand. I dropped the keys. He grabbed them and took off with the car. Two of my fingers got cut halfway off, and I'm waiting to see a hand surgeon to see if he can save them."

I was in shock, but I was so grateful that he was okay.

"Are you crazy? You could've been killed! I'm so thankful you are okay!" I responded, hugging and holding him.

His coach showed up at the hospital to check on him. "This never happens here. I just can't even believe it."

He then reassured Luke that he wouldn't lose his spot on the team. "We will be here when you are ready to come back; do what you need to do so you can play again."

"I just don't even know. I don't know if I'll even be able to hold my stick. What if my hand is ruined? What if I can never play hockey again?" Luke said in complete despair.

"Let's not jump to the worst, hon. You're gonna be fine. The doctor will fix you up, and you'll do what you need to do to get back to playing. You got this!" I reassured him.

I could tell he wasn't hearing me.

The coach sensed it too. "I'll check on you tomorrow. Hang in there, buddy."

By the time Luke was out of surgery the next morning, his parents had arrived.

"We told you guys, this is no place to live. You don't belong here. We're getting a U-Haul and getting you out of here as soon as they discharge you," his dad insisted.

They both demanded that we come back home.

Luke agreed without any discussion.

I didn't want to leave, but I needed to support my husband. So, we dredged all those heavy weights, the baby stuff, and our furniture back down to another truck, picked up Delilah, and drove back home.

Now what? I wondered.

I was supposed to start school the following week. I was about to go to my first college class, and now we were back living in Luke's parents' house.

Luke was not sleeping; he was having nightmares about what happened. He became scared of every little thing and constantly worried about one of us getting killed.

That event changed him. It changed our relationship.

He wanted to buy a gun. He didn't want to go anywhere, and he didn't want to play hockey.

His fear led him into a dark place, and we fought constantly. He talked about not seeing any point in living in such a horrible world. One night, he acted on it; he took all the pills he could find in his parents' bathroom. When I found him a short time later, he was barely responsive and refused to tell me what he had taken. His dad rushed him to the hospital, and they pumped his stomach and saved him. He was admitted for observation and had a psych evaluation.

How did it turn out to be him in this situation and not me? I thought to myself.

When he was released, he was forced to go for counseling.

Later, he told me that Alicia had visited him when he was in the hospital.

At first, I was upset and jealous. But then he explained that she'd told him she had tried to commit suicide recently and could relate to what he was going through. Apparently, she'd just had a baby and gotten married, but they were already talking about divorce because he was cheating on her. She told Luke that she didn't feel like a loving mom and was trying to figure out what was wrong with her. She'd heard what happened to Luke and just wanted to be there for him.

"She was talking really fast. She was all hyped up and didn't make a lot of sense, but it was nice of her to come see me, ya know," Luke said.

I thought it was a little strange that she didn't reach out to me, since I was once her best friend. She and Luke had never been close, but I tried to tell myself that it was good for him to have someone. I didn't call her because, obviously, she didn't want to talk to me about her issues. I felt really bad for her, though. I had always worried about her mental health because of having an abortion at such a young age and not talking about it.

I soon regretted not calling her.

Alicia killed herself in her living room: gunshot to the head. As soon as I heard, I ran over there. Her living room had a large picture window, and you could see right into her house. I stood across the street and watched as the police taped off the house like a crime scene and then took pictures of her—brains splattered all over the living room walls and ceiling. The next day, I returned to watch as people cleaned up her remains off the ceiling. My heart was broken for her and her family.

All my sorrow and heartache and confusion made me want to go back to church, so I decided to go that Sunday and talked Luke into going with me. I needed God to help me understand why people hurt each other, why they give up, why they feel the need to end their lives, why some live and some die.

My heart ached for Alicia's family, whom I watched across the pews as they cried and prayed, with confusion and sadness all over their faces. Then, Monsignor asked the congregation to bless all those who had passed on during the previous week. I held my breath, waiting to hear, "And for the family of Alicia Kriton, may they find peace."

But he finished without ever saying her name and moved on to the next part. I was mortified. Luke and I looked at each other in shock, then I stared at my beloved crucified Jesus on the cross; the same Jesus who had comforted me so many times in my life.

I started yelling in my head: *How could Monsignor not acknowledge her death? Her poor family is standing there grieving, and he didn't even acknowledge them. I don't give a shit if she committed suicide, which is supposedly a sin. Her family are the ones suffering, not her. She's in heaven with You and no longer suffering. He should acknowledge her family, who come faithfully every week, give their money, and did nothing wrong. Dear Jesus, You know depression is a sickness. She didn't commit suicide to go against You; she obviously felt alone and wanted to stop her suffering. What the hell happened to forgiving people for their sins? Why is my church not following Your teaching?*

I was so outraged that I walked out and planned to never return. That day, I realized that my church and my religion did not represent my faith. Yes, I was a Christian, but I definitely could not be a Catholic, not like that. I could not support a church that would turn its back on its own people during the worst moments of their lives.

By not acknowledging Alicia's suicide, the church wasn't punishing her; instead, the actions of the church punished her family and loved ones, who were already grief stricken and trying to forgive her for leaving them behind. She left us all behind—her little baby was without a mother, her new husband was without a wife, her siblings were without their sister, her parents were without their child, and I was without my childhood friend. Her loved ones needed the power of forgiveness from the church so that they themselves could forgive her and move forward in their lives.

I believed that God sent Jesus to this earth to teach us unconditional love and forgiveness, and the purpose of our lives was to try to be like Him, however impossible that might be with our imperfect sin-filled minds. The church should have set an example and showed unconditional love for Alicia and forgiveness for her sins, but instead it placed blame and perpetuated the shame and fear of mental illness as something she could have controlled.

When will they understand that it's an illness, not a sin?

I refused to be a part of that hypocrisy and ongoing cycle of mental abuse.

Unfortunately, that not only pushed Luke away from the church but also from God—completely. He lost his belief in the hope that Jesus brought. That fear and disbelief unintentionally pushed him away from me and everyone else. He questioned everything and believed nothing.

We were no longer seeing things in the same light. In fact, he couldn't see the light at all. He focused on the darkness. He would say things like "I don't like people; they suck."

I, on the other hand, was still very much a social being, and

I continued to see the good in humanity. His view of people and the world changed significantly. We were becoming completely different people as we entered adulthood. We were no longer just the jealous little teenagers we had been when we met.

Humanity

Once life calmed down a bit, I started taking classes at the community college back home and got a job working as a nurse's aide in a nursing home. That turned out to be one of the toughest jobs imaginable—physically, mentally, and emotionally.

Working there changed me.

Every day, I was responsible for ten to twelve elderly people, most of whom were too frail to walk. With my 105-pound frame, I had to lift them up off their beds, put them in their wheelchairs, transfer them on and off the toilet, transfer them on and off the shower commode, and get them back into bed. I had to change their clothes and bedding, clean up their soiled bottoms, brush their dentures, cut their nails, give them enemas, and feed them—just to name some of my duties.

It was hard on my body, but even harder on my heart. Some days, I went home angry at the system for allowing such a situation to exist; some days, I cried for their suffering; some days, I left feeling accomplished and full in my heart for the interactions I'd had with those beautiful souls.

Those people were lonely, afraid, miserable, and sometimes confused.

Beulah was a frail, miserable old lady who couldn't care for herself at all. She was so angry at her situation that every morning when I came in to get her up, she would hit me, try to bite me, and scream, "Leave me alone! I want to die! Why don't you just leave me alone? I want to die!"

It broke my heart that I couldn't give her the peace she longed for. Instead, I had to turn her from side to side and clean up the diarrhea that she lay in. She never had normal bowel movements and had no control to use the toilet. The diarrhea would go up her back and even into her hair sometimes. I knew she was humiliated and felt she had no more reason to live, but there was nothing she could do about it. I always treated her with the upmost respect and reassured her that I wanted to take care of her and be there for her. I would ask about her childhood to try to distract her, and for a few moments she would calm down and say something that didn't involve her being miserable.

Margaret wasn't as old as Beulah, but she'd had a severe stroke. She was completely immobile and also mute. I had to use an actual syringe to feed her because she didn't have the motor skills to chew, and she always tried to push the mush back out with her tongue. Even though she couldn't talk, she made it clear that she did not want to be fed.

I knew that, in her head, she was screaming the same things that Beulah always did, but all that came out was a wretched wailing from deep in her throat, accompanied by a painfully scrunched-up scowl on her face. Her spastic arms would then try with all their might to push that syringe away. Feeding her felt inhumane; it felt wrong. I wanted to take care of her, but that wasn't at all what she wanted or needed.

Emotionally, that job was exhausting and scarred my heart.

Taking care of the men was usually more difficult because of their general size and stubbornness. Richard was a good example. He was angry and mean. He wanted to be left alone, but he couldn't take care of himself. Once, I tried to get him to come down for dinner, and he trapped me in between his bed, the wall, and himself in his wheelchair. He hit me with his cane and yelled, "I don't need your help!"

I had to climb over his bed to get free. There was no reasoning with him. I finally figured out that I had to bribe him by telling him which dessert they were serving that day. His sweet tooth usually got him to go.

There were funny times, like when poor, confused Millie sat in a chair in the hallway after lunch and watched as we wheeled her roommates back to their rooms. She said, "Here comes the horse and buggy to deliver the milk. Watch! The milkman is going to stop and steal a kiss from Ma."

I laughed and said," What are you going to do after the milk comes, Millie?"

"I'm going to go get penny candy with Jack. What else would I do, of course?" she responded with a big toothless grin, as if she were five years old again.

Little glimpses like that into their childhoods gave me pause.

They were once vibrant, happy, and young. They had once been like I was now. They had relationships and lives just like I did. They must have had dreams, desires, pursuits, and secrets. Now they were just broken shells of the people they had once been. *Did they get to accomplish all the things they wanted to? Did they feel love and passion, excitement and success? Or, were they regretful, remorseful, and saddened about wasting their lives?*

Ironically, in those very old people, I found youth.

They gave me energy. I found my passion to help and care for others. I realized that I wanted to help people live their best, most fulfilled lives. I didn't want people to suffer the way Beulah, Margaret, and all the others did. I desperately wanted to create change. I wanted to change their lives for the better, the way they were changing my life. I was starting to realize my purpose.

True Support

I got a second job as an assistant in the biology lab. My professor and boss, Dr. Feldpausch, taught science in a way that was applicable to life. For the first time, I was able to appreciate the earth, the human body, and nature in all its wonder. The finite details of microscopic bacteria coexisting within the human body for function and survival truly amazed me, and the fact that people were smart enough to figure it all out impressed me even more. I wanted to understand the anatomy and physiology of our bodies, together with the psychology behind our behaviors, and also the magical part of how our souls worked with our bodies and minds to create each individual in the most unique way.

Dr. Feldpausch was also a pastor and saw science as God's work. It all made perfect sense to me now. The way a single cell could develop into a living organism and affect the world around it could only be seen as a miracle. This strengthened my faith and pushed me toward my purpose. I realized that gaining knowledge gave me the power to change my life.

I was starting to realize that I had abilities and talents. They might not be obvious, like my mom's sewing or my dad's cooking, but I had something that I needed to cultivate.

Subconsciously, I probably wanted to figure out how the mind and body worked so that I could intervene and change that—at least with my own. I still hated my body and was afraid of my mind. I actually felt better once I began to understand the human body, the human brain, and the reasons why humans do the things they do.

Unfortunately, Luke became jealous of my relationship with Dr. Feldpausch. He thought I had a crush on him, and he didn't like me spending so much time with him. Looking back now, I understand. He knew I had lied and betrayed him before, so it was hard to trust me. However, I truly was there for the right reasons. Dr. Feldpausch didn't ever allow for any inappropriate talk or behavior; he elevated me to better behavior, and I appreciated that. It felt safe to be around him, and I was able to focus on learning. He never commented on how I looked, he never behaved inappropriately.

I was learning how to let go of the superficial concerns in my life. The more I learned and succeeded, the more I felt empowered. He helped me to stay focused on Delilah and Luke and my future.

He believed in me.

Because I was at a community college for nursing, most of the students there were nontraditional students: older women who already had families and jobs and who were going back to school to better their situations. It was so much easier to relate to them than it had been with the students at the university or my coworkers at the pizza shop.

One day, I was talking to other women in my lab class about our birthing experiences. We all took turns describing our horror stories of ten- and twenty-hour labors, and how we'd felt powerless during that time. Their doctors, like mine, didn't seem to care what women wanted; they were all very paternalistic.

I was all fired up about my doctor having treated me so poorly just because I was young. Dr. Griffin hadn't explained things to me or given me options during my pregnancy or childbirth. We didn't have discussions regarding risks or benefits, and he definitely didn't allow time for me or make me feel comfortable enough to ask questions. I wished that it didn't have to be that way for young women with unintended pregnancies—or for women of any age or circumstance, for that matter.

"I wish I could change health care. I wish there were more female doctors to take care of us women because I think women would be more respectful and understanding. These old white-men doctors think they know best, and they don't care what we think."

The ladies all agreed with me.

Later, Dr. Feldpausch and I were cleaning up the lab. We started talking about how doctors still practiced paternalistic medicine, and I shared my experiences of working in the nursing home. I told him that I was feeling frustrated about becoming a nurse.

"I don't want to just carry out orders some old man gives me. No offense, Dr. Feldpausch. I just don't think I can do it." The little jab was just so I could get the I'm-not-old glare from him. He was probably only in his early forties. "I wish I could be the doctor and help women have a voice. I wish I could be the one to help them. I would listen to them, respect them and their situations, give them options, and help them decide what is best for them instead of just telling them what to do."

"You can be a doctor—if you really want to," Dr. Feldpausch responded.

I was stunned.

"Um, no, I can't. I'm a high-school dropout with a kid; becoming a doctor is not even possible," I replied.

"Sure it is," he insisted. "If you continue to get all A's, like you have been, you could apply for a scholarship and go back to the university. They have a medical school. I would write you a letter of recommendation."

"Are you serious? You think I am smart enough to be a doctor?" I said in complete disbelief.

"Yes. Yes, I do," he replied in all seriousness.

I went home, still shocked by what he had said. He believed in me, just like Mr. Cage and Mrs. Diebold had. I had accomplished what they believed I could, so maybe I could pull off the impossible.

I immediately told Luke, and he agreed with Dr. Feldpausch.

I thought to myself, *Are these people crazy? I'm white trash, a slut, a loser, a cheater, a liar—you name it—but a doctor? No way!*

Then, I told a few ladies at school, and they quickly supported me and said they had no doubt I could do it.

It felt amazing that people believed in me.

My little voice inside came back, louder than ever: "Of course you can do it; you can do anything you put your mind to! You want to do it, so make it happen. Show the world what you're made of!"

I quickly got used to the idea of taking on such a feat. I talked myself into doing it, not realizing what I was actually getting myself into: six years of undergrad, four years of medical school, and four years of residency.

I finished my second year at the community college with a 4.0. I had reapplied to the university, and I was accepted and received two scholarships.

Luke finally rehabbed his hand enough to get back into the minors. He had to move to Minnesota for the next season. That fall, I moved into family housing on campus—just Delilah and me. The apartment complexes were full of little children. Delilah always had someone to play with; she loved it there. There were a few white families, but everyone else was from all over the world: Argentina, India, China, and Africa, in our building alone.

It was truly an amazing experience for us, especially Delilah. They had an elementary school and day-care center right behind our building, and she was one of only three white kids in her kindergarten class. Our apartment was small, but it was a wonderful time.

When I got there, I was so proud of myself, but then I had to take a math placement exam, and I was told I had to restart at the beginning. It was looking like I would have to take three to four years of classes to get a premed bachelor's degree, instead of just two more years. My two years at the community college gave me the ability to get to the university, but the classes themselves didn't count toward much because they were for nursing.

I didn't let it get me down.

I went back home for Christmas break, and I ran into a high-school friend who was working at Kmart. I bravely told her that I'd transferred to the university, was going to become a doctor, but still had four years to go before I could even start medical school.

"Wow, you have to start all over? That is going to take forever. How are you going to pay for that? I would never waste ten years going to college. You're gonna be like thirty when you get done!" she replied in the typical, negative, small-town, defeated way.

"What else do I have to do?" I responded. "It'll be worth it."

As I walked away, I thought to myself, *Damn straight, I'll be thirty, but I'll be a doctor. When she's thirty, she's still going to be working at Kmart, wishing she had done something with her life.*

The words of Pearl Jam played over and over in my mind:

I changed by not changing at all
Small town predicts my fate
Perhaps that's what no one wants to see
I just want to scream hello

"Fuck that!" I answered in response to the song's suggestion that I couldn't be successful.

I felt more determined than ever to prove that I could do it. I made a conscious effort to believe in myself and to ignore all the skeptics. I'm not sure whether they didn't believe in me or just lived in fear, the fear of failure.

I refused to live in that fear.

It's impossible to succeed at anything if you are worried about failure. I had plenty of years of failing, and I was still standing. Now I was getting another chance. *Why would I waste my time worrying about failing? I know I'm going to fail sometimes; I'm human. When I do fail, I will just figure out a different way to succeed. I'll retake the damn college math class, just like I retook that damn eighth-grade math class, and then I'll move on to bigger and better things. I'll do what I need to do and not worry about stuff I can't control. I will do my best until my best is good enough.*

And, God help me, that was exactly what I did.

I busted my ass trying to learn physics and chemistry with such a limited background of knowledge. I had to look up a lot of stuff and teach myself foundational things that I should have already known. I didn't let it stop me. By the time I got to organic chemistry, I had to ask for help. I was embarrassed and started to think that I wasn't capable of learning that stuff. *It's just too hard*, I thought.

But there was a tutor lab available to everyone, so I went. I walked in to get help, and the place was packed. I quickly realized that I was not the only one struggling; kids who had gone to prestigious, affluent private schools needed help, just like I did. I didn't need help because I was a high-school dropout; I needed help because it was such a difficult subject.

The tutors were grad students who were really good at explaining and teaching the most complicated things. They taught me *how* to learn and study. I was never really taught how to do that. I felt empowered and excited to continue on my journey. I wasn't going to let a little organic chemistry scare me. I enjoyed the challenge, and my competitive side really started to come out. I not only wanted to survive and pass my classes, I also wanted to kick ass and prove that I belonged there and was as good as all the kids who'd been given opportunities and had a stronger foundation from which to start.

I majored in physiology for premed and was assigned a school counselor. Dr. Hunt was the head of the department and very accomplished. I took a class that used a textbook that Dr. Hunt himself had written. He had white hair and a white beard, wore sport coats, and carried a leather briefcase. He was the quintessential professor.

I was so nervous the first time I went to his office. It was in the Physiology building, which was very old and architecturally beautiful. His office was made entirely of dark cedar. It was dark and cold inside and smelled like really old books; it was almost dingy. He had large cedar cabinets, and glass cupboards and little apothecary drawers covered the walls. There were stacks of papers everywhere. I waited almost twenty minutes for him.

I was about to leave when he finally showed up. I felt like a nuisance and was afraid to even speak, for fear he would realize I didn't belong there—that I was just white trash trying to fake my way through college.

But that was not at all how it went.

He apologized for being late, explaining that he needed to deal with his son, who suffered from schizophrenia.

I shared my lifelong fear of mental illness (schizophrenia, in particular) and my desire to understand the mind and give people a compassionate, listening ear.

He was kind and seemed genuinely interested in my life story, my background, and my desire to become a doctor. "Your story is so unique. Your passion to help people and make a difference is so refreshing. I don't care if you can't make a 4.0 and haven't done tons of research in undergrad; you have life experiences that most other kids your age don't have. Those experiences are invaluable. You are special, and you will make an excellent doctor someday."

I left that meeting feeling appreciated and empowered.

Dr. Hunt had acknowledged me as a person of value. He saw the good in me and believed I was capable of great things. He believed I could get into medical school, become a doctor, and make a difference. He validated my dreams and all my hard work, embarrassment, struggle, and sacrifice. What a beautiful gift he gave me simply by listening to me and supporting me.

That boosted my ego and gave me the confidence to start my junior year. Classes were becoming even more challenging. Meanwhile, I was still a wife and mother. Delilah started school, and I joined the PTA. Okay, not only did I join, I also became the secretary. My new friend, Brooke, who was the president, talked me into it. It was very important to me to be an active mom. I spent time in the classroom, listening to the kids read aloud; I helped organize the book fair and a bake sale; and I helped create celebrations for Christmas, Hanukah, Kwanzaa, Omisoka, and other holidays.

For Halloween, I took Delilah trick-or-treating in the dorms on campus. The college kids decorated their halls every year and passed out candy. It was a fun, warm way to trick-or-treat, since we didn't live in a real neighborhood. It was an awesome experience for her, but it kind of bummed me out. I had to see all the college kids, who were the same age as I was, dressing up and partying, having fun, blowing off steam, and enjoying life. Meanwhile, I had to be a mom, taking my kid home and putting her to bed by 9:00 p.m. I tried to make the best of it and just enjoy life through my daughter, but I couldn't help feeling like I was missing out.

When Luke was with us, he didn't want to hang out with friends or go out. To make matters even worse, he didn't like me having friends. I couldn't help it. As a social being, I enjoyed being with people and wanted to have friends. Looking back now, I realize that he objected to my social life because I didn't make him feel loved and irreplaceable. He didn't feel secure in our relationship. We were so young and dysfunctional. It took me another fifteen years to truly understand how to have a healthy, mature partnership.

When Delilah started kindergarten, I met Sarafina, the mom of one of Delilah's new friends. She had many girlfriends and encouraged me to hang out with them. They got together every morning for coffee in Brooke's apartment, after the kids left for school. I was able to go twice a week, on the days when my classes started later. They were completely different from any girlfriends I had ever had. They were all about empowering and celebrating other women, not judging them or cutting them down.

They listened to chick music like Sarah McLachlan and Paula Cole, they went to Lilith Fair, and they burned patchouli oil and candles while they drank wine and enjoyed each other's company. It was all so different to me, and I loved it.

I went from listening to the angst of Pearl Jam and Nirvana, to listening to the empowering voices of women. The messages in their songs were about being strong, overcoming obstacles, and being resilient. Prior to that, the only other female whose music I had listened to was Tori Amos. She was like a savior to me through tough times, but no women I knew listened to her. Music had always been a powerful message in my life, and when I listened to Tori, her songs opened my eyes.

Tori's voice and her piano told painfully true stories. I related to her struggles with men, her body, feeling objectified, the hypocrisy of religion, and her doubts about God. I felt like Tori was singing about my life, my thoughts, and my fears. Secretly, she was my voice. I found strength by listening to her.

Until I met Sarafina, I had kept that a secret. It didn't feel safe to celebrate women out loud. When I was alone, I would indulge in listening to Tori. I would drive along, belting out the lyrics, with tears streaming down my face as I felt the power of Tori's words:

I've been looking for a savior in these dirty streets
Looking for a savior beneath these dirty sheets
I've been raising up my hands
Drive another nail in
Just what God needs, one more victim
Why do we crucify ourselves?

Up to that point, I had believed that women were strong but that we were supposed to show our strength quietly, in a stealthy manner. I had a big mouth and was always getting into trouble for it, but my strength was one thing I wasn't ever loud and obnoxious about—and I should have been.

No other women in my world, up to that point, had been outspoken feminists, for lack of a better term. Women in my life were strong. They did whatever was necessary to keep their families together, to keep their husbands from drinking themselves to death, to keep their kids out of jail, to keep their electricity on, and so forth. But they never came right out and demanded to be treated better. They were cheated on, abused, used, ignored, dismissed, ridiculed, and objectified. I was taught, indirectly, by watching women deal (or not deal) with those situations, that you find your strength to get over it, and then you pray it doesn't happen again. *Maybe that's why I cheated, lied, stole, and did all those horrible things. I couldn't accept the idea of a man dictating my thoughts and actions. Maybe that was my way of defying the expectations.* Just a thought.

Well, we all know how it turns out when women don't speak up for themselves and demand respect—the dysfunction just continues. The vicious cycle doesn't end; it gains momentum and plows down all those women in its path.

Becoming friends with women who supported me as a woman and wanted to see me succeed really refueled my fire and refocused my pursuits. I also wanted them to succeed and conquer the world. I wanted to be a part of social change and advancement for women. I wanted to be the role model for Delilah that she would need growing up.

I took sociology classes and learned about strong women like Eleanor Roosevelt, Harriet Tubman, and Marie Curie. These women weren't afraid to stand up to men and do what they believed in. Instead of feeling disadvantaged and second rate, I started to feel proud to be a woman. Even more so, I started to feel proud of myself and my story. It was my strength, and it made me unique. I had always been ashamed and had seen it as a disadvantage and a roadblock, but I was starting to see it as an asset and a building block.

My Foundation

My foundation (built from my childhood experiences, relation-ships, failures, successes, hopes, and dreams; made of my person-ality, my soul, and my purpose) was not your basic four layers of cement block, laid out perfectly plumb and level, with matching grout. Mine was made from leftover, broken cement blocks that other people had tossed aside. These blocks were different colors and sizes, had big chips taken out of them, and didn't always seem to fit together. Old rocks were used where the blocks didn't line up. There was a scant amount of mortar used to hold the bricks together, and moss and vines covered the places that were never completed or tended to. The whole thing looked dingy and old. It was a hot mess.

Nonetheless, I built my life on it.

At first glance, it looked ugly, sloppy, dangerous, and weak, but once I started to build a meaningful life on it—and, later, remodel it—you couldn't deny its strength, beauty, and longevity.

Over the years, I occasionally spent some time repairing my foundation, as best as I knew how. I dealt with my depression, my body-image issues, my lack of parenting and respect for authority growing up, and, now, my strained marriage.

Unfortunately, I had to chisel away at a few rocks and blocks, and, eventually, replace them with new ones. I had to add mortar to some areas, and I tried to make my foundation appear more respectable. But I did it with care, so as to not completely destroy the foundation and the life on top of it. I fixed the areas that needed fixing so my life would look better and be safer; so that my foundation would be stronger to continue to build upon and to temporarily house others, if need be.

For so long, I had coveted others' beautifully perfect foundations and the lives that sat upon them. The more women I met and interacted with, the more I was able to see inside their foundations. There were huge cracks, some with attempts at repair using Scotch tape or superglue, some that had been completely destroyed and entirely rebuilt, and some, sadly, left crumbled and in ruins. Sometimes the foundation was a complete facade. From afar it looked beautiful and perfect, but if you accidentally got through the gates to get a closer look, you could see that the bricks and mortar were actually drawn on thin paper, which collapsed as soon as the inhabitants tried to build a life upon it.

Some women even went so far as to leave their own foundations sitting there while they built their lives on someone else's foundation. Unfortunately, most people do not have enough room to accommodate another person long term. They eventually collapse or kick them out at the first sign of weakness.

I liken that to raising children. While they are growing and building their own foundations, we, as parents, must guide them on how to construct those foundations, giving them supplies and tools with which to work. We need to show them how to finish each layer properly before moving on to the next. We need to show them how to examine their work and check for plumbness and levelness. They should be shown how to use certain blocks at certain times, like corner pieces that connect different sides and continue the foundation to completeness.

We shouldn't just allow our children to stay on our foundations where it is easy and already done for them. Then, there is no room for them to build their own lives. If they try to build atop of yours, your life (your house) will become overloaded and buckle at the seams. They won't have something to be proud of or call their own. I had to learn to not judge people superficially and assume their foundations were strong just because they looked good on the outside. I had to learn to quit wanting what others had and, instead, work on making what I had be the best it could be.

Thinking back, I tried to run before I could walk. I tried to teach before I learned. I tried to love before I loved myself. I tried to grow up without guidance, and that caused me to grow up without a sturdy, proper foundation.

My ignorance had traded in my innocence.

As a child, I had desired love, attention, and acceptance. I had wanted to feel empowered and important as a human being. I had wanted to feel needed, and I had wanted to feel worthy of the unconditional love that Jesus seemed to give. At that time, boys made me feel loved and needed. Looking back now, I realize that I thought my worth was physical. I lived as though the only thing I had to offer was my body, and the pleasure it gave. Even so, somewhere deep down, I knew I had something more substantial to give; my little voice inside told me so.

I believe Tori Amos obviously felt the same way. When I heard her song "Girl," it all started to make sense:

She's been everybody else's girl
Maybe one day she'll be her own

During that time of personal growth and girl power with my new girlfriends, unfortunately, my demons couldn't be killed. I still struggled with wanting physical perfection. I hated my body, especially my saggy, empty, ruined boobs. I hated being twenty-something and feeling too ashamed to wear a bathing suit or a bra that wasn't padded. I exercised, whitened my teeth, constantly tried to change my hair, baked myself in the tanner, and sought the attention of guys.

I needed validation.

I needed to hear that I was beautiful and good enough. I wanted to hear that I was still worthy of appearing in the *Sports Illustrated Swimsuit Edition*. I tried to make those thoughts disappear. I tried to love myself as I was. I tried to be comfortable in my own skin the way my new girlfriends seemed to be, but I couldn't get there.

I focused on the superficial alterations to give me that contentment. I wasn't looking inwardly at my soul for my beauty. I continued to look outward, and so I continued to be disappointed and frustrated. I felt ugly and thought I was a failure.

Luke was well aware of my issues, and when I told him what I wanted to do, he supported me. "As soon as I get paid at the end of the season, we'll get you boobs!"

His support solidified in my mind the need for me to do this. *I know he wants me to have nice boobs and look like Pam Anderson; he's agreeing to it, so I'd better do it*, I thought.

I honestly thought that I would like my body after that, and I did for a while.

I struggled with the idea of Delilah finding out and then not feeling good enough or liking her body. More than anything, I wanted to spare her this curse. I wanted her to love and accept herself. Ironically, getting breast implants gave me the confidence to help my own daughter appreciate her body. In my mind, I finally looked like I was supposed to look, like I'd wanted to look all those years. Yes, with plastic in my body, I felt like myself again. I wasn't comfortable with my ruined body, and no matter how hard I tried, I couldn't come to terms with it.

What do I do when I don't like something? I change it. So, that's what I did.

It may be freeing and empowering to love yourself as you are, but it is also freeing and empowering to do what you need to do to make yourself happy. I didn't want to perpetuate the idea of women as sex objects, but I did not want to deny my sensuality either. God made us beautiful, with bosoms and voluptuous curves, and that was the type of body that symbolized femininity, strength, beauty, fertility, and power in my mind. The women in my family were big busted, and that was my ideal of a woman's body. So, I struggled on many levels with the idea of altering my body. I saw it as replacing the body that pregnancy had stolen from me, not as changing what God had given me.

I wanted to be a good role model for my daughter, and I wanted to send the right message to society in terms of how women are seen and valued. But I also wanted to be happy. I wanted to love myself, which included loving my body. I wanted to quit feeling shame and self-disgust.

Losing my prepregnancy body had also made me lose my ability to have intimacy. I was never comfortable enough to be naked in front of my husband. I was too busy judging and hating myself to even connect with someone else—and, believe me, I tried. I tried with other guys because I thought it was Luke's fault. No matter the situation or the person, I couldn't get comfortable in my own skin.

So, I had a breast augmentation, and I felt beautiful. But now I had a new problem. I felt ashamed.

I didn't want anyone to know, especially my feminist girl-friends, that I was that shallow and superficial. I knew I wasn't, but I didn't think I could explain my reasoning in a way they could understand. We had so many conversations where they bashed celebrities or everyday women for having plastic surgery, especially breast implants. For women who don't suffer from body-image issues, it is easy to misjudge the women who do it and not understand their reasoning.

I was also terrified that I would end up like Alicia. She had surgery, and it obviously didn't help her love herself more. It reminded me that loving my body and loving myself were not one and the same. I also acknowledged that I most likely suffered from depression, as Alicia did, and that depression was what led to her demise, not plastic surgery.

I finally decided that *because* I loved myself, I would do whatever it took to love my body as well. My body didn't define me, but it did change how I behaved. It was destroying my marriage, and it kept me from enjoying life to the fullest. I knew I needed to fix that so I could get on with my life.

Yes, having fake boobs helped me get real. I don't know what else to tell ya.

All my life, I had always wanted more. I had always wanted what others had, and I'd never felt content with myself or my situation. How could I learn to love and appreciate what I had and who I was? I realized that it was partly a choice of focus and it would take work. I needed to put the effort in to make myself better, make my situation better, make my life what I wanted it to be.

It wasn't going to just automatically happen. People who lived amazing lives, who affected other people and made a difference, worked hard and sacrificed. They did not seek material possessions or superficial love and attention. They had a purpose.

I knew I had a purpose, so I must do something about it. I needed to make it happen.

My next big obstacle to getting into medical school was taking the MCAT (Medical College Admission Test), a seven-and-a-half-hour exam covering biology, physics, chemistry, physiology, psychology, statistics, and the list goes on. It is a requirement when applying to medical school, and if you want to get into a decent medical school, you need to get a competitive score on the MCAT. I spent two months of intense studying, beyond taking my regular classes, to prepare for this exam. It was very time consuming, emotionally draining, and somewhat challenging. But, guess what? I was up for the challenge.

Whenever I felt like giving up because I couldn't figure it out, I would remind myself of where I would be if I quit: *Well, you could be working at a gas station back home, bored out of your damn mind, or you could shut up and become a doctor! You can't fail. You need to make your family proud and keep your word, for once. You'll be able to help them out of debt and change their futures. You need to prove that you're not white trash. You need to prove you can do anything you set your mind to.*

I definitely wasn't nice to myself, but that was what worked. It gave me the motivation I needed to continue on.

Many nights, my motivation came while reading bedtime books to Delilah. I remembered how my mom read to me when I was little and what a gift that was. She taught me to love books and to not be afraid to read. I would lie there, reading to Delilah, dreaming of how much better her childhood was—and would continue to be—because I was breaking the cycle. I got us out of Nowheresville and was creating opportunities she wouldn't have otherwise had.

I made sure Delilah went to preschool, took dance classes, gymnastics, and swimming lessons. I just always took my books with me to study while she was doing her thing. In the summer, she did YMCA camps, so she could do something positive and make friends. I didn't want her to sit around with nothing to do all summer; that was how I'd gotten into trouble. The nuns had always said, "Idle hands are the devil's playground." They were right.

I knew that if I succeeded, I would make enough money to help my parents out more. I was already helping them pay bills and get their cars fixed, just to name a few things. I loved that I could do that for them. I felt indebted to my parents for stealing from them and being such a difficult child. I wanted to make sure my parents never suffered again; that was my goal.

I had all these good intentions to give my family a better life, but this what I learned after many painstaking years: you can't make people change or do what's best for them. My parents were notorious for making poor financial decisions, but it wasn't because they were dumb. On the contrary, they were very smart, but their decisions were guided by their huge hearts. They listened to their hearts and did what was best for others, not what was in their own best interest. It was a beautiful thing. When they did stuff, I always imagined they asked, "What would Jesus do?" And that was what they would do.

For so long, I found it frustrating because I wanted better for them. I wanted them to put themselves first, for once, but they always took care of their children instead. Eventually, I realized they would never put their own needs above others', and I should just love them for the truly gracious, selfless people that they were and figure out a different way to help them.

Their generosity definitely shaped who I became.

I loved to give too.

I couldn't even count the number of people that I'd helped over the years, without any plans to get anything back.

I always remembered something my mom told me when I came home crying that Vanessa lost my jeans that she had borrowed. "You should never give someone something if you expect to get it back. You will only be hurt and resentful. If you give something, give it because you want to help someone out. If they give it back, great. If not, they must need it more than you do, so let it go and don't hold it against them."

I have made a conscious effort to live like that. To this day, I don't have any pent-up resentment against anyone, and I don't feel like anyone owes me anything. I made the choice to "lend" two hundred dollars here, fifteen hundred dollars there, etc. In the back of my mind, I thought, *I hope someone will allow me the same grace if I ever don't pay them back or show them gratitude.*

Karma can be a beautiful thing.

Anyway, I finally took the MCAT, and I kicked butt, in my humble opinion. My score was good enough for me to apply to the university medical school, and that was where I wanted to go. In addition to excelling academically, I had to show that I was a well-rounded, caring person with community involvement. Medical-school applicants were expected to volunteer their time, talents, and treasures, as well as have a healthy personal life.

I worked in the bioengineering research department a little bit. I volunteered with the premed group and the American Red Cross. I regularly staffed the homeless assistance office. Now, that was an uncomfortable situation and really opened my eyes.

I would be there from 6:00 p.m. to 10:00 p.m., which were the hours that any homeless person could come in for toiletries, clothes, blankets, or help finding a place to stay. I was always busy. So many different people came in every night. We had three homeless shelters that we could call for a bed for them, and two hotels that we could write vouchers to cover them for a few days. There were all kinds of rules, and getting people to abide by those was almost impossible. There were many regulars who lived in the system for years.

One man had been kicked out of both city rescue missions for thirty days, and he was angry that he had nowhere to stay or any way to eat. It broke my heart, but it also frustrated me that I couldn't get him to change his ways. I tried to get him to see that he needed to play the game and follow the rules. I told him, "Personally, it took me many years to figure that out; but, once I did, my life blossomed. Yours can too!"

All the while I was trying to be a good citizen and an active member of the community, I was still struggling with being a good parent. I tried to be like Charlie's mom, Lauren. I would think to myself, *How would Lauren handle this?*

She was always so good about holding her children accountable and lifting them up. She exposed them to all life had to offer and encouraged them to work hard and succeed. That was the kind of parent I wanted to be for Delilah. When she wanted to quit dance because it was too much work, I made her finish out the year. When she got bored with gymnastics, I encouraged her to find new ways to enjoy it each week and got her to finish what she started. When she did simple things, like her nightly homework, I encouraged her to do her best by taking her time to focus and write neatly. "Your work represents you, Delilah."

It was really important for her to finish what she started and to follow through with her commitments. "That is an attribute that successful people cultivate. They don't give up, they don't let other people down, and they do the hard work."

I taught her that discomfort is just your mind and body's way of showing you that you're making good changes within yourself. "When a caterpillar decides to build itself a cocoon, it has to stay in there patiently until it's time to emerge. Then, it has to do the hard work to get out of the cocoon and set itself free as a butterfly. All of that struggle is worth it because it ends up living a new life—beautiful and free. I want that for you, Delilah. I want you to become a butterfly."

It was hard figuring out the appropriate balance between letting her have some autonomy while at the same time not letting her just give up when things got tough. I wanted her to have the freedom to imagine, experiment, and fail, like I had had, but with closer supervision and accountability.

As a child, I often walked a figurative tightrope and swung like a trapeze artist without a safety net. I wanted Delilah to "walk the tightrope" without fear, like I did, but I needed to give her a safety net in case she fell. The tricky part was not letting her necessarily see the net and rely on it. I strongly believe now that my successes and most enjoyable moments in life have happened when I wasn't living in fear. I also believe that most of my bad behaviors and decisions happened because no one was there with a safety net to catch me when I fell.

I wanted her to find that courage inside her heart, but I wasn't capable of completely looking the other way. Was I, as a parent, living in fear? Or was I being cautious and wise?

I realized this early on, when Delilah was learning to ride a bike. Luke was coddling her and trying to protect her from ever falling off the bike, but I argued with him that falling is inevitable, and she'd never learn to ride if didn't let go of her bike. He was living in fear, and I was not about to let her learn that stifling behavior.

I took over teaching her how to ride, and he went in the house, all pissed off. I gave her a pep talk, then reassured her that I wouldn't let go until I was sure she was ready. I ran up and down the street, probably ten times, holding her seat and yelling, "Look up! Keep pedaling!"

I finally let go, and she rode all the way to the corner, then ran into the curb and fell over. She cried for a minute, but then she said, "Hold me again!" all excited as she climbed back onto her bike.

She knew she could do it and that falling wasn't the end of the world. The joy of riding was worth the little fall.

Her dad ran out of the house. "Good job, sweetie. You did it!" he yelled to her.

"Yes, I did. I taught her to not live in fear," I replied to him with a smirk on my face.

"You're lucky she didn't ride right into the intersection," he snapped back.

"Oh, good Lord. Relax, Luke. You can't protect her from

everything, every minute of the day. You're not doing her any favors by smothering her with your safety net."

That was one of many struggles Luke and I had while trying to raise Delilah. I believe that if you don't make them try when they are scared, or If you let them give up when things get tough, then they won't know how to accomplish things, follow through, or finish anything. They will never experience pride or come to know their self-worth. They will not become independent, productive members of society.

Likewise, if you don't make them share their toys and cookies, they will never sacrifice and make true friendships. If you don't hold them accountable for their little white lies, they will grow up to live an inauthentic life. If you teach them to only do things for material or monetary gain, then they won't have kind, caring hearts. We must teach our children to do difficult things, to do things for others, and to just do what is right—for no other reason than to turn them into be good human beings.

When children do the right thing because they know that's what's expected, the feeling of fulfillment they get in their hearts is a much greater gift than any material or monetary thing you could ever give them. One great example of that came when I volunteered with a group who was providing basic health care to local migrant workers and their families. We checked their blood pressure, provided physical exams, and treated them for minor medical problems.

When I saw the children of the workers, I realized that they didn't brush their teeth. Not because they didn't want to, like my kids, but because they didn't have the tools required or the knowledge of how to do it. No one there had ever owned a toothbrush. I asked the adults if they would be interested, and they smiled at the idea.

The next day, I went to the Red Cross distribution center and got two huge boxes of toothbrushes and toothpaste. I took them to the migrants and showed them how to use them. They were so excited to have something of their own, and you could see that they appreciated my kindness.

I brought Delilah with me. She was about seven by then, and she gave the kids some of her toys and stuffed animals. She gave the girls her clothes that no longer fit. The migrant children were happy and thankful, but her giving of herself, no doubt, gave her so much more in return that was beyond measure.

Teaching our children to be givers is much more important than teaching them to ace a test or win a game. My parents taught me to be a giver, unintentionally, by just being who they were. They may not have hounded me about homework or given me a curfew, but they led by example when it came to being a good person toward others.

My mom was such an honest, good person. Once, we went to Walmart and bought a kiddie pool. We loaded it up in the car and drove home. I was so excited for little Delilah to have a pool to play in, but when my mom went to fill it up, she realized there were two pools stuck together. She insisted we drive the other pool back to Walmart and return it because we didn't pay for it—mind you, it was probably like a six-dollar pool. We packed Delilah back up in her car seat, drove there, and gave it back. The kid working there laughed when my mom walked in with it and told him what happened, but I guarantee that her honesty stuck with him, like it did with me.

I wish there were more people like my mom in the world.

And even though my dad may have cheated, I have only known him to be an honest, caring, completely selfless person throughout my life. He would give a stranger the shirt of his back, without hesitation.

I strive to be as selfless and thoughtful as he.

Somehow, I made it through those four years and was going to graduate with a bachelor's degree with honors. I would be the first person on both sides of my family to graduate from a four-year college. It was a huge accomplishment, and my family was so proud of me. They all made the long drive across the state to come and cheer me on when I received my diploma. I felt special. For so long, I had just wanted them to be proud of me. I finally made it happen; it felt amazing.

It was a very stressful time because I only applied to one medical school. Yes, I put all my eggs in one basket, because I believed in myself. I had done everything that Dr. Hunt told me to do, and I even spent time shadowing the medical students there to make sure it was a good fit for me. I just knew in my heart that I would be accepted there; it was where I belonged.

I could see my path being laid out before me.

So, I applied and waited. In the meantime, I got a job at the Red Cross. I really enjoyed my year there. I worked with so many interesting people in different stages of their lives. Some were younger and using it as a springboard; some had been there thirty years and climbed the ladder; some just worked for the paycheck to survive. I appreciated being with real people who struggled and lived the way my people had. It felt like home.

The letter finally came in the mail:

October 22, 1998

Dear Mrs. Jansen-Evans:

Congratulations! It gives me great pleasure to tell you that you have been admitted to the College of Osteopathic Medicine.

How surreal.

Crabby Cathy was going to become a doctor! We visited back home soon after and took my letter with me to show my family. My parents said it was great but didn't ask many questions.

My older brother, Steve, read it and said, "Wait, is this even a real medical school? Are you going to be an actual doctor?"

"Yes! Yes, I am!"

He said that because it was an osteopathic school, and he didn't know what that meant. I explained to them that DOs are equal to MDs; they just have a different philosophy about health and medicine. "They see the body holistically. The mind, body, and spirit are all interconnected; each affects the other. DOs learn all of the same science and evidence-based medicine as MDs, but they approach health and healing with an all-encompassing mind-set. They believe that the body's structure and function are reciprocally interrelated and that the body is capable of self-healing."

I was excited to learn how the mind affected our body (how it could cause physical pain, and vice versa) and how to treat and help prevent disease. Subconsciously, I probably longed for the knowledge to use on myself. I wanted to understand how to control my depression and make sure I didn't develop schizophrenia or the like. Of course, more than anything, I wanted to help women and make a difference in their lives.

Fear

During this time, Luke and I continued to struggle and not work on our relationship. We became like roommates who were raising a child together. He had gone the last two hockey seasons without getting picked up by the minors, so he was doing the stay-at-home dad thing. I could tell that he was miserable and looking for a new path. He mentioned that he dreamed of being an actor, like Brad Pitt. When I encouraged him to entertain the idea, he got upset and acted like he had no choices in life and couldn't possibly do such a crazy thing.

"I will happily apply to medical school in Los Angeles. We can move out to LA, Delilah can try child modeling, and you can try the acting thing, I replied with total encouragement. And I meant it.

"Stop being ridiculous. You know we can't move there. My parents would kill me, and I need to start working and get a steady paycheck to take care of you guys," he said.

"Stop worrying about money. There's more to life than money! I want you to do something you're passionate about. If you want to keep working on getting into the NHL, then let's do it; but if you want to pursue acting, then I am ready to support you 100 percent, right now! I need you to find your happiness again," I insisted.

"Drop it!" he snapped as he walked away.

His fear frustrated me.

I couldn't understand why he let fear paralyze his life and

squash his dreams. I had repeatedly refused to let fear stop me, and, up to that point, my persistence hadn't let me down. I looked at him and thought, *Why can't you see that conquering my fears has worked for me and that you should pursue your dreams?*

I had a hard time feeling bad for his unhappiness. I knew what he needed to do, but I couldn't make him do it. I started losing respect for him, however screwed up that might have been. I wanted him to be strong enough to go after his dreams.

Soon, I started medical school, and my first year was challenging as hell! I would study until 3:00 or 4:00 a.m., take a nap, then get up and go to take an exam at 7:30 a.m., on all the material I had just stuffed into my exhausted brain. This went on at least two to three times per week, for two years.

I was working my ass off to make shit happen, while Luke continued to stay home, watch TV, and work out. Okay, he was also cooking, cleaning the house, and taking care of Delilah much more than I was. He was supporting me so that I could do what I needed to do, but we weren't a team. We weren't on the same path toward the same future, and it was becoming obvious.

Looking back, I wish he would have been more selfish and nurtured his own needs a little more. What he did for me was a great thing, but he cheated himself. I wish we could have chased our dreams together, found success together. Him living only for Delilah and me was not healthy, and it really ruined us.

The harder I worked and the more I accomplished, the more he came to resent me. I couldn't be the attentive, loving wife he needed. I kept telling myself and him that all the sacrifice would be worth it. The concept of delayed gratification became our saving grace. "It will all be worth it when we are sitting by our pool, I would say regularly to pacify him.

"I'll be a stay-at-home dad and be your pool boy."

"Perfect!"

Even though he was in shape and attractive, I was too busy and too tired to have any interest. He was also very jealous and didn't want me to have friends. I had many events with my class to get to know each other, and many included spouses so that people could make friends and have support, but he didn't want to be a part of that.

Toward the end of my first year, we were invited to the wedding of my good friend, Tina. She was my study buddy, and we hung out together every day since the first day of medical school. She invited the entire class and their significant others. I dragged him there reluctantly, and, as predicted, the night ended in a fight.

When we arrived, many classmates, some of them guys, greeted me with hugs. I thought nothing of it because that was how they were at school, but I got an evil look from Luke. (Later in life, I realized that was a very common way to say hello and good-bye, but where we came from, it was not.) A little later, I went onto the dance floor and was dancing with two girls. I saw that Luke was not happy, so I went over to him.

"I can't stand all the guys looking at you, and why do they think they can touch you?" he asked.

"They're not looking at me, and so what if they are? I'm here with you, I replied, but that didn't help.

"I'm ready to go."

"Okay."

And, sadly, we left, without saying good-bye to Tina—or anyone, for that matter—because I knew any more hugs would have pissed him off even more.

We had a huge fight, and he expressed how he didn't want us hanging out with my class because many of them were single guys. I was not okay with that. I wanted to fit in and be a part of my class. We, as medical students, were going through one of the most difficult things together, which only someone who experiences it can understand. I needed their support and friendship.

There were things I could only talk to them about, things like trying to accept the fact, during anatomy class, that we had our hands inside the bodies of dead people. Real people who had lived and breathed, dreamed and loved, laughed and cried; real women who had carried children in their uterus during their lifetimes and had thick C-section scars distorting their anatomy to prove it. Those days in anatomy lab, breathing in formaldehyde while contemplating their lives and stories, was, at times, overwhelming. Those people had made the selfless decision while they were still alive to donate themselves for the betterment of educating future doctors. It was a beautiful thought. There were many moments of gratitude for the experience, but also moments of feeling our own mortality, which only someone experiencing it could understand.

There were funny times, like when we opened the shaft of an old man's penis and there was a penis pump.

It was a surprise, and the guys laughed, saying, "Wow, he must have had a great life!"

I thought about the fact that he must have suffered from impotence, and I wondered if it had impacted his marriage. Now he had twenty medical students inspecting it.

I realized that so many people had stories to tell, and so many probably never got the chance to tell theirs. Maybe they knew that donating their bodies to science would be a way to tell their stories, at least in part. I felt it was my duty to be respectful and appreciative of those people who had donated themselves for the betterment of medicine. Their donations would help me become a doctor. Looking back, I see that their selflessness helped me become the great surgeon I am today.

So, back to Luke. We were growing up and were no longer the same people we had been when we got together in high school.

Actually, I realized I was never my true self around him, and now it was getting harder to hide that. Shame on me for trying to be the person he wanted me to be rather than who I truly was.

I was afraid of rejection.

I also felt indebted to him for supporting me, so I felt like he had a say in what kind of doctor I would be. Originally, I imagined myself becoming an obstetrician/gynecologist. I had a strong desire to take care of women and make sure they had better experiences than I had. I wanted to give women a voice and empower them to take control of their health and their birthing experiences, become educated as to their choices, and just overall improve their lives.

However, shortly after I started medical school, Luke and I went to an informational meeting and heard people's opinions about the different specialties of medicine, like family practice, internal medicine, emergency medicine, and OB/GYN. These were mostly from residents who were currently in the middle of the most difficult times of training.

The OB/GYN residents complained about how painfully long the hours were, how they got stuck staying after hours to finish a delivery they were managing all day, and how they had to do four or five months of night rotations. They talked about how often OB/GYNs get sued and how stressful the specialty was.

In contrast, the ER residents bragged about how they only did fourteen shifts per month and when their shift was over, they got to go home. They explained that the attending physicians got all kinds of time off to be with their families, while OB/GYNs had to take calls in addition to working all day. The ER residents did a good job of making it sound glamorous, like they got their adrenaline-junkie needs fulfilled from traumas that came in, but that they had all kinds of free time to enjoy life.

It was very appealing, and Luke really pushed the idea for me to become an ER doctor. He made it clear that he didn't want me being on call, going in to deliveries in the middle of the night, and not being home when I was supposed to be. "The ER lifestyle will be much better for our family," he insisted.

Internally, I went back and forth with what I wanted. I wanted to do what was best for my husband and family, but I didn't feel that being an ER doctor would be the most effective way for me to help people. Deep down, I knew that I had gone down this path to do something great and make a difference in women's lives. Nonetheless, I went with the idea of it for the time being. I didn't have to decide my specialty for another year, so I decided to give ER a chance. I became the vice president of the emergency medicine club, which was a ton of fun. It was mostly guys—adventurous, single, thrill seekers; basically, who I would have been, had I been born a guy. Luke didn't realize that part.

As we learned how to suture and tie knots, I realized that I could become a seamstress of sorts, like my mother, but I could sew and fix people the way she did with dresses. When I told her that, she was excited; she got a real kick out of that. I liked the idea of being a surgeon. I was truly enjoying medical school and wanted to learn and do everything I could. It was empowering, gratifying, and, at the same time, exhausting, draining, and just plain hard.

It definitely didn't give me much time to focus on my marriage. I didn't usually share anything about school with Luke because it all seemed to upset him. The times I tried to tell him stories about my day ended up in a fight. He would be jealous that I had to interact with guys or that I was doing something cool. Sometimes he said, "Maybe I should go to medical school."

"You should. You would be a great doctor, I responded with enthusiasm.

"But I don't really want it like you do. I could never study the way you do," he protested.

"I have no doubt that you could do it if you wanted it bad

enough, but you don't really want it. I think you want to do something, but that's not it. If it is, then I support you 100 percent."

"I don't know what I want. I want to be an actor. I want to be in action movies and get paid to work out and do cool stunts."

"Then let's go to California, like we should have more than a year ago. I'll do my residency in LA. I'll apply where ever you want; nothing is holding us back," I said excitedly.

"My parents would kill us. We're not going anywhere," Luke said shortly, so as to end the conversation.

I wish now that he would have taken me up on that offer. I believed in him, and I would have gone anywhere to help him follow his dream. Again, I couldn't understand letting fear paralyze you and prevent you from doing what you wanted to do.

The only fear I understood was regret.

We continued to grow apart, and we didn't talk about much more than Delilah or groceries. The only time we spent together was watching TV or going to hockey games. I was lying to myself and him, thinking I could give him what he wanted. And I was getting to the point where I couldn't deny who I was and what I wanted. We hadn't gone to bed at the same time in at least two years. He always stayed up and watched TV, while I stayed up to study in another room. We only had sex when I felt guilty or after a fight.

We only really hung out on weekends during hockey season, when we went to games with his parents. He seemed happy during those times and really got into it. I wanted to hang out with my classmates at the games, but he didn't want to, so I really didn't enjoy going. I preferred to spend time with Delilah or study instead.

We were really good at hiding our problems. Everyone thought we were the perfect couple. I never talked bad about him to anyone, because I didn't want to be disrespectful, and I didn't want to admit to myself that we were broken. Both sets of our parents stayed together, whether they were happy or not. His parents were masters of denial. You could feel the annoyance and even disgust at times, but they never talked about it. They would never even consider divorce. God forbid! That wasn't an option in the Catholic church. The same mentality was expected of Luke and me.

The event that ultimately broke my heart to the point of no return was when my uncle Jack died. I was overwhelmed with sadness and grief for my family. I couldn't handle thinking of how great their suffering was. The only other family member who had died was my great-grandma Holliday, but she was very old, and so it was expected. My uncle Jack was young; his kids (my cousins) were my age. The thought of losing one of my parents was unbearable. Needless to say, I was a mess. I needed my husband to be understanding and supportive, without question. When I told Luke the details for Jack's showing and funeral, he said we wouldn't be able to go.

"What are you talking about? We have to go!" I insisted.

"You weren't even that close with your uncle. You haven't even seen him in like four years," he reasoned.

"You have no idea what you're talking about! I love my uncle Jack very much. He was very special to me. And I love my family. I'm sure my dad is heartbroken, and so is my aunt Kim and my poor cousins and all of my aunts and Grandma and Papa. How would I even think of *not* being there? I can't believe you don't understand my need to be there! That is my family!"

From that moment on, I never again felt truly loved by Luke. I needed him to console me, hold me, tell me how sorry he was that I was in pain, and bend over backward to get us to that funeral. But he didn't do any of that.

I realized that he and I felt differently about "family." I knew he didn't want any more children and that he didn't necessarily like being around my family, but this was beyond unacceptable in my heart.

It gave me pause.

How was it that we had such different priorities, beliefs, desires, and plans? How did we grow so far apart? Why did we never see eye to eye?

I realized that I wanted to be close to my family, I wanted a big family of my own, I wanted to adore and respect my partner in life, and I needed that unconditional love. He could never be the way he was when I met him; I had hurt him too deeply, and, besides, we were just too different.

Fortunately, or unfortunately, I was no longer able to live like that. I came to a point where I wanted out. I tried not think about it. I just focused on Delilah and school.

Change

My second year of medical school started, and I became a "blue coat," for extra money; that meant I was an anatomy tutor to the first-year students. I was assigned to teach the heart. I would have five or six people around me at once, listening to me explain what I was showing them with an actual dissected heart.

Kevin Landing was one of those first years. He was funny and flirty, and he made me feel smart. Soon enough, Kevin was everywhere. He made it known that he was infatuated with me.

He would often tell me, "You are my dream woman."

Kevin's compliments happened all the time. We might be in the break room, playing foosball; or, I might be quizzing him on heart anatomy.

One day, we in the break room, playing foosball, and, as usual, I was self-deprecating, saying, "I don't need to eat lunch; I'm a fat heifer."

"Why are you so mean to yourself? Wouldn't you be pissed if someone else told you that you don't need to eat because you're a heifer?" he asked in all seriousness.

What the hell? I thought.

He stopped flicking his little stick-guys at the ball and looked me in the eye. "Don't be so mean to yourself. You are the coolest, most beautiful woman I have ever met."

"Whatever!" I said, dismissing him with my signature eye roll.

"I am serious. You are amazing."

"Yep, I'm amazing," I responded with complete sarcasm and whacked the ball into his goal.

Kevin taught me how to play Ping-Pong and made me listen to the Dave Matthews Band. That music was so captivating and full of life that I couldn't help but see all of his fun, loving, energetic qualities. He dreamed big and didn't live in fear. He was a lot like me. When he wanted something, he went for it and made it happen.

Kevin seemed to appreciate everything about me, when I wasn't holding back or trying to impress him. I was just being completely myself, no holds barred. And he insisted that I love myself. He insisted that I acknowledge all of my amazing attributes and let myself shine, without any shame.

"I can't believe you have a ten-year-old daughter. You are an amazing mom for working so hard to give her a better future. I really admire all your maturity and strength. I would be honored if you were my wife. Your husband would be a fool to not realize what he has," he told me when we talked about our lives.

That gave me pause.

Here was a man who accepted me and loved me for me. He loved my competitive drive to win every Ping-Pong game and be the best in my class. He loved my loud, boisterous personality and my fucking sailor mouth. He laughed when I burped loud enough to shake the walls, unlike Luke, who would give me unaccepting looks of disgust.

I didn't really share my feelings with Tina, because I knew I should be ashamed of myself. I was cheating on Luke, in my heart. I didn't think she would understand. However, at that point, fate intervened.

Tina was having intense abdominal pain while we were studying our gastrointestinal class, but she blew it off as mental, like she had Munchausen syndrome. We laughed because in every new systems class we took, someone would insist they had the disease we were studying. I'm sure that many in my class worried that their diarrhea was undiagnosed celiac disease or their heartburn was esophagitis or their persistent cough was actually tuberculosis—or other crazy things.

It turned out that Tina wasn't imagining it or being paranoid; she ended up actually having appendicitis, which required emergency surgery. She was gone for over a week. So, for the first time, I was alone at school. During that time, Kevin and I let our feelings get the best of us. By then, I knew that I had to leave Luke; it was completely unfair to him.

I spent many nights not being able to sleep or study because I was so distraught over the state of my marriage. I almost flunked endocrine class. My professor told me I only passed the exam by one question and that he would let it slide once, but that was it. I felt myself becoming deeply depressed and withdrawn. I became almost nonfunctioning. I lay in bed, in the mornings, while Luke got ready for work and Delilah got ready for school. I stayed in bed until it was time for them to come home. It took everything I had to get myself out of bed and start making dinner.

"Didn't you go to class today? I feel like you've missed a lot of class recently," Luke said.

"I don't need to go. I get the notes; it's fine," I lied.

I wanted to tell him how miserable I was and that I felt like our marriage was over, but Delilah was always around. The thought of ruining her world broke my heart.

Tina called me and asked, "Why didn't you come visit me after my surgery?"

"I'm sorry. I'm such shitty friend. I haven't really been going to class 'cuz I don't feel up to it."

"What the heck is wrong with you? You love school," she reminded me.

"I don't know. There's just a lot going on in my head, and I feel lost."

"Well, I'm coming back to school tomorrow, so you'd better be there. We can talk after class. Okay?" she insisted.

I was able to force out of myself a hint of happiness. "Okay. I'm glad you're all healed up. I miss you. I'll see ya tomorrow."

When I didn't show up the next day, Tina knew something was really wrong. She came over after class. I dragged myself out of bed and let her in.

I told her, "I just don't want to do any of this anymore. I need to focus on Luke and my marriage. If I don't do that, we're going to end up getting divorced. The problem is, I don't want to be with him anymore. I just want to give up."

"Cat, I think you should see a therapist or psychiatrist. I think you need counseling and maybe some meds," Tina said.

"I'll be fine. I just need to stop being so weak. I need to get my shit together, and I need to do it soon."

"You know it doesn't work like that. You are depressed. You can't just talk yourself out of it. Obviously, or you would have shown up in class today, like you said you were going to. Aren't you afraid of failing out of school?" Tina asked.

That moment was eye opening. I realized I was scared to admit that I needed help. This was the one area of my life where fear got the better of me. "I'm so afraid that if I admit I need help, I will spiral down into some crazy mess!"

"I hate to tell you, but you are already there," she said in all honesty.

"Fuck!" I shouted in defeat as I slammed my hand on the table.

"It's okay, Cat. You are the strongest girl I know. You will figure all this out; you just need some help getting your mind out of the deep, dark hole that it fell into. I will email Professor Sawyer and ask who you should go see. Okay?"

"It's not okay, but I guess it has to be. Right?"

"Right."

"Thank you for checking on me. I don't deserve to have such an awesome friend."

"No more crazy talk, Cat. Go take a shower. We're going out to lunch."

I gave Tina an extra-long hug. I felt so grateful that she was trying to pull me out of that deep, dark hole. She found me a psychiatrist, and I was able to get to see her that week. I poured out my heart. What did I have to lose, besides her diagnosing me as bipolar or something.

She didn't say anything scary. She just told me what I already knew. "I think you have underlying depression, and your situation brought it out. I think you can start to feel better if you exercise for stress relief, confront your personal issues with your husband, and get better sleep. You should probably start on some Prozac. It will help you feel better so that you can do those things. We are starting to understand that people with depression have low levels of serotonin in the brain, so giving you Prozac should help your brain get the serotonin you need. Prolonged periods of stress, like impending divorce, studying in medical school, and sleep deprivation deplete your serotonin levels, which exacerbates your depression."

It all made sense to me. It was exactly what I had learned as a first year, but admitting that it was happening to me was a completely different thing. For so long, I had believed that I was strong enough to overcome my depression on my own. Now I was realizing that I could help control it by making healthier choices, but it wasn't about being strong or weak. It was a chemical imbalance. It was a scientifically based medical problem that deserved to be treated as such. It wasn't a choice to feel this way, and it wasn't something to be ashamed of.

The psychiatrist likened it to thyroid disease. "When your

thyroid isn't producing enough thyroid hormone, we give you Synthroid to replace it. When your body isn't making enough serotonin, maybe you need to take something to replace it."

Within a week, I was functioning again. I wasn't going to end up in psych ward, needing electroshock therapy, like Sylvia Plath— at least not this time. That entire experience was actually empowering. Once I started feeling like myself again, I was ready to take control of my life. I wanted to find happiness, peace, and truth again. I wanted to be the amazing person that I dreamed I could be.

I asked Kevin out to lunch and told him everything I had gone through.

"I'm so relieved that you are okay, Cat. I really care about you, and you deserve to have an amazing life. I hate the thought of you being depressed. You are way too fun and loving to be locked in your room all day!"

I told him that I wanted to get a divorce, but I didn't know if I would survive. He insisted that I would. He told me that his parents got divorced when he was young, and his parents and their respective spouses were actually friends and hung out with each other.

"That will never happen with Luke," I told him.

"No, but maybe you can be amicable, raise Delilah in a happy, loving way, and quit hurting each other," he explained.

After our food came, he asked if he could say a prayer.

"Of course," I answered, quite stunned.

"Dear Lord, please help Cat find the strength to do what is in her heart. Please let her see how strong and amazing she is and that people will love her no matter what. Dear Lord, just please look over her during this time. Amen."

"Amen," I repeated.

My heart was full. Not only did he show me unconditional love and live without fear, but he also had faith and was proud to show it. That sealed the deal. He had just reminded me that I needed Christ in my life. That was what was missing from my marriage and my life.

So many times, I had wanted to be active in a church again and raise Delilah with some faith. I realized I was failing her with the most important job there was. She needed to know Jesus's unconditional love. I hadn't given her the foundation of faith, which had been the cornerstone of my foundation.

From then on, I prayed that giving her and teaching her love would be enough to make her foundation strong, sturdy, and safe. I also prayed that it wasn't too late for her to accept Jesus as her Savior.

I realized I could get an apartment and take care of Delilah while still kicking ass in school.

Kevin promised that he would help me, and he made it clear that he wanted to marry me as soon as I was free.

"Well, according to the law, you have to wait six months to have your divorce finalized when there are children involved," I explained.

"You just tell me the date!" he replied.

Now I had to tell Luke. I was scared to death.

I sat Luke down and told him how depressed I had become because I was miserable. I told him I couldn't live that way anymore. "I don't want to end up like our parents. I don't want to look back at my life and feel regret. I want to be in a happy and loving relationship. I want to show Delilah that she should do whatever it takes to be happy and live without regret; that means living an authentic life—being true to who you are."

"So, you want a divorce. Is that it? Is that what you're trying to tell me?" he asked, trying to stay calm.

"You're not miserable?" I asked sarcastically.

He eventually agreed that we were miserable together, but I

could tell he wasn't ready to change his situation. Part of me didn't want to leave; my heart was breaking in half. I felt like a failure, but I also felt finished. The only reason to stay, that I could come up with, was Delilah and our parents. But I realized that Delilah deserved to see an example of a loving, respectful marriage, not one of complacency, denial, and resentment. For so long, I had stayed out of obligation and guilt.

Since when did I do anything I didn't want to? For everyone's sake, I had to leave.

I gave him the silent treatment for an entire week because I wanted him to think about what he really wanted, without any discussion. I wanted him to face his truth and not feel like he could rely on me to ignore it and just say, "Never mind; we'll work on it." We had done that too many times already, and it never got better. We were good at having drag-out fights, followed by deep, meaningful apologies, exchanging many big promises of changing, only to renege within days. We had proven over the course of many years that we were not capable of making those changes.

I was finally ready to admit defeat and try something new. Kevin made it look so appealing—he was fun, accepting, encouraging, driven, and fearless, just like I was. My heart responded to that.

He loved me for me. He embraced the real me and insisted he couldn't live without me. I was finally getting everything I had longed for.

I was also getting a second chance to be a great wife. There was no baggage, no bad memories, and no heartbreak—only a future in which to try again and do it right. I wanted to live with integrity and honesty. I wanted a partner in life; someone who would make me a better person, and vice versa.

Luke and I had never really grown up as a couple or gotten over all the hurt we had caused each other; we were never able to be who we needed to be together. We didn't make one another better, the way partners should. We both deserved a chance to have that. I wanted someone to love him the way he deserved to be loved. I wanted someone to love the real me, and not feel ashamed or worried all the time that I was embarrassing him, pissing him off with my actions, or just was not good enough.

Luke and I finally agreed that our marriage was over. I told him that I would move out and that I would leave everything for him. I wouldn't take anything except my personal things. We agreed to joint custody and promised to always put Delilah first. We promised to never speak ill of each other. We decided to tell Delilah together.

I will never forget that painful moment. We sat her down on the couch, and Luke said, "Your mommy and daddy are getting a divorce."

Before he could say anything else, she screamed and cried out, "*No!*"

She sobbed harder than I had ever heard her cry before. My heart was completely broken at that point. "No, please don't get divorced. I can't handle that," she pleaded.

He continued, "We both love you very much, and you will still be with both of us, but we won't be together."

I hugged her and held her and didn't let go. I cried even harder than she did. I couldn't believe I was breaking up our family. How could I be so selfish? I wanted to take it all back and take all of her pain away, but I knew that if I did that, there would be ten times more pain to come. *Rip it off like a Band-Aid*, I thought to myself.

After she calmed down, she asked, "Can I at least be with one of you like Sunday, Monday, Tuesday, and Wednesday? Because I want it to be fair. I want weekdays and weekends with both of you. I don't want to see one of you just on weekends."

"That is a good idea. We are very proud of you for being so

mature and strong. We both love you so much, and that will never change," I replied, and Luke agreed.

A little later, Delilah and I were petting Gracie, one of our two cats, and she said, "I think Gracie should live with you, and Hunter can live with daddy, so Hunter can't be mean to Gracie anymore. I think Gracie will be very happy moving out with you. And I can have kitties at both places, so I don't miss them."

"I think you're right; Gracie would be very happy to have a new place without Hunter," I agreed, thinking how fitting her analogy was.

Hunter didn't like Gracie and always picked on her, and Delilah could understand her wanting to get away from that, because we had failed at changing Hunter's behavior toward Gracie. Our cats' relationship helped Delilah understand and deal with what her parents were going through.

The next few months were very difficult. Kevin helped me find an apartment, move my things, and get settled. I had a bedroom for Delilah and tried to make it special. Kevin built her a mermaid bed and painted a sea-life motif on the walls; she thought that was really cool. He stayed with me the nights that I didn't have Delilah. Those nights were really hard for me. I missed her so much, and I hated the thought of not lying in her bed and reading to her every night.

I had agreed with Luke that we wouldn't have anyone live with us unless we were remarried. Kevin bought a huge, fancy diamond ring and proposed to me the weekend my parents were coming to meet him. He told them that we planned to get married in August, before my third year started, because this would be our only break from school until we graduated, and we didn't want to wait years to get married and go on a honeymoon.

My dad was quiet and standoffish because he didn't approve. My parents never really saw Luke and me fight or not get along.

We always made sure we looked like the perfect couple. I rarely told my parents anything of substance, so when I told them I was divorcing Luke and had met Kevin, they were shocked and not happy. I'm sure they expected Luke and me to stay together, no matter what, like they did.

Maybe I was just a failure or a quitter. I'd like to think that I was an imperfect human who made mistakes and wasn't capable of fixing them, so I was going to make the best of things and salvage what life I had left. We had exhausted all efforts trying to make our marriage work, and so now it was time to try something new.

Not only did I see a future where happiness and love were possible again, but I also loved Luke deeply, and I wanted that for him as well. I felt a huge amount of guilt for hurting him and letting him waste his life supporting me when he had bigger fish to fry.

"Go to Hollywood and become an actor. Be selfish; do what you've always dreamed of. You are free now. Go live your life," I insisted.

I wanted to see him succeed.

In those months following, I made sure I was an active, loving, and attentive mom on the days I had Delilah. The other days were spent at the coffee shop with Kevin, studying until all hours, drinking more coffee than any human should possibly ingest. We were a great team. We quizzed each other and pushed one another to do our best.

Soon enough, Kevin and I were planning a huge, elaborate wedding. He really wanted to have a big wedding back in his hometown. "I've never been married. This is going to be my one and only time, and I want everyone there to witness our love. I want to give you the princess wedding that you deserve."

"Only if you really want to. I don't need that, but if you do, then let's do it," I agreed.

We invited more than 250 people. Most of my extended family

came, from all the way across the state, booked hotel rooms, and partied the night away at an extravagant reception. We pulled it off on our tight, school-loan budget. We were able to save money on almost everything because Kevin and his mother seemed to have connections for everything. They knew the jeweler, the florist, a cake lady, and the guy who rented out the hall, and his family cooked all the food and got the alcohol cheap from Canada. You'd never know it, because it turned out beautiful.

Delilah was my maid of honor; she looked like my little mini me. And my girl Charlie, my BFF from second grade, was a bridesmaid, along with Tina, and my sisters. My mom made my wedding dress from scratch, along with all the bridesmaids' dresses and her mother-of-the-bride gown.

My wedding to Kevin was a clear example of how amazing my family truly was. They always lived in love. When I took Kevin to meet Grandma and Papa Jansen, they welcomed him with hugs and complete acceptance.

"If you love our Cathy, then we love you," Grandma said.

Even though I hadn't seen many of my family members in years, I think almost every one of my extended family came, and Kevin welcomed them with open arms. My family just wanted me to be happy. My dad took a little longer to come around, but when I told him how Kevin treated me and how he had a strong faith in God, he accepted him. My dad was just being protective of his daughter.

Kevin planned an elaborate honeymoon to Belize. I had never been out of the country, not even Canada. He was well traveled—he had backpacked through Europe, traveled the US, and had gone on mission trips to Mexico. He spoke fluent Spanish and took care of everything. I was not used to being with a man like that. He was so confident and thoughtful. He was also so friendly and outgoing; he made me look shy, which is saying a lot. I enjoyed being taken care of and pampered.

I had brought my old tankini bathing suit, with its boy-short bottoms and a top that covered my stomach. He said that suit was completely unacceptable. He talked me into going bathing-suit shopping when we got there. The suits were so skimpy, with nothing but strings and triangles. I was mortified at the thought of wearing something like that, but he insisted I try some on. He handed me a bright-pink suit, and I reluctantly tried it on. I was surprised that I didn't hate it. *Maybe I can pull it off if I get tan enough,* I thought.

"You are stunning! You are the hottest woman ever!" he declared.

I was embarrassed and uncomfortable, but I wanted to make my new husband happy, and he seemed to think it looked good. He bought it, and I wore it every day. He took pictures of me by the pool, in the room, and did a mini photo shoot in the ocean. He made me feel like a *Sports Illustrated* swimsuit model. Was this really happening?

My confidence was growing exponentially because of him. Over the years, my stretch marks had faded from dark purple to white, and my fake boobs had made me feel sexy again, but was his attention and complete acceptance boosted my self-esteem more than anything else.

Did I mention that, when we were intimate for the first time, I cried in shame? I didn't want him to feel my boobs or know that they were fake. I was so afraid to get naked, but he was patient and continually reassured me that I was the most beautiful woman he'd ever seen.

When I started crying, he became so concerned. "What's wrong? Why are you crying?"

I finally mustered up the courage to tell him, because I knew I wanted to have a completely honest and open relationship. I was going to do it right this time, and never keep anything from him. "I'm just really ashamed. I need you to know that, when I had

Delilah and breast-fed her, it ruined my breasts. I was eighteen years old and left with nothing but deflated, scarred-up skin. I looked disgusting. I tried to not let it bother me, and I lived like that for years, but I finally broke down and got a breast augmentation a few years ago so that I could quit hating my body."

"It's okay. I know they're not real," he said in a sweet, gentle tone. "You don't have to be ashamed. My stepmom has had like three boob jobs. It's not a big deal, Cat. I love you no matter what. You should always do whatever you need to do to feel good about yourself."

"Thank you for understanding and accepting me. I don't deserve you," I replied.

"You deserve the world, more than anyone. You've worked harder and struggled more than any other girl I've ever met, and you appreciate it. You are special, and I knew it as soon as I met you."

His love and acceptance gave me a renewed sense of confidence. I was ready to conquer the world.

I do deserve the world, I told myself.

My Purpose

I started my third year of medical school, which consisted of me doing various specialty rotations, which changed every four weeks. When I made my schedule, I listened to my heart and signed up for an OB/GYN rotation as soon as I could.

I was assigned to work with Dr. McDaniels. For my four-week OB/GYN rotation, I would be in his office every day. When I arrived the first day, he gave me attitude for being five minutes late. I apologized profusely and promised it wouldn't happen again. He proceeded to quiz me about Pap smears and HPV (human papilloma virus). I must have given the right answers, because he let up and started telling me how fun it was to be an OB/GYN, and how much money he made.

"I just ordered a Porsche 928 sports car. Do you want to know how much it cost?" he said proudly.

"Nope," I replied.

"It was a hundred thousand dollars, and I had to special order it, so I don't even have it yet. If you want to be poor and drive a Honda, then you should do internal medicine, like Phil Zuckerman. If you want to be able to buy a Porsche with cash, then you should be a gynecologist, like me."

I had just finished my internal-medicine rotation with Dr. Zuckerman; apparently, they were friends in med school way back when.

"Did Phil check his stocks every day when you were with him?" Dr. McDaniels asked, smiling.

"Yes. How did you know that? He was always worrying about what his stocks were doing," I explained.

"Guess how often I check my stocks?" Dr. McDaniels asked. "Never. I know what I'm doing, and they're making me rich, so I don't need to worry about it. That's the difference," he answered, laughing.

I quickly saw that Dr. McDaniels was very cocky and sarcastic, but, just as quickly, I also realized that he was a good doctor. He had reason to be; he enjoyed what he did, and his patients loved him.

Every patient who came to his office was happy to see him, and he acted like they were best buds. He made them feel important and cared for. I admired his confidence and his ability to make naked women feel comfortable during the most uncomfortable of moments.

I shadowed him every day, and we saw all kinds of women. It reminded me of why I had chosen to go to medical school in the first place.

One Tuesday afternoon, he said, "Meet me at the hospital in the morning. I have to do a C-section on a lady, and I'm on call."

"Really? Do you think I'll be able to watch?"

"You can do whatever I tell them you can do, so, yes. You might even get to see a vaginal delivery," he said in his usual cocky tone.

I was so nervous. I hadn't worked in the hospital with him yet. I thought, *What if I love it? What if I realize I really want to be an OB/GYN? He makes it seem so great. I guess we'll see what happens.*

That next day, I made sure I wasn't late. He gave me scrubs to put on, and I followed him around like a lost puppy. He introduced me to his patients, saying things like "This is Dr. Jansen, my cute and, hopefully, smart student." He always got a laugh. He made his patients feel good.

Then, we met the OB residents. He made them feel bad. "This is Dr. Jansen, my hot student, who has shown in two days that she is much smarter than all of you. She is going into the C-section, so help her out."

I wasn't sure how the residents felt about him, but he obviously didn't care. Unfortunately, they gave me major attitude, like I was invading their space and hogging their attending.

Dr. McDaniels must have sensed my concern. He said, "Don't worry about them; they're just jealous."

The C-section was incredible. I couldn't believe how gruesome and barbaric it really was. There was cutting and ripping and pulling. Amniotic fluid shot out like a geyser, and blood poured out and down the sides of the table.

After he pulled the baby out, with great force, he announced, "It's a girl!"

"What the fu—?" the patient started to say from behind the curtain.

Dr. McDaniels cut her off. "Sorry! There's his penis; it's a boy!"

He knew damn well what he was doing. He loved to joke around and get a rise out of people. The entire OR team roared with laughter and shook their heads at his inappropriateness. I thought it was refreshing and awesome. That was a story the parents would tell for decades.

Then, he took the uterus out through the incision and placed it onto her abdomen. He dug inside the uterus a few times, while squeezing and massaging it.

He showed me her bowels. "And here's her guts," he announced, more joking than teaching.

He sutured layer after layer, then finally put everything back the way it belonged. All the while, the patient was talking and enjoying her baby, her husband, and her experience.

How is he possibly making this woman, who is cut wide open, with her internal organs outside her body, comfortable and happy? I wondered. It was incredible and so impressive. *I would love to do that.*

I was aching to scrub in, feel those organs, and suture that uterus closed.

I listened as he criticized the resident who was doing her side of the surgery. He was harsh with her.

Could I handle that? I wondered, but then I answered inwardly, *Fuck, yeah!*

After the C-section, we went to the cafeteria for lunch. He told me to get whatever I wanted. I got the salad bar and saw a vanilla pudding, just like I had served at my dad's restaurant back in the day. We sat down and started eating. He looked at my plate, then at me, and snickered. I didn't know what to think, so I ignored it.

After I finished my salad, I took a big spoonful of the pudding, and my entire face puckered in disgust. It was mayonnaise! I looked up and he had a huge smile on his face.

"How's your mayonnaise taste?"

I grabbed my napkin and spit out the mayonnaise, wiping my tongue.

"You suck!" I started laughing from embarrassment. "Why did you let me eat that?" I asked in a snotty tone.

"I wanted to see your reaction. I couldn't help myself." He laughed even harder.

There I was, a third-year med student trying to impress my attending, feeling out of place and over my head, and I had just humiliated myself. *Don't show him how mortified you are,* I told myself. *Be confident and laugh it off. Show him you can take whatever comes your way.*

That afternoon definitely made up for lunch. A patient of his showed up in labor and said that I could be in the room. It wasn't her first baby. She and her husband were a little older and seemed so happy. She had a natural labor, and her husband coached her through the pain. The delivery was quiet, controlled, loving, and truly magical. Dr. McDaniels was gentle and, at the same time, funny. He kept the mood happy and seemed to truly enjoy his work.

When that little girl came out, I saw the instant unconditional love in their eyes, and it gave me flashbacks to Delilah's birth. I cried tears of joy and felt honored to be able to be a part of the most intimate, most important moment in their lives.

This was my purpose.

This was why I had busted my ass for so many years, sacrificed time away from my family, missed holidays, and gone into significant debt—I was supposed to be an OB/GYN.

When I got home that evening, I couldn't wait to tell Kevin how amazing my day had been. I excitedly proclaimed, "I know what I'm going to do! I am going to be an OB/GYN, just like I originally planned. I'm sorry that the hours are long and invasive, but this is my calling."

Kevin reacted in the perfect way a supportive, loving partner should. "That is awesome! There's nothing to be sorry about. Being doctors is what our life is going to be about; it's not just going to be our jobs. You are special, and women are going to be blessed to have you as their doctor."

I was beaming from ear to ear. I couldn't wait to change my other rotations to focus on becoming a doctor for women. I needed to be a great surgeon, I needed to understand sexual health, mental health, and internal medicine. It felt great to reclaim my purpose.

I was feeling strong. I was ready to take on Dr. McDaniels and the other attendings. I knew that I had to kick ass and impress them, because I had to get accepted into that residency program. I wouldn't be able to move, because I had joint custody of Delilah. That really limited me. It was the only OB/GYN residency in town, so I needed to make it happen. I had only applied to university medical school, and I had gotten in, so I knew I could do it again. I knew it would be hard, but, luckily, I had no idea just *how* hard. If I had truly known ahead of time, I wouldn't have made it through.

Getting picked for residency was more about my personality than my grades or intelligence. There were sixteen residents at a time, four people for each of the four years. There was only one guy in the program. In addition to being accepted by fifteen female residents, I needed to be liked by the forty-plus nurses who worked in the department. They were very vocal, and the attendings listened to them when they had opinions.

I'd had an awful experience with one of the nurses during my very first day in the hospital with Dr. McDaniels. I had walked into the room of one his patients. She was in labor. I introduced myself to the patient and her husband, thanking them for letting me be in there, but, as soon as I walked out, the nurse followed me and grabbed my arm. She got right in my face and said, "Don't ever walk into my room again without talking to me first."

Apparently, I should have introduced myself to her first.

"I'm so sorry," I said. "Dr. McDaniels told me to go in and say hi to them."

"That is my patient and my room. You will talk to me first. Got it?" she said sternly.

"Yes, definitely," I replied in a defeated, confused way.

I told Dr. McDaniels, and he told me to not worry about it. "Just act like the nurses have the power, and your life will be a lot easier."

You'd better believe I remembered that on my first day of my OB hospital rotation a few months later. I needed the nurses to like me. I needed the residents to like me, and I needed to impress the attendings. I only had two months in which to accomplish that and make a good, lasting impression.

Most of the residents were really awesome and encouraging.

They taught me how to deliver a baby, suture real skin closed, present a patient to the attending over the phone at 3:00 a.m., check a cervix for dilation, and identify trichomonas under the microscope. John, a second-year, gave me the scalpel at the start of a C-section on a health-department patient and let me cut the patient open. He talked me through it, and I performed a large part of the surgery.

It was exhilarating.

I loved every terrifying moment of it. Being a surgeon seemed natural. I loved feeling the warmth of the patient's blood pumping under my hands; I loved being the first person to touch another human being as that tiny person entered the world.

I was entrusted with people's lives. What I did or didn't do could affect them for the rest of their lives.

What an honor and a privilege!

One attending, Dr. Wannabe, was mean and relentless from the get-go. The first time I met her, I mistook her for a nurse, and there was no way she was going to forgive me.

"She hates you," one of the residents told me when I asked him why she was giving me attitude.

Great. She hates me for no reason, I thought. Trying to win her over was useless, so I tried to avoid her like the plague. When I had to deal with her, I tried to kill her with kindness, but that just made her even snottier and more unaccepting of me.

So, instead of dwelling on it, I focused on things I had control over. I read as much as I could. I stayed late to follow through with deliveries I was in on. I rounded on patients I didn't even help deliver, just to help out the residents.

Once those rotations were over, I tried to talk to the OB residents whenever I saw them in the OR and cafeteria, and I made them all rock candy and cookies at Christmas time.

Then, fate intervened.

I met the GYN oncologist, Dr. Lewis, and he agreed to let me rotate with him as an elective toward the beginning of my fourth year, right before I had to apply to the residency program. He didn't usually take students and seemed to have little patience for the residents, or anyone who wasn't on their A game.

He was hard on me, but he let me get my hands dirty, from day one. He made me do colposcopies (looking at the cervix with a microscope) on cancer patients, debride abdominal wounds in the office, and catheterize post-op patients who had bladder injuries. And then, he took me to the OR and gave me a scalpel. I quickly learned that when he asked me if I could do something, I should always answer yes, because, then, he would let me do it. He respected confidence. Insecurity and hesitancy meant the kiss of death around Dr. Lewis.

Fake it till you make it, I would tell myself.

He would intervene if he didn't like what I was doing; or, he would just redirect me. As a medical student, I was assisting with vulvectomies (surgically removing the cancerous skin of the external female genitalia), ovarian cancer debulking (surgically removing cancer in the abdomen and pelvis that has spread from the ovaries, panniculectomies (surgically cutting off an obese patient's hanging belly fat), and anything else he let me do.

"Where the hell did you learn how to tie? You do this stupid thing with your thumb every time. Cut it out!" he insisted.

"You're just seeing it wrong. My tying is perfectly fine. Just admit that I'm a good surgeon, already!" I sneered.

"I will, as soon as you become one," he snarled back.

I could see his eyes smiling behind his mask.

"I'm only a fourth-year student! Just wait until I'm your age. I'm going to be so much better than you; you'll wish I was your partner," I insisted.

Traditionally, gynecologists avoid abdominal anatomy at all cost, and if they have to deal with it, they call in a general surgeon or a urologist for help. As a GYN oncologist, Dr. Lewis was trained to handle all of it. I studied his every move in the OR and tried to mimic him. He taught me to not fear the bowels or the ureters—or any other anatomy that most gynecologists feared.

I wanted to be like him. I wanted to be able to take care of anything I encountered in the OR and be able to fix anything I had injured. My time with him was invaluable. As fate would have it, when I started residency, he started working there as well, instead of the competing hospital across town.

After my rotation, I asked Dr. Lewis to write me a letter of recommendation. He wrote me a very nice letter. I was so proud of myself. When I read what he had written, I knew I had a great shot at getting accepted into that residency program: "She has great hands. Her surgical skills are well advanced for a student."

Dr. McDaniels wrote me a letter as well. He also praised my surgical abilities: "She is confident in surgery and has great skills."

I was so proud of myself for succeeding in something so important, something that had nothing to do with my looks. I was using my body for something important; I was using my hands to serve.

So, in typical Cat fashion, I only applied to one residency program, and I was accepted. A girl named Amanda, who was in my medical-school class the first two years, a guy named Anthony from Nebraska, and a guy named Lenny from Florida were the other three accepted for the next year's class.

The funny thing was that Amanda and I didn't really click with each other in med school. During our interviews, she told the other candidates the story of the first time we met. Apparently, I had forgotten all about it. I didn't know what she was going to say. She got all fired up and started telling the story. "We were making small talk after our first test, and then I said, 'By the way, I'm Amanda.'"

Apparently, I had responded, "Oh, you're the one from State? You're nicer than I thought you'd be."

"Yeah, and you're Cat from University, right? You're smarter than I thought you'd be," she had snarled back, as she told it now.

I laughed hysterically when she told this story, saying, "I really said that to you? That's fucking hilarious!"

"Yeah, ya did. I thought you were a bitch," she stated sharply.

The other interviewees laughed at our banter.

Amanda lightened up and laughed too. "Oh, Lord, they'd better not pick both of us. I don't think I can handle four years of you, Jansen."

She was only half joking.

Well, they did pick both of us.

Amanda and I were about to embark on an amazing journey together, one we later called *hell*. Anthony, the only other male resident who was chosen for our year, didn't even last three months. He had succumbed to the stress; he threw a few temper tantrums and eventually quit because he couldn't handle it. Honestly, I'm not sure how anyone survived. It was completely dysfunctional and malignant.

The idea that his mind got the best of him and so he quit really pushed me to be even better. I insisted that I could handle the stress, degradation, sacrifice, sleep deprivation, and constant judgment. I had made it this far in my life without completely succumbing to mental illness. I was still taking Prozac and seeing a therapist twice a month. *Mind, don't fail me now!*

Amanda and I became each other's saving grace. We relied on one another, supported one another, and pushed one another to be better. Every morning at 7:00 a.m., we had sign-out, where the night residents relayed all the information on the patients they were in charge of: the ones in labor, the ones being triaged for a complaint, the ones admitted with a medical problem, the ones who were postpartum (meaning, "already delivered"), and all the patients who'd just had surgery or were admitted from the ER.

When Amanda explained a probable diagnosis or treatment plan that I disagreed with, I would call her out on it, and a heated discussion would ensue. She did the same to me. It became a regular thing for us to question each other to the point where the other residents got sick of it.

"You're done," our chief resident would say.

We hated that. Even though our discussions got heated, we thrived on challenging each other and calling bullshit on the status quo. Sometimes residents would give their plans, and when I asked where the evidence was to back that up, they would say shit like "That's how we always do it" or "That's what Dr. Wannabe said to do."

I learned the hard way, during my first month of residency, to never answer like that. Dr. McDaniels almost ripped my head off in the OR when I told him, "That's how Dr. Wannabe does it." I never answered like that again.

Those reasons weren't good enough. We needed to hear that it was an ACOG recommendation or that Wilsons obstetrics said so; something with some evidence behind it. We didn't want to just learn tradition and hand-me-down medicine, which a lot of obstetrics was. We wanted to practice evidence-based medicine, which was a relatively newer concept in obstetrics, mostly because, historically, ethics had forbidden research and studies on pregnant women.

There was also a misconception that women and men were alike as far as medicine was concerned. Most evidence-based medicine came from men studying men, and the results were just extrapolated to women. In reality, women are nothing like men, so medicine was not so exact when it came to understanding and treating women, especially pregnant women.

Obstetrics, in particular, is fraught with myth and fear. Much of what is known was learned from poor outcomes and disasters, at the sacrifice of women's and children's lives. I was not okay with letting women suffer, and then just learning to do it differently the next time. I also didn't want to experiment on patients. I wanted to make their lives better, in the here and now. It was a complex situation with no easy answers, and I felt up to the challenge.

As residents, we each would do block weeks, day after day, either doing obstetrics or GYN surgery, or night after night of running the entire department on our own. As first-year residents, we had a senior resident with us for backup.

One night, a very obese Polynesian woman presented in labor. She hadn't had any prenatal care, so we didn't know anything about her. As soon as the nurse got her in a bed, IV placed, and baby monitors on, she started having a seizure. Julie was my senior resident, and the nurse called out for us. We ran into the room.

Julie ordered, "Get four grams of magnesium, call Dr. McDaniels, the anesthesiologist, and the pediatrician—*now!*"

She immediately grabbed the bed and rushed the patient to the OR. By the time we got into the OR, the patient had gone into cardiac arrest. We called a code blue, and Julie opened the emergency C-section tray, ripped the patient's gown open, splashed betadine on her abdomen, and quickly made a big incision.

In less than ten minutes from calling for help, she had pulled out a baby girl. The baby cried, and we all took a breath.

The internists and anesthesiologists had started CPR and were resuscitating the woman in the meantime.

Once Julie delivered the baby, the patient regained a pulse and eventually started breathing on her own.

Julie went from sleeping in our lounge to saving a baby and her mother, all in the span of about twenty minutes.

I just kept thinking, *Holy crap! Could I have done that if Julie weren't here with me? Well, someday, I'm sure I'll have to!*

I was so proud of her. Seeing her be able to perform like that as a third-year resident gave me confidence that I was in the right place and that I was going to end up becoming a great doctor. It seemed like a miracle, but it was a lot of smart, quick, brave actions on the part of a lot of young doctors just trying to do their best to save someone.

There were, however, other experiences that were completely devastating and out of our control. This solidified the fact that doctors are not God; we are just God's hands to serve.

We residents managed the county health department's women's clinic, with one of our attendings overseeing us. A typical day in the clinic involved seeing OB patients who were on Medicaid, either because they were young (like I had been), or they were poor. Some were from other countries and didn't speak any English. We had all the resources they needed, all in one place. It was so rewarding to be able to provide care to them and just show them some compassion and empathy.

One day, I saw an Indian patient and her husband. She was past her due date, and it was their first baby. I tried to explain that I wanted to check her cervix and that we should consider inducing her if she didn't go into labor soon. Her husband declined for her. They were agreeable to letting me look with the bedside ultrasound to at least make sure the baby was head down and still had a normal amount of amniotic fluid. I did the ultrasound, and the baby's head was well applied down on the cervix. There was a normal amount of fluid, the baby was moving and doing practice breathing—all reassuring signs that the baby was doing well. They agreed to come back in three days for a nonstress test, which was standard to do at forty-one weeks.

The next day, that Indian couple presented to the hospital because she was having contractions and green discharge. The nurse took her into a room to hook her up to the monitor, but she couldn't find the baby's heart tones. The nurse came out and told me to get the ultrasound machine.

"I'm sure the baby is fine; she was great yesterday in the office, and she's head down," I reassured the nurse as we walked into the room.

I smiled at the woman and her husband, and they looked relieved to recognize someone.

"Ah, you saw us yesterday," her husband said in his broken English.

"Yes," I said, smiling. "Let's see that sweet baby again," I explained as I put gel on her belly and started looking with the ultrasound probe.

There was the baby's heart, but it wasn't pumping at the normal 140 bpm. I was straining my eyes to see movement and wanted to believe I was seeing some, but I knew it was only the patient's own blood pumping that caused the slow motion on the screen.

I stared at the screen so long, praying that my eyes were deceiving me, that the nurse finally nudged me and whispered, "Should we call for a formal ultrasound?"

"No need," I said, heartbroken.

I looked into my patient's eyes, and she knew.

"I'm so sorry," I said.

She looked at her husband, and he said to me, "She told me the baby was not alive. She is right?"

"Yes." I nodded, my eyes welling up.

She cried silently, eyes closed, tears streaming down her face. He laid a small rug down on the floor next to her bed, got on his knees, and started to pray out loud in his language, bowing his head to the floor over and over. Surprisingly, his voice did not sound angry or like he was questioning anything. He sounded sad but grateful.

The nurse and I left the room to give them, and me, time to

process. For, soon, I had to explain that we needed to induce her to help her deliver her dead baby.

Their faith was so strong that they seemed completely at peace with everything that had to happen. They thanked us, and she never protested once. I encouraged her to get an epidural so she wouldn't have to feel physical pain; I imagined her emotional pain was overwhelming enough. Luckily, she didn't have to push very long. There were no excited shouts at her to push, no smiles of anticipation. It was quiet and somber, and when that baby girl came out, it felt surreal.

She had thick, silky black hair with curls on the ends. Her eyelashes were extra long and gorgeous. She looked like a beautiful, sleeping baby. I had delivered other stillbirths, but they usually were small, preterm babies who were already becoming deformed. This baby was more than eight pounds, and she looked completely healthy and perfect, except for a large true knot in her umbilical cord. That knot was her demise.

Her parents held her and loved on her for an hour or so. They prayed over her and seemed at peace. They thanked me and hugged me, as if I had done something good. I had given them their dead baby.

How can they possibly be thankful for me? I was so humbled by their faith and their unquestioning acceptance of life and death.

That gave me pause.

What a beautiful lesson that perfect little girl was for everyone. I wondered if I would be that gracious and forgiving to God if I were in their place.

Obviously, I had dealt with death during my internship and even working in the nursing homes. I had to pronounce people dead, tell their families, and prepare their bodies to be seen before they were taken away. But they were always elderly; they had lived their life, and so death made sense.

Seeing a brand-new baby not even getting a chance to take her first breath was different. What an incredible job I had. I realized that my calling was deeper than just making sure women were given options and a voice in their care. I was expected to help people during their most joyous, and also most devastating, moments in life.

What an honor, but I couldn't possibly be qualified!

Life was telling me otherwise.

I realized that I didn't have to experience all those terrible things myself to be empathetic. My patients needed compassion, support, a listening ear, and someone to help them focus on finding peace and forgiveness. I learned so much from caring for my patients. I should be thanking them, instead of them thanking me.

Appreciation and Exhaustion

That day, I went home and hugged Delilah for a long time and told her how grateful I was to be her mommy. I tried to be attentive and loving to her. I never wanted her to feel like my career robbed her of her mother. I wanted her to be proud of me and understand my sacrifices.

We regularly went to the mall to hang out. I liked buying her cute clothes, even though she would protest, saying, "You don't need to buy my love, Mom." She didn't understand my motivation. That wasn't it at all; I was trying to connect with her. When I was her age, I enjoyed clothes, and so I wanted to give her all the cute stuff that I would have wanted. Apparently, that wasn't really her thing; or, because it was my thing, she made sure she wasn't interested, in typical young-girl rebel fashion.

We often went and painted pottery, which we both enjoyed. It gave us alone time to just talk and connect. Part of her resisted connecting with me. She was angry at me for a long time, but once her dad got remarried, she started to be okay with things. She really liked Luke's new wife and family, which helped a lot.

Kevin was a loving stepfather. He tried to interact with her and make her feel special, and, secretly, I think that she liked how he said grace before meals. He always wanted to include her and make her feel important, which I really appreciated. We tried to always make her feel loved and wanted. We did everything we could to give her the opportunities that I never had. She was a great kid and a great student—basically, she was nothing like I had been. During my rebellious teenage years, my mom would yell at me, cursing me by saying, "I hope you end up with a daughter just like you!"

In fact, I got the complete opposite. Was this because her upbringing was so different from mine, or did we just have such different personalities that I had sought out mischief while she avoided it? I like to think it was both.

Somehow, even though Kevin and I were both in residency, we found time to live life outside the hospital. I appreciated that he was so full of adventure and passion for life, but he often took it to the extreme. He was obsessed with skiing and other daredevil, adrenaline-filled adventures, like skydiving and rock climbing. He would encourage me to find a hobby, but I knew that we both couldn't be off doing fun stuff. Someone had to be home taking care of the responsibilities of owning a house and having a child.

Since I had Delilah, it was easy for me to stay home. We usually watched Disney Channel shows on Fridays nights, and I would be out cold before the night was over. I was beyond sleep deprived. I dedicated all of my extra time to her. I spent many Saturdays going to her soccer tournaments out of town.

Speaking of sleep deprivation, mine was so bad that it was often dangerous for me to drive. That was definitely the case during the week. I slept at the same stoplight by the gas station, every morning. I trained myself to wake up when the light changed to green. My mind noticed the color difference through my eyelids. It was scary, but I couldn't help it. I tried rolling down the windows, playing music, and pinching myself, but I was so sleep deprived that I just learned to power nap.

Some days, instead of scarfing down lunch, I napped sitting up against a wall for twenty minutes. I took it however I could get it. I even fell asleep standing in the OR, holding a laparoscopic instrument.

"How is that even possible," you ask?

Well, sometimes the OR is dark; all the lights are off so that you can see the camera monitor. You are warm because you are wearing a gown, gloves, a hat, and a mask. And when you are a first-year and the low man on the totem pole, you get the menial job of holding something still, for painfully long periods of time.

When you are sleep deprived, that is a welcome reprieve; well, at least, until you accidentally jerk yourself awake and almost hurt someone. I guarantee I'm not the only resident who has experienced that, and I guarantee it wasn't the only incident at the operating table.

Truthfully, becoming a doctor is one of the unhealthiest things a person can do. In addition to being sleep deprived, any good eating habits you once had go out the window; you're lucky if you have any time or energy to exercise or have sex, you get mentally berated on a regular basis, and sometimes you get physically abused.

Being hungry was a sign of weakness, and it definitely wasn't a priority if you wanted to please your attendings. We ate whatever doughnuts or pastries were on the table at morning report. Our main focus was getting coffee; or, for some, Red Bull.

Sitting down to eat lunch was a perk. If you were doing surgeries or deliveries, then forget it. You might be lucky enough to scarf down the graham crackers and peanut butter from the patient kitchen; or, sometimes we would try to take care of each other, and a resident would bring you lunch from the cafeteria, because they were on office or triage that week, so they had time to walk down for food. The day shift didn't end until 6:30 p.m., so by the time you got home, dinnertime would be over.

One day, I realized that my attendings were living the same unhealthy way we were. They were the ones perpetuating this vicious cycle of self-abuse. Dr. Fleshing, in particular, would get very inpatient and nasty when she was hungry. I honestly hated working with her. I was assigned to her surgical cases for the day.

By the third case, I was thinking how awesome it was that she hadn't kicked me or yelled at me today. That turned out to screw me over because I let my guard down. I was joking around and enjoying her company, until we started the third case, and the laparoscope kept fogging up. Her mood flipped a switch, and she became annoyed and impatient. I tried joking around to lighten the mood, and that really ignited the flame. She must have pulled the laparoscope out of the trocar twenty times to wipe it off so that she could see, but, every time she put it back in, it fogged up again, making everything look blurry.

She was annoyed because she planned to get lunch before the cafeteria closed, and it was supposed to be any easy hysterectomy. The scrub tech encouraged her to just be patient, but she didn't like being told what to do.

"It's fine; hold this," she said as she handed me the camera.

She took the bipolar grasper (an instrument that is used to burn blood vessels closed) and picked up a pink/tannish tubular structure.

The fog was slowly blurring our vision, and I thought, *Are you sure that's the round ligament?*

Ching, ching, ching, ching, beep went the bipolar machine, and a thick plume of smoke completely covered our view. She removed the grasper, cleaned the camera in a huff, and then, when she slid it back into the patient, my stomach dropped. The scrub tech gasped. Dr. Fleshing started looking around the pelvis frantically, in disbelief.

No one said a word. She let go of the camera and went and sat on a stool in the corner.

I motioned for the circulating nurse to come over.

"Get the general surgeon in here—*now*," I ordered her in a quiet, polite tone.

I just stood there, feeling sad for the patient, until the general surgeon came in.

"What did you do now?" he said in a snarky, joking manner.

My eyes bugged out of my head. "I didn't do anything," I emphasized to him. "She accidentally burned the patient's small bowel."

"Well, Fleshing, get over here, and help me fix this!" the general surgeon demanded.

They were friends, and he didn't think much of the situation.

All of a sudden, she came back to life, so to speak, and started talking about how bad the equipment was, how it got foggy, and how it wasn't really her fault for burning the bowel.

I wanted so desperately to not be in that case. I was sick to my stomach. All I could think was *This coward is going to twist it around in her mind and blame me. How can I protect myself? I couldn't even protect this patient.*

I felt like I had failed the patient. She was supposed to go home the same day, with three tiny incisions and minimal pain. Now, she had to have a bowel resection, with a temporary colostomy bag attached to her abdomen, then go back to the OR for a second surgery with a large incision from above her belly button down to her pubic bone. She was there for a total of twenty-nine days.

Surprisingly, Dr. Fleshing was super sweet to me after that case. She forced me to eat lunch with her and was trying to be my buddy. "These things happen, ya know. Now we just need to make sure we keep her comfortable and happy, so she doesn't sue us. I want you to kiss her ass. Got it?"

"Yes, of course," I replied.

The next day, I was late and didn't get a chance to round on my patients before morning report. In morning report, I explained what had happened, and, luckily, the residents knew it was her fault. They knew her all too well. So, after report, I went upstairs to round.

Dr. Fleshing was at the nurse's station, and you could almost see flames shooting out of her nostrils. She grabbed my arm and yanked me into the corner. "Why the hell didn't you see my patient this morning, or last night, for that matter?" she demanded.

"I'm so sorry. I'm going right now. I thought you would have rounded on her last night to explain what happened," I said; regretting it the moment the words left my mouth.

"That is your responsibility! I told you to kiss her ass and take care of her. You are absolutely worthless. She could be septic or dying, and you wouldn't have any clue! Your ass should be rounding on her at least twice a day and calling me with updates. That is the *least* you should do."

Dr. Fleshing was being irrational and projecting, as usual. I didn't bother explaining that I called the nurse and checked on her as I drove in that morning and that I reviewed her vitals and labs as soon as I got to the hospital.

So, I rounded on her twice a day for twenty-eight days, kissed her ass, and kept Dr. Fleshing from getting sued.

Truthfully, *she* should have seen the patient that first night and apologized to her. Seeing as I was only a first-year resident, *she* should have brought me with her, so I could see how to tell a patient bad news and how to handle a malpractice situation. But, alas, she wasn't capable of that; her ego was too big.

I can't say she didn't teach me anything; she taught me lots of things. She taught me the importance of being patient, eating before the "han-gry" kicks in (a combination of *hungry* and *angry*), and how *not* to treat other human beings. What little respect I had for her was now gone. I felt sorry for her patients. They were always an afterthought to her.

That experience reaffirmed my desire to give women better

options for who they went to. I cringed at the thought of a few of my attendings taking care of me. It shouldn't be like that, but that's real life. Just like there are many bad electricians, accountants, etc., there are many bad doctors, nurses, and others in the medical profession—all of whom, unfortunately, are trusted when they should not be.

As a child, I lied, stole, and cheated, but I wasn't trying to be malicious. I was trying to figure out how the world worked and how I fit into it.

Once I knew better, I did better.

The thought of even being capable of doing those things now is foreign to me. I wouldn't be able to live with myself, and I have no reason to do those things. For me, growing up meant developing a conscience. I realized that sinning not only hurt the people I loved, it also hurt my soul.

When you sin, you become less complete; you lose a part of you. Your whole being consists of integrity, grace, forgiveness, joy, empathy, honesty, love, and faith. Broken people have lost one or more of those necessary attributes, which causes even more breakage. It's impossible to be whole if you are consistently lacking some of those pieces.

As difficult as residency was, there were aspects that I cherished, like the relationships. Kevin and I were couple friends with Bill and his wife, Emily. Bill was a year ahead of me. He was an ER resident. Emily was an accountant, so she got annoyed whenever the three of us talked about work or medicine.

She and Bill were adventurous, fun, and brave. I had a lot of my "firsts" with them. They taught us how to kayak and white-water raft on the Upper Gauley, in West Virginia. We went skydiving by Niagara Falls. And, the first time I even smoked pot was with them. I couldn't stop belly laughing, for probably an hour.

I know, I'm just as surprised as you are that I was almost thirty before I ever really smoked pot. The thought of it never appealed to me; probably because my dad did it, and he and everyone else I knew who did it, craved it and made it a huge part of their life. I didn't want that crutch. Somehow, I was able to quit smoking cigarettes when I got pregnant in high school, and I never became addicted to alcohol. Addiction runs in my family, so that thought always worried me and kept me in check. I was very fortunate to not get the addiction gene.

Anyway, Emily got baby fever and became pregnant. I had the honor of delivering her. It was a long and difficult labor. Her baby was stuck asynclitic, occiput posterior (aka, coming down crocked and wrong). I had to work hard to slowly help the baby turn into the correct position. I finally got him to turn, and I helped Bill deliver his firstborn son. It was such a beautiful moment.

I cherish those moments.

Following her delivery, I delivered quite a few of the wives of my fellow residents; I felt so honored that they trusted me to be a part of their most intimate times. I loved bringing babies into the world, and I also loved seeing how their siblings reacted. My younger siblings were inseparable. It was a special unique relationship that I didn't really get to have, because Steve was so much older than I was, and the others were so much younger.

I always felt bad that Delilah didn't have any siblings and that she would never experience that relationship. She and my youngest sister were close when they were young, but since they didn't see each other very often, they eventually grew apart. Delilah often said she wished she had a little sister, and I really wanted to give her one, but there was never a good time. Luke had never wanted more kids, and Kevin and I were too busy.

Then, I got baby fever. I had always wanted to have more kids, but I was very afraid of having another vaginal delivery like the one I had with Delilah. I dreamed of having many children to laugh with, to support and encourage, and to watch grow into awesome human beings. I also loved the idea of having a baby to snuggle with and give all my attention to, so I finally mustered up the courage and made an appointment with one of my attendings, Dr. Middleton.

I told her about my fears of having another fourth-degree tear and my hesitation to go to an attending in our residency. "I really want to have a more kids, but only if I can have a planned C-section. I don't want to rip all the way through my ass again. And I really want to breast-feed, but I don't know if I can because I had breast implants about eight years ago. I don't want anyone to know, so can you please not put that in my chart? I'm ashamed of that decision I made so long ago."

I cried when I finished telling her all this. It felt overwhelming to finally acknowledge my fears and embarrassment out loud.

She relieved my fears. "Of course we can do a C-section. You know better than most people the risks of surgery, so if you want to do that, then I'd love to do it for you. And don't worry about the other stuff; it's no one's business. You shouldn't be so ashamed. I feel bad seeing you like this. I won't tell anyone, but it's okay, because no one would think any less of you. I'm glad you confided in me."

"Thank you. I definitely want you to be my doctor. I trust you and appreciate your understanding," I responded.

Dr. Middleton put my mind at ease. I decided to no longer live in fear. Kevin and I were ready to start our family. We agreed that life had been too much about delayed gratification and working endless hours for some pie-in-the-sky hope that we would, some-day, be able to start our "real life."

I was done putting my life on hold. I told myself that I could handle my last year of residency being pregnant, and then I could take some time off to enjoy my baby before I became an attending.

Looking back, I think that was sleep deprivation making me delusional. Just kidding!

So, we tried to get pregnant for a few months, and, by the third month, I was. I could hardly contain my excitement. By the time I could see a little gestational sac with the ultrasound, I was telling everyone at the hospital. There wasn't even a baby yet, but I couldn't keep it to myself. The nurses laughed at my inability to keep it a secret.

"I can't help it; I'm just so excited!" I exclaimed.

I loved coming to work every day, because I got to look at my little baby growing inside me, using the ultrasound machine we had in the department. By the time I was four months along, Natalie, one of the residents, would joke about the size of my baby's penis whenever she caught me looking with the ultrasound. That led to jokes through the whole department.

"I have a huge penis inside of me right now!" I would say during morning report or during a stressful situation during the day to help relieve the tension.

Everyone would burst out laughing and respond with statements like "How does that huge penis feel today?" and "How can you work with that big penis in there?"

That kind of stupid stuff got us through some rough days.

I had a lot of extra responsibility as the chief resident that year. I had to make the rotation and work schedules for all fifteen residents for the year. I had to be fair and supportive and consider everyone's requests and life events. I often had to listen and play mediator between fighting residents or upset attendings who felt like they were getting the short end of the stick.

I couldn't believe that Dr. Slayton, my program director, picked me for this job. I felt honored, but, at the same time, very humbled and a little inadequate. People seemed to like how I handled things, which boosted my confidence. I started to feel like I could handle anything thrown my way, until one day, when I snapped.

For four years, I did everything I could to make Dr. Wannabe happy, and, at times, I saw a glimmer of hope. There were times when she loosened up and treated me decently. When I became chief, she actually started talking to me with some respect; that is, until the day she caused me to snap.

Another attending, who used to be a resident, was Dr. McPhail. One morning, he was complaining to me that there wasn't a resident taking care of his labor patient.

"All the residents are going to lecture for the morning, just like they do every first Monday of the month for the past decade, which you know because you just finished residency, like yesterday," I snarled.

I gave him attitude because, somehow, he had forgotten what it was like to be a resident. He turned into an egomaniac. He started yelling at my junior resident, Pam, blaming her for his patient not going into labor quickly enough. Then, Dr. Wannabe jumped in with her complaints and accusations. They were ganging up on Pam as she was trying to leave for lecture.

I snapped.

I whipped my pen at the desk, sending pieces of it flying. I looked at Dr. Wannabe, and screamed, "Stay the fuck out of this! This has nothing to do with you! Why are you always so mean?"

My blood was boiling, and my entire body was shaking.

I continued yelling at her as I stood up, my pregnant belly leading the way, and stormed off into the back sleeping quarters. I cried and cried. I felt out of control. All my years of pent-up anger toward that miserable woman came pouring out for the entire nurses' station to see and hear. I didn't care anymore. I was done.

Dr. Slayton, my director, came and found me and consoled me. He knew how difficult Dr. Wannabe was to deal with, so he wasn't upset with me. I apologized, and he assured me that everything would be okay.

I felt sad for my baby. I didn't want to subject my unborn baby to such anger and intense emotion. I was worried that I might have damaged him because I was still taking my antidepressant medication, even though the evidence said it was probably safe. I felt guilty. I wanted to give him the perfect start to his life, but I was broken and had issues, and perfect just wasn't possible. I made the conscious decision to let go of my anger toward Dr. Wannabe. I would kill her with kindness—or die trying!

Live in love, I told myself.

I'm Cathy, the Patient

I was filled with so much anticipation the day he was born. I couldn't wait to meet my baby boy. Somehow, I knew he would love me more than any man ever could. I prayed he would be a happy, healthy baby. I prayed that the antidepressant I had been taking hadn't harmed him. I tried so hard to not let the guilt and fear consume me.

As I lay there in the hospital bed, hooked up to the monitor and an IV, I focused on how sweet it would be to smell his head and snuggle him while he nuzzled my neck. I couldn't wait!

Because I was so excited to get the show on the road—and, honestly, because I didn't want my "lady bits" out for everyone to see in the OR—I had the nurse put the catheter in my bladder while we were waiting for Dr. Middleton to arrive. To clarify: normally, we wait until the spinal is done and the patient is lying on the OR table, numb, before we place the catheter, but then the patient is spread-eagle for all to see.

Boy, was that the dumbest idea ever! Dr. Middleton was late; I mean, really late. My C-section was scheduled for 7:00 a.m., and at 8:00 a.m., the nurse finally called her and woke her up.

About twenty minutes later, Dr. Middleton came flying through the door like Kramer from Seinfeld, hair all wild, apologizing profusely. "We got back really late from skiing up north all weekend. I must not have set my alarm clock. I'm so sorry."

"It's fine, except that I had Samantha put the Foley in already, and it's driving me crazy!" I whined.

"Oh my gosh! Why would you do that? Let's get going! Tell anesthesia I'm ready!" she blurted out as she flew back out the door, introducing herself to my family in one long breath.

"That was Dr. Middleton, my doctor. I love her," I explained.

"Yeah, she seems very sweet," my mom replied.

Almost everyone was there to meet baby Fischer Landing: my parents, Grandma and Papa Jansen, Kevin's mom, Grandma Landing, and soon-to-be big sister, Delilah. My siblings came later that day, along with many aunts, uncles, and cousins. As usual, my family showed up and celebrated with me. I knew I could always count on them.

The OR was just as packed. Almost every OB nurse working was in there, the anesthesiologist, two anesthesia residents, the pediatrician, the pediatric resident, Dr. Middleton, with Dr. Slayton and my girl Amanda (aka resident Dr. Strongworth) assisting, the scrub tech, and the six OB residents who were working that day. You can see why I didn't want my legs spread wide open for everyone to see when I was on the table.

I sat up for the spinal, which went smoothly. They lay me down and proceeded to cover me with sterile drapes. They tested me like we always do, by pinching the abdomen with big, sharp pickups.

"Do you feel anything sharp?" Dr. Middleton asked.

"Nope," I replied.

As I lay there, I felt pressure and movement happening, and because I had performed a thousand C-sections, I was able to tell exactly what they were doing to me. "You're cutting my fascia, aren't you? This is surreal. I can't believe how weird this is! Anesthesia is the greatest invention womankind has ever known."

I couldn't get over the idea of it all. It was almost an out-of-body experience.

"Ah! You're separating my rectus muscles, aren't you?" I shrieked as I felt my tummy being pulled apart.

It didn't hurt, but, because I knew exactly what that looked like, it kind of freaked me out. "You're okay, Mama," Delilah whispered in my ear as she sat beside my head.

On the other side sat Kevin. The anesthesiologist patted Kevin on the back. "Stand up and watch your son be born."

Just as fast as he stood up, he sat back down.

"I didn't need to see that! It looked like they were going to pull Fischer's head off trying to get him out of your cut-open belly," he muttered, shaken and pale. (He was a resident physician too, mind you, but I guess seeing your wife cut open and bleeding all over the place is different than seeing a patient.)

I looked over and saw the pediatrician drying off a big crying baby with red-tinged hair. I saw Delilah walk over and extend her hand to her brother. Fischer immediately grabbed Delilah's finger and wouldn't let go. It was the most beautiful sight I had ever seen.

Finally, Delilah had a sibling.

Soon enough, he was swaddled up like a burrito and given to Kevin. He held Fischer's face to mine, and I smelled him. It was even better than I had dreamed. It was worth every moment of discomfort.

I took eight weeks off from residency to stay home with Fischer. It was a precious time that I wouldn't trade for the world. I spent most of my hours feeding and sleeping. I tried really hard to have him on a schedule of nursing, interactive time, then napping. I slept when he slept. After he was done nursing, I put him in his swing or on the floor, then I hooked myself up to the double breast pump and pumped out another few milliliters of breast milk to freeze. By the time I was done with that, it was nap time. I would lay straight back on my recliner couch, and Fischer would sleep on my chest.

I loved it.

For the first few weeks, my mom, Kevin, and Delilah were around a lot to help give me a break so I could at least shower and eat. But then reality set in, and it was just me and Fischer for eight hours a day, and nursing every two to three hours during the night. My C-section incision was becoming less painful, but my jelly belly was still there. It was definitely not comfortable to wear regular clothes. My body was definitely not returning to its prepregnancy size the way it did after I had Delilah.

After about six weeks of nonstop nursing, pumping, changing diapers, being repeatedly woken up from sleep, and not leaving my house, I felt lonely and miserable. I was still taking my antidepressant, but it wasn't helping. I had been in my jammies 24/7 for an entire month. I needed to get out and interact with grown-ups, get my hair done, and wear regular clothing.

I needed a break.

I was thankful that I was already on medication for my depression and that I was well educated about postpartum depression, because I could have easily slid into a severe state of psychosis. Kevin saw the warning signs and made me call Dr. Middleton. She increased my medication, and I started going to counseling again. I got out of the house on a daily basis, either going to dinner with Kevin or grocery shopping by myself. Those little events felt wonderful. For an hour, I didn't feel like a milk machine; I felt like I owned my body again. Carrying a child for nine months and then caring for it 24/7 is completely draining. I just wanted my body to belong to me again. I gave all that I had, and then some.

But, really, there's no real break when you have a baby, especially when you are a doctor who has had a baby. So, you find ways to recharge, to keep giving and keep going. Counseling reminded me of ways to make myself a priority, and ways to make healthy choices to get my body healthy enough to protect me from worsening postpartum depression.

When I went back to residency, I was still breast-feeding, so I needed to pump every three hours. Let me tell you, that was nearly impossible. When you are managing labor patients or scrubbed in doing surgery, you don't get to decide when there is time to pump. You have to wait until the patient's needs are met first. (So much for making me a priority.)

Once, I was in the middle of doing a vaginal hysterectomy, and my breast milk was letting down. It was a fierce shooting pain down my breasts into my nipples. I felt my chest getting warm against my completely stretched-out Victoria Secret bra. Then, I felt wetness overcome me. My bra was now heavy with engorged breasts and milk-soaked pads.

But could I leave and take care of the situation? No. I had to ignore my own discomfort and potential embarrassment, and finish the surgery. I was trained to always put the patient first; which meant holding it when you needed to pee, going hungry and skipping meals, not returning personal calls, and just pretty much ignoring personal needs. Residency was about training yourself to work and stay focused on the needs of others, while ignoring the hunger pains, cramping bowels, ready-to-burst bladder, backaches, headaches, and any other screaming signal from your body.

Becoming a physician is a hazard to your health.

Somehow, I survived. I had to go an extra eight weeks after graduation to make up for my maternity leave, but it wasn't terrible. I enjoyed being chief resident and wasn't too excited about going out to practice.

I didn't have many options, because I had to join a group in town. Kevin was still in residency, and Delilah was still in high school, so we couldn't move. Amanda and I had vowed not to join the groups of any of our attendings, even though that was what most residents did. Everyone joked about how inbred our program was because, once you came in as a resident, you stayed on as an attending.

I had one attending whom I really admired for her surgical skills and confidence. She was inbred, so to speak, but she went out and practiced on her own for a few years before she came back to be a teaching attending. This meant that she was forced to do surgeries by herself. She had to rely on her skills and knowledge to get through cases, which made her become the excellent surgeon she was. I wanted to be that way. I enjoyed teaching residents, but I wanted to be able to do my own surgeries.

As a teaching attending, you should let the residents do the case as you guide and assist them. If you have never done the cases on your own without someone overseeing you, then you shouldn't be overseeing someone do a case. It's a setup for complications, misguided training, and handing down of bad surgical habits. I wanted to go out on my own, without my trainers or fellow residents to rely on.

Unfortunately, there weren't many prospects in town. I interviewed with a small practice in the next town over. Their office was beautiful and had an upscale aesthetics spa attached, which the doctors worked out of in their spare time, for cash. The patient population was very affluent, all white, and overly educated.

There were a few red flags during my interview that I shouldn't have ignored, but I needed a job close to home. Everyone in the office was very formal and treated me like a queen. "Good morning, Dr. Jansen. What would you like in your coffee?"

I didn't fit in there. I wasn't comfortable with people waiting on me or treating me like I was more important than they were. If there's one word to describe me, it's *real*. By which I mean *authentic*. I'm not pretentious, and I don't expect to be treated any different than the medical assistant, the secretary, or the janitor. I think it's a slippery slope to think that your education, profession, or paycheck puts you on top rung of the ladder. If I'm on the top, then someone has to be on the bottom, and I will never be okay with that.

I will always be Chatty Cathy sitting in the hall with my desk in third grade, feeling inadequate—the person on the bottom rung of the ladder. So, I'd rather not have anyone ranked, period. We are all just human beings trying to make it through the day, do the right thing, and be happy. My education, profession, and paycheck don't make me who I am. I am successful because I am kind, caring, selfless, thoughtful, considerate, determined, hardworking, sacrificing, and fearless!

If I lost everything I have worked so hard for, I would still be all of those things. You cannot rank personality traits, so I don't have to worry about falling down the ladder. I am who I am. In the words of my dear friend whom I haven't introduced yet, Anastasia Cartwright, "I am enough."

I'm Dr. Catherine Jansen

So, my next adventure, as an attending physician, began. Unfortunately, it wasn't what I hoped it would be. I thought I'd be seeing patients all day long, doing surgeries every week, and delivering babies. Instead, my days consisted of seeing a few OB patients and one or two new-patient referrals for basic issues like needing a physical exam or birth-control pills.

I tried to discuss the issue with my partners.

Their response was "Your OB patients will become your GYN patients. It takes a long time to build a practice."

This frustrated me because, when I interviewed with them, they told me I was replacing their partner and would be inheriting an established practice with a good patient base. Now they were telling me something completely different. As a new attending, I needed to do surgery and gain experience, to keep up my skills. That was not going to happen the way they set me up, and they weren't apologetic.

Meanwhile, I found out that the office staff was being directed to not give me referrals that would lead to procedures or surgery, because my partners got paid based on production. I was being paid a straight salary for the first two years, but their paychecks were determined by what they billed out. This is called the "you eat what you kill" mentality. So, they were preoccupied with making as much money as they could. Sometimes I would question if a procedure or surgery was necessary or if they just wanted to do the higher-paying procedure. I was very much against this. I thought, *Your paycheck should never guide how you practice medicine or care for a patient.*

Sometimes insurance companies and hospitals force physicians' hands to increase the bottom line, but physicians should never be persuaded to guide the patient toward the more profitable direction just to benefit their pocketbooks. When you talk to physicians about this topic, they usually agree that it is potentially dangerous, but they all deny being swayed by it. I don't buy it. I've seen it time and time again. Proponents of it say that it causes fair competition so that physicians don't become lazy or rely on their partners to do all the work. They say, "You should get paid for your work, and if you work harder, you should get paid more."

I agree with that statement; however, it's not that black and white. Medicine is partly science, but it is also very much an art. Every patient scenario is unique. Decisions the patients make regarding their care are based on many complex factors, including their finances, their home life, the type of work they do, whether or not they have support from family and friends, their thoughts and beliefs about medicine in general, and their previous encounters with doctors. On top of that, add the physician's schedule, experience and expertise (or lack thereof), and feelings about treating their patients. If you also add to that how much the physician will be paid for each of those decisions, the physician has the opportunity to become biased in terms of how they present options to their patients.

Whose needs will be put first, and how can we come to a compromise where everyone is happy? Remember, physicians need to feel satisfied to continue to come to work every day and give of themselves beyond what is expected. When that is no longer the case, physicians become burned out and patients become disgruntled. It's a complex, ever-evolving mess.

Okay, I'll get off my rant now. I just want you to understand that physicians are only human. They have needs, desires, and faults that get the best of them. I was witnessing this on a daily basis, and I had no way to change it. I knew in my heart that I didn't want to end up practicing medicine that way. I would do everything possible to avoid that.

That situation was wearing on me, so, one day, I tried to broach the subject during a lunch meeting with my partners. They became very defensive and told me to not make waves as the new girl.

One partner said to me, "You're lucky we gave you a job when no one wanted to hire you, so you need to be quiet and just worry about what you're doing."

I was speechless. *Who the hell did she think she was talking to?*

Then, I regained my voice and said calmly, "You are *not* that important. You are *not* my boss. We are partners, and I don't care if I started two months ago or today; I will not be treated this way."

I got up and walked out. By the way, I was pregnant again, so I was feeling feisty. I was feeling empowered and wanted to be in control of my life. I wanted to grow a practice; meaning, I knew I would be taking care of my patients for most of their lives. I was slowly starting to build those relationships, but the thought of working with those doctors much longer seemed like a miserable and unsafe idea. I was losing my surgical skills because I wasn't getting any surgical referrals. I needed to do something to change the direction of my professional future.

I ended up meeting with the practice manager to ask for her to release me from my contract. I explained how unreasonable my partners were, how I didn't trust them, how selfish they were when it came to decisions regarding the practice, and how I could no longer work there.

Surprisingly, she was very understanding. I assumed she dealt with them enough to know. She commented on how hard it had been to get anyone to join their group. She ended up voiding my contract, including the noncompete clause, which was the most important part. Normally, when you quit a practice, your contract says you cannot work anywhere within a thirty-mile radius, so you can't steal patients and take them with you to your new job. But she felt so bad for me, and she knew I had been given very few patients, so she dismissed the noncompete.

I left that meeting feeling like a rock star. I wanted something to happen a certain way, I asked for it kindly and graciously, and what I wanted happened exactly the way I wanted it to.

It gave me pause.

It's amazing what you can get if you just ask for it.

Now I was pregnant and jobless, and my husband still had another three years of cardiothoracic fellowship to finish, which meant staying in that town indefinitely.

I had a standing offer from the hospital where I did my residency, so I called the CEO. He offered me a great contract to join the teaching attending group. Financially, it was a tempting offer, but I would have to share call with Dr. Wannabe, my archnemesis. My little voice inside told me not to do it, but I didn't know of any other option if I was going to support my husband and his dream of becoming a heart surgeon.

So, I went in and signed on the dotted line. He shook my hand and gave me a signing bonus check of twenty thousand dollars. I left feeling uneasy about my decision. The problem with me staying there and starting another practice was that I knew I would want to leave when Kevin finished his fellowship, so that wouldn't fix the real problem. I was trying to avoid leaving another practice after becoming established. I didn't want patients to get comfortable with me and rely on me, only for me to up and leave them. I wanted to build long-lasting, meaningful relationships with my patients, and I knew I didn't want to live there long term.

Before I quit my job, I had applied for a position at a small hospital close to my hometown because I was curious to see what they could offer me. They knew I was available, so they kept calling me to come interview.

I loved the idea of being close to my family again, because that meant my babies could grow up seeing their grandparents and extended family.

When I explained my situation and concerns to that little hospital, they bent over backward to accommodate me and help me figure out a way to have it all. They offered me a house to live in with my babies (Fischer, and Kensley on the way), they said they would find me good child care, they agreed to a signing bonus, and they promised that I would have a ton of patients and be doing surgery again.

Kevin loved the idea of living there—eventually—so he agreed that I should go for it. He would come see us on the weekends that he was free, and then he could move there once his fellowship was complete.

How is all of this possibly going to work out? I thought.

Delilah was actually graduating high school the following month and going off to college, so she didn't see a problem with it. She was on to bigger and better things. She was excited about her new life as a soon-to-be adult. I was so proud of her.

I had broken the cycle!

Delilah was going to graduate high school without getting pregnant, and she was going to college. She was going to be the independent young woman that I had worked so hard for her to become.

So, after we all agreed that I should go for it and take that other job, I remembered that I had one issue: I had already signed that other contract. Thankfully, I hadn't yet cashed the check. Nervously, I called the CEO, to make it right. I said to myself, *Just ask for what you want, tell the truth, and he will understand.*

I explained that my long-term goal was to not stay in town and that it broke my heart to think of starting another practice only to up and leave. "I shouldn't have signed the contract. Is there any possible way that you cann*ot* hold me to it? I haven't cashed the check," I explained, crying with regret.

"You don't have to cry. It's not a big deal. If it's not what you want, then I don't want to force you to do it. Just rip up the check and contract like it never happened," he responded.

I was stunned. I couldn't believe it was going to be that easy to get out of it.

"Thank you so much for understanding. This has been a terribly difficult decision, but it's my career. I just left a bad situation, and I don't want to do something that doesn't feel completely right."

"I respect you for that. Take care, Dr. Jansen."

"Thank you. You too." And I hung up.

Wow! I was free to move. I loved the idea of working somewhere that you could get to know your patients, you would potentially take care of coworkers and their family members, and you would run into the babies you delivered at the grocery store. It all sounded perfect, except for the moving-without-your-husband part.

For the time being, I didn't worry about it. I was going to have a high-school graduate, a newborn, and a toddler, all while starting a full-time career in a new city, without my husband.

Well, when I read it in print, yes, it sounds crazy.

But, I squashed my fears and relied on my little voice inside, which told me it was the right thing to do.

Cat's New Life

The birth of Kensley was so wonderful! We were all very excited to meet our sweet baby. I felt proud of myself for creating
so much love. I was able to give Delilah the siblings I thought she
deserved, and I loved the idea of Fischer and Kensley having each
other to grow up with. They would never have to go through tough
times alone. Growing up with two huge families showed me how
truly important and necessary family is. I told myself, *When I am old,
Delilah won't have to take care of me or make difficult life and death decisions
alone. When I am long gone, they will still have each other.*

The Jansen and Robbins families might not see each other that
often, but if someone needed something or there was something to
celebrate, you'd best believe they would show up.

Knowing you can rely on your family is an amazing feeling.
It gives you security and strength. Hey, maybe that's why I'm so
fearless. I know that, no matter what, they will always be there for
me and never forsake me.

I was blessed to have so much time to spend with my babies.
I had left my job when I was two months pregnant with Kensley,
and I didn't go back to work until I moved almost ten months later.

When I moved there, it snowed a ton of beautiful white snow
every day. I bought knee-high boots and walked through my backyard to work every day. It made me smile. Everyone in my new
office welcomed me with open arms. They were so friendly and

accommodating. They tried hard to show me how much they appreciated me. Apparently, the doctor I was replacing was a complete bitch, and impossible to work with. One of my partners got sick my second day there, so they threw me right into seeing patients. I loved it. This was what I was meant to do. It had been so long, I was worried I would forget everything, but it all came back to me. It was like riding a bike.

I hired two young ladies to nanny for me. I needed someone to "sleep for dollars," meaning I paid her to sleep at my house in case I got called into a delivery during the night. During the day, Fischer and Kensley went to a day care in town.

I was too busy to worry about my husband not being there, and he was too busy as well. He would drive over once a week, on three to four hours sleep, just to see us. He was constantly "running on empty."

Honestly, Kevin didn't know how to slow down. He believed he was indestructible. He often refused to admit that he needed sleep or food like a normal human being. He always had something more important to do. There wasn't much room in his life for us. It's common knowledge that heart surgeons often end up with God complexes. I was afraid he would become a narcissist, especially with me not there to keep him grounded.

I was starting to feel guilty for taking his children so far away. I worried that they wouldn't develop the relationship they needed to because he wasn't around much. I would pacify myself by thinking, *The kids are young. He'll be here when they are old enough to need him. They will be fine.*

Some nights, he would get sad and call, saying he missed them, but when day came he was raring to go and had every minute of his day booked with other things to do.

Then, he started running and training for a marathon. That was very time consuming. He said it was a good thing because it distracted him from missing us and kept him occupied. It also gave him a way to relieve stress and get healthy. I was envious. I wanted time to take care of myself. I couldn't even go to the bathroom without my kids, let alone go running for hours on end. Maybe someday. Being, essentially, a single mom working full time was exhausting, to say the least.

Thank God, my kids were little. They didn't have much concept of time, so when I was with them, I made the most of it; but, honestly, I worked a lot. I ended up hiring a daytime nanny named Marilyn because I couldn't even get the kids to day care in the morning, let alone take care of my household. She ended up being my saving grace.

She got the kids ready in the mornings and took them to day care. Then, she came back and did all the laundry and cleaned up the house. She kept my household running while I was working. I was so grateful for her. She treated them like her own grandchildren. She was funny, loving and supportive of everything they did. She invited us to her family functions and always bought them gifts. She gave my children some consistency and normalcy.

In addition to working my normal forty hours per week, I had to take call more nights than not. I had many pregnant women who wanted me to do their deliveries, which meant working more than just the nights I was on call. I "specialed" way too many patients, meaning that if they presented in labor when I wasn't working, the nurse still called me, and I took care of the patient and did the delivery. This made my patients very happy, but it really drained me.

Women are often highly selective when it comes to choosing their OB/GYN. Many will scrutinize, judge, and challenge their physician before accepting them. And that's the way it should be. Women *should* question things when it comes to their health and well-being and the well-being of their unborn children. I encourage them to be active participants in their health care. The days of the doctor telling the patient what to do, and the patient doing it without question, are over—as they should be.

However, that made my job harder because I was trying to please everyone and give them what they wanted and needed. I tried to spend enough time with each patient, giving whatever they each required. If it was a fifteen-minute appointment, but they needed forty minutes, I listened. I tried not to rush them, praying that the next few patients wouldn't need extra time and that they would understand my running behind. I told myself, *This is an OB/GYN office, after all; women should expect some delays.*

For example, an appointment scheduled as a vaginal-infection check turned into a counseling session because the patient was recently divorced and had concerns about STDs and painful inter-course; she really just needed to vent.

Women often scheduled appointments under the guise of something else. The patient didn't want to explain to the sched-uler that she was cheating on her husband and needed secret birth control, or that she didn't want to take care of her newborn or even get out of bed.

I was never fazed by the many surprises of the day. I tried to roll with it the best I could, while keeping upset patients happy, and trying to create understanding among other patients who actually did just come in for a simple fifteen-minute appointment and ex-pected to be in and out without delay. Every day was a juggling act, and the days I was on call magnified that by a hundred. It seemed like as soon as I would catch up and start running on time, the birthing unit would call and tell me to rush over for a delivery; or, the ER would call to tell me a girl had an ectopic pregnancy and needed to go to surgery because she had an abdomen full of blood.

That variety was one reason why I loved my specialty. It never got boring or predictable. I had to be able to adapt and switch up the plans at a moment's notice. I had to multitask all day, every day.

If I ate lunch, it would be while I charted (did paperwork) during the ten minutes I had available, because I almost always was still seeing patients through my "lunch break." I was used to living a fast-paced life and putting myself last; that was what residency had trained me to do.

So, on the random days that day care called and said, "Fischer has been throwing up. Can you come pick him up?" or "Kensley has a fever, so she needs to go home," it really threw a wrench into my day. Somehow, I got through it.

In those moments, I felt resentment for Kevin. I would think of him working all day, knowing he didn't have to worry about taking care of sick kids, picking up the kids by 6:00 p.m. when day care closed, cooking and feeding them dinner, or doing the bedtime routine. He only had to take care of his patients and himself. He was running every day, going on ski trips with his buddies, and enjoying life. Meanwhile, I was gaining weight, struggling with my depression, and living to meet everyone else's needs.

Somehow, God knew I needed to be lifted up, so what did He do? He sent me a project to lift up others.

Paying It Forward

My medical assistant at the office, Carrie Oakey, became my new best friend. She was full of life and wasn't afraid to have fun. I called her "the brunette me." She saved the day for me, on a regular basis. She picked up my kids from day care when I worked late or got stuck doing a delivery. Eventually, she came to be known as my BFF-MA-PA-PIC (best friend forever, medical assistant, personal assistant, and partner in crime) because she always went above and beyond to help me out.

Carrie's brother, Joe, was a teacher at the alternative high school in town. This school was such an awesome situation for kids who were struggling and needed a more flexible, understanding, supportive approach to finishing high school. I had never heard of it, but I definitely could have used that when I was in high school.

One day, Carrie mentioned that she had told Joe and his friend Nate, the school's principal, my life story, and Nate said that wanted to meet me. He was interested in talking to me to hear more of my story. So, I gladly went to meet him a few weeks later.

"Hi, I'm Nate Sutton, the principal at Alternate Paths High School," said this very nice man as he reached out and shook my hand.

"Catherine," I replied. "Nice to meet you."

He went on, "I'm so excited to meet you and talk to you. Joe told me a little bit about your story, and I think you would be the perfect person to talk to my kids at graduation."

I felt honored and embarrassed at the same time. He explained that the alternative high school helped kids finish high school when they hadn't been successful in a regular high-school setting. Some had issues with bullying at their previous school; others were homeless and not able to get to school. Some had learning challenges and needed extra guidance. Quite a few of the girls had become pregnant and needed support catching up on missed classes or getting child care to be able to attend classes.

I gave him the five-minute lowdown of my life, and he seemed very interested in what I had to say. He encouraged me to share my story. When I finished, he said, "I'd like you to give this year's commencement speech."

Of course, I said yes. I explained, "Part of my success is because people stepped up to help me, and I would love to have an impact on these kids—even just one kid. I would love to pay it forward."

This invitation to speak at graduation reaffirmed why I had sacrificed and struggled all those years. It gave me a new challenge. Could I empower these young people to see inside themselves and realize their worth and potential, the same way I somehow had?

Then, I realized, *I have to do this! This is part of my purpose!*

Next, came the tough part: I had to write a really good speech. I had to connect with them, motivate them, and resonate with them. I needed to think about my life and what gave me the ability to overcome my obstacles, move past them, and succeed. I needed to figure out how to condense that into a ten-minute speech that would inspire these kids to continue seeking change and succeed in their lives going forward.

What a huge challenge I was taking on!

So, I started at the beginning, with my earliest important

memories, and figured out how and why I was able to persevere and succeed despite my odds.

Soon, the newspaper called me for an interview. They ran a nice article in the paper a few days before graduation that highlighted the importance of Alternate Paths High School in our community. They mentioned that I, the keynote speaker at the commencement, would be sharing my story of having been a pregnant teenager and high-school dropout who eventually got her GED and went on to become a successful doctor.

Of course, I had to work the day of graduation, and I was almost late because I was seeing patients in the office, giving them the extra time they needed. When I arrived, the auditorium was packed. I was greeted by the superintendent of the school system, the mayor, the principal, nurses from the OB department, Kevin, Delilah, Carrie, the women from my office, and many of my family members. I felt blessed.

I saw four rows of students wearing caps and gowns, along with nervous, excited, proud smiles. All of a sudden, I felt really important. I was there to do a very important job, in front of all those people. I needed to connect with those kids and make them feel like the most important people in the room, because they were.

Principal Sutton did an amazing job, speaking about each and every student. He then went on to say, "It is my honor and privilege to introduce to you a woman who was once in your shoes. She has an amazing story of success that I want her to share with you. Please give a huge welcome to Catherine Jansen."

I purposely asked him not to introduce me as doctor, because I had put that at the end of my speech, for dramatic effect.

I thanked the principal and then began:

> Hi. My name is Catherine, and I have been given
> the honor of speaking to you on your big night. Your

awesome principal, Mr. Sutton, kindly asked if I would come speak to you, the graduating class, because he thought you might relate to my story. A few years ago—okay, maybe twenty—I was a lot like you, except that there wasn't a supportive high school like this one to help me graduate.

I grew up in a town a lot like this, but without all the resources. My mom and dad worked seven days a week and had five kids. I was the middle child, the black sheep of the family. Growing up, my family called me "Crabby Cathy" because I was never happy. I was never content. I always wanted more—more things, more opportunities, more adventure, and just more out of life. In my mind, they were disregarding my dreams, my imagination, and my desire to do anything.

I went on to tell the condensed version of my life: my struggles, my lack of opportunities, and my setbacks. I could tell the kids were listening and thinking of the hardships they themselves had overcome. I became so emotional that I could barely finish my speech, but I continued, for their sake:

I took nursing classes at my community college, kicked butt in my classes, and started to be considered really smart. People I met were impressed that I was doing all that while raising a baby. I could go on all night, because I have fifteen-plus years of hard work, sacrifice, and determination to describe, but I'm going to cut to the chase. After two years, I transferred to the university, with scholarships. I got a bachelor's degree with honors, and then I got accepted into medical school. I kicked butt in med school, survived four years of a very grueling surgical residency, and am proud to now be called Dr. Catherine Jansen.

What I came to learn was that just because people say or think things about you doesn't make it true. If you believe otherwise and trust the little voice inside you, you'll realize you're right. If you desire more from life than what has been laid before you, then do whatever it takes to create that life you so desire. Don't settle. Don't let fear stop you. Don't waste another day thinking life is just going to automatically get better; it doesn't work that way.

Tell yourself you are as good as anyone else out there doing great things; you just have to work harder at it. Your path may be extra long, have hurdles to jump over and pot holes to avoid, or even seem like a dead end, but there is *always* another way. No way is the right way. It's all in what you make of it.

Your sitting here tonight is a huge accomplishment, and I am very proud of you! I have no doubt that you can be way more successful than any of us in this room, because you have shown us your strength and desire by graduating tonight, despite your difficulties in life. These struggles only make you a more awesome person; struggling builds character. Character isn't defined as how you act on your best days, when life is a breeze and you're crowned homecoming king or queen; it's defined by how you act on your worst days, when you're embarrassed to death because you have to use food stamps to buy your kid's food, and your former classmate is the cashier. Yes, the day that happened to me, I vowed to myself that someday I would make so much money that my taxes would cover someone else's food stamps. I would repay society for paying for my teenage pregnancy, my food stamps, my rent, my college grant money, etc.

Life is about seeing what you're made of, accomplishing things you never dreamed possible, and then, when you're enjoying the good life because of all your hard work, *paying it forward*. You will then be able to help others succeed, to realize they are more than what people may call them at some point in time. You can go from Crabby Cathy, to white trash, to smart and impressive, to doctor—to whatever— *if* you believe in yourself!

Just remember, there's no room for fear when you're trying to conquer the world! Okay?!

As the tears flowed down my face and the faces of the graduating students, the entire auditorium burst into cheers and applause, rising to their feet to give me a standing ovation. It was a beautiful moment. I thought, *If I spoke to just one of those students and pushed him or her to the next level in life, then my struggle will all be worth it.*

I stayed up on the stage as the students' names were called and they each walked across to receive their diplomas. I could feel their excitement and pride. I had key chains engraved with the words "No Fear," and I gave one to each student. Every single student hugged me and thanked me. My heart was filled with joy.

That moment gave me pause.

By taking the time to give those kids what they needed, I, in turn, got what I needed. This lesson wasn't lost on me.

Time and time again, when I have felt worthless, empty, spent, selfish, or materialistic, God has given me an opportunity to lift someone else up, lend my last dollar, extend my efforts beyond what I thought was possible—always with my own reward being far greater than I could have imagined.

When those lessons come into my life, I could easily complain and say, "I'm too busy" or "I don't have enough money to give" or "That sounds too difficult, and I don't really want to go through all of that discomfort right now," but, because I accept the challenge and care about other people, and because I honestly want to be a good person, I choose to acknowledge my responsibility and put others first. I've found that the more often I live in this mind-set, the more my life feels blessed and my heart feels full.

I received so much wonderful feedback from giving that speech. It solidified my desire to be a permanent part of that community. I knew I had found my place.

Heartbreak

Now I just needed to get my husband to finish his fellowship, move to where the kids and I were, and start our purposeful, grown-up life as prominent members of our community, making a difference and paying it forward.

I acknowledged my resentment toward Kevin for living apart from us, and I actively tried to let that go. I realized that his life wasn't great; he missed his wife and wasn't able to watch his kids grow on a daily basis. That caused him to have resentment toward me as well. He didn't verbalize it at the time; maybe he didn't even realize it. Regardless, it manifested into emotional distance between us. Eventually, we got to a point where we no longer leaned on each other for love or support.

When he finally finished his fellowship, he moved in with me and the kids. He had secured a great position at the big hospital nearby. He started their open-heart surgery program. This made him a huge asset, and, therefore, they treated him like a king. They made him his own OR suite and bought all the new equipment he wanted. He had a special team of nurses and techs just for him. I was very proud of him for doing such important, advanced work, but it quickly went to his head. All the attention and special treatment fed his ego, and he quickly fell into the trap of the heart surgeon with a God complex, just as I'd feared.

Within the first two months of him moving in with the kids

and me, the shit hit the fan, so to speak. Kevin had a crazy, dangerous guy calling him in the middle of the night, threatening to kill him. It turned out he was the husband of a nurse Kevin was having an affair with. I was terrified that the guy would kill Kevin, or hurt me and the kids.

After a few nights of this guy torturing Kevin, I got on the phone and said very calmly and directly, "Kevin told me everything. He doesn't want anything to do with your wife. He will never talk to her again, and she needs to stay away from him. She is not innocent in this either. If you ever call here or even try to threaten my husband again, I will fucking hunt you down and make you and your wife very sorry."

He tried to interrupt me, wanting to tell me details about the affair and make Kevin out to be a dirtbag, but I shut him down. I was going to fight for my family. I was not going to allow this drunken lunatic to threaten to kill my husband and ruin my children's lives.

Now I had to deal with my heartache.

Kevin confessed everything and begged my forgiveness. He admitted to getting caught up in all the excitement of his new professional status. He insisted he completely regretted what he had done and that he was committed to me and the kids. "I just need to get back to the good man that I know I am, and focus on you, Fischer and Kensley. When you met me, I would have done anything for you. All I cared about was your happiness and your love. I want that back. Please forgive me."

"What choice do I have? I've waited for so long to have this family, and it's finally becoming a reality. I don't want to lose it already. Please figure your shit out," I said, feeling emotionally exhausted.

Much of that year was a blur to me, but I was 100 percent committed to strengthening our marriage and trying to make it work.

Intuition

As if dealing with all my personal struggles weren't enough, I was still a doctor, and I had to be able to check my feelings at the door at a moment's notice and deal with others' emergencies. I was put to the test—mentally, physically, and emotionally—on a regular basis. A simple labor and delivery could quickly turn into a near-fatal experience, without warning. Unfortunately, that happened to me more than once.

For example, I had a wonderful patient who had seven girls and was pregnant with her first boy. She and her husband and their daughters were so excited. Her delivery should have been an easy, beautiful event. She had been dilated for two weeks and was nervous about her water breaking before she got to the hospital, because she knew she would deliver fast.

I saw them in the office, and she said, "I'm feeling nervous about this delivery. I think I should have this baby soon."

We discussed admitting her to the hospital and breaking her water to induce labor in a safe, controlled environment.

"Do you want to come in tomorrow morning, and I'll just break your water?" I asked.

"Yeah, I think that is a wise plan," she insisted, looking at me with concern in her face.

"You look concerned. Do you think we need to do it today?" I asked.

"No, tomorrow is fine, but I just think we should move forward with the delivery sooner rather than later," she said.

When a patient tells me about any feeling regarding her pregnancy, I always stop to listen. Patient intuition is wiser than any textbook I can reference.

The next morning, she came in for induction. She was put on the monitor, had her blood drawn and an IV started, and was noted to be contracting.

Without warning, she said to the nurse, "I think my water just broke."

Nurse Jen noticed that the fetal heart tones decreased—always a concerning sign. She quickly thought to check the patient's cervix and felt an umbilical cord in the vagina. She called out to the desk for me. I came running into the room, she told me the situation, and I called for an emergency C-section. Nurse Jen was smart enough to keep her hand in the vagina, pushing the fetal head upward to keep pressure off the umbilical cord. Compression of the cord from this prolapse situation can cause fetal death in minutes.

We rushed the patient on her bed, nurse attached, into the OR, and I proceeded to splash her abdomen with betadine and make an incision. I delivered their eighth child, and only son, within four minutes. He came out crying, making everyone in the room cry tears of joy and relief.

Had her water broken outside of the hospital, in any other circumstance, they most likely would have lost their son. Somehow, my patient knew she needed to be in the hospital that day and entrusted me to take care of her and her unborn son.

What a privilege.

Unfortunately, these dramatic events happen all too frequently in obstetrics; hence the reason we do deliveries in the hospital in this day and age. I learned early on that when the adrenaline kicks in, I need to stay calm. I actually feel a sense of calm and control come over me. I am able to focus and do what needs to be done, without even thinking. My instincts and training kick in, and I just do whatever is required. There is no worrying about my discomfort or being sued; my only thoughts are of saving the lives of both of my patients, mom and baby, and trying to keep the mom (and dad, if present) calm and informed. I try to give them the ability to consent to my interventions, when possible, and to make them as physically comfortable as possible. The last thing I want is to cause PTSD (post-traumatic stress disorder) from a traumatic delivery, although sometimes that does happen, despite my best efforts.

Each time I hold someone's life in my hands, I feel humbled, and I remember what an honor and responsibility I have been endowed with. I do not take that lightly.

That day gave me pause.

My patient and her husband were so grateful, and I felt so competent and sure of myself. Well, professionally, at least.

Wow, I can save a life, so why can't I save a marriage? I thought.

Kevin and I were planning a trip with our friends just a few months later, so the guys could go fishing and the girls could hang by the pool.

"I'm excited to go back to Belize with you," I said. "We should renew our vows while we're there, since that's where we went on our honeymoon ten years ago."

Kevin responded with something like "Yeah, maybe we can make that happen."

I took that to mean he would make it happen, the way he always made things happen when he wanted something.

Alas, we were there, and no such thing happened.

While we all were watching the sunset our last night there, I whispered, "I really thought you would have set up something for us to renew our vows."

"I'm sorry. I didn't realize you really wanted me to do that."

"I wish *you* wanted it," I replied.

"I want to get to that point again, I really do," he said, making it seem that reconnecting was not his priority, so I dropped it.

He seemed preoccupied on the trip, especially in the airport there and back. He was on his phone constantly "for work." He filled every moment of every day with something to keep him busy. He never stopped. He was slipping further and further away from me and the kids. If he wasn't running or hunting, he was at work.

Shortly after that trip, he got up with the kids early one Saturday and told me to sleep in. I thought it was weird, so I went downstairs and caught him texting someone. He insisted that it was innocent and nothing. I was almost angrier at the fact that he should've been on the floor, playing with the kids and giving them his attention, than the fact that he was lying to me.

As a gesture of effort, he started going to marriage counseling with me. That brought up a lot of pain and undealt-with issues. Things continued to be rocky, and I was struggling to work, cover call, and be a mother to my children. I couldn't focus on my marriage as much as I needed to, and Kevin didn't seem to truly want to focus on us either.

Death Begets Life

Just when I thought life couldn't get any more devastatingly challenging, it did.

I am now fully aware that, as an obstetrician, I am just functioning as God's hands to serve. I do not decide who lives or dies; I am just a vehicle through which God works. I do everything I know how to humanly do, and then I have to be okay with the outcome. It is not my choice. I do whatever I can and leave the rest up to God.

I know this now, but I didn't know it then. This truth became painfully evident one December day while I was taking care of my pregnant friend, Cynthia. She was an awesome person. She was loud, outspoken, funny, confident, and successful. She was a young, caring teacher who was very active in the community. She was married, and they had a little boy who was in day care with my Fischer. That was how we met.

Cynthia was a great person, and I was enjoying her company that day. Her husband, Ken, wheeled her into the birthing unit. She was huffing and puffing and swearing, shouting at the nurse to give her an epidural. Once she got that and her contraction pain was gone, she became her sweet, pleasant self once again. She and Ken cracked jokes most of the day. Cynthia had an infectious laugh that made you laugh.

I told them about the awesome New Year's surprise plans I had made for Kevin. "I got tickets to the University outdoor hockey game. I guess you have to wear snow pants and mittens and every-thing, because it's so fucking cold. Then, we are staying at a hotel that has a New Year's party with dinner and dancing all night. He'd better love me, 'cuz it's expensive, not to mention pretty fucking awesome of me!"

"That does sound awesome!" Ken assured me.

"Wow, he's spoiled! He's going to love that! You are really a great wife for planning that. I would never sit in the freezing cold to watch some game; I don't care how much Ken would love it!" Cynthia said, laughing.

"Yeah, we just really need to reconnect somehow. I want him to have a good time and enjoy being with me. He's in Vermont right now, skiing with his buddies. Hopefully, he'll have enough energy for me when he gets back," I joked.

They knew that Kevin and I had lived apart for three years and that we needed to work on our relationship, but they didn't know the extent of the damage. I really didn't share our difficulties with anyone, not even my closest friends, Carrie and Anastasia. I was embarrassed that he cheated on me. I was ashamed that we couldn't get our shit together and figure it out.

As we were hanging out and talking, Cynthia said, "I feel funny."

I asked her what she meant, but before she could answer, her eyes rolled back, and she passed out. She wasn't outright seizing; it was more of a flexing and stiffening (in medicine, we call it "decor-ticate posturing"). The different diagnoses ran through my head: eclampsia, stroke, amniotic-fluid embolism.

"Cyn, Cyn, can you hear me?!" I yelled as I tried to arouse her. "Get mag sulfate!" I called out to the nursing station, praying it was eclampsia and not an embolism.

Before I could even give her the magnesium, she came to, looked me in the eye, and said, "Where am I? I feel weird."

"Cyn, stay with me. Do you know where you are?"

"I'm here, having a baby," she said with much effort as she gasped for air. Then, she was gone again.

I felt for a pulse and couldn't find one. I called a code blue. "We need to get the baby out—*now!*" I commanded as I quickly wheeled her down the hall.

The code team met me in the C-section OR and started resuscitating her. I splashed her abdomen with betadine, opened the emergency C-section kit, threw on some gloves, and made the same cut I had made so many times before. As I was getting to the uterus, Cynthia's body was going up and down as they performed chest compressions and bagged her lungs. I finally got to the baby's head and delivered a beautiful, pink, crying baby girl. Baby Abby was delivered within three minutes of me calling the code.

I expected Cynthia to "come to" once the baby was out, like the patient did for Julie during residency. When Cynthia didn't respond to her baby being born, I knew it wasn't an eclamptic seizure or stroke; it was the most terrifying event possible in obstetrics—it was definitely an amniotic-fluid embolism.

Fuck. Fuck. Fuck! Cynthia, you cannot leave us. You need to come back and be the mother you're supposed to be! I screamed in my head as I delivered her placenta and started to suture her uterus closed.

The code team was doing an amazing job; she was intubated, central lines placed, lifesaving drugs pushed many times over, blood products given to replace all she had lost. I had completely sutured her back up and covered her incision with a dressing, and they continued on.

Soon after, we saw thin, pink blood pouring out past her dressing, her central line, and then from her nose and mouth. She was going into DIC (disseminated intravascular coagulopathy), and I needed to do a hysterectomy to try to stop her bleeding. I opened her back up, removing all the sutures I had placed. As I entered her abdomen, large blood clots poured out. Her uterus was big and mushy, not firm and round like it was supposed to be. I stayed focused and performed the steps of an abdominal hysterectomy. That procedure can be challenging when there is a lot of bleeding, but now I was trying to do it while her abdomen went up and down with each chest compression. I had to coordinate each pass of my suture needle to hit the right spot, while avoiding stabbing myself. Once I got through that and had secured all pelvic blood vessels that could possibly bleed, I closed her up once again.

As the team continued working, I went out and talked to Ken and her family. As soon as I started talking, I broke down. Trying to hold back my agonizing tears, I said, "We are doing everything humanly possible to save her. We are breathing for her and trying to replace the blood she has lost, but she continues to bleed."

"Well, do whatever it takes," Ken's dad replied.

"I already did!" I cried and fell to the floor in exhaustion. "I put her all back together, and she still bled; I did an entire hysterectomy, and she is still bleeding. She just won't respond to anything. She's gone. She's really gone."

Ken came down to the floor and held me, and we cried together for the loss of his wife, his children's mother, my friend, and a woman loved by so many.

I finally collected myself and stood up. "Do you want to see her to say good-bye?"

"Yes," Ken said. He was in complete shock.

As the nurse took Ken and his family in to see her, I tried to call Kevin, but he was on the top of a mountain. I needed him more than ever. I looked down and realized that I was still wearing my street clothes. I had on jeans, my gray, knit Ugg boots, and a sweatshirt. I was all sweaty and covered in my friend's blood. To this day, there is still a small spot of Cynthia's blood on the tip of my boot. I can't bear the thought of having them cleaned.

Despite my broken heart and physical exhaustion, I was still the physician on call, and there was another patient who just rolled in the door and needed a C-section. Somehow, I had to go back into that OR and do my job. I had to get control of all my emotions and not think about the details of what had just happened in that room. I had to move on to the next person who needed me, and give her my full attention. This was more difficult than I can explain. I had to care for this person the same way I would have if I hadn't just lost Cynthia.

"You are amazing," said the nurse who had just arrived to relieve the previous OR nurse.

"No, I just don't have a choice. I have to do what I'm here to do," I replied, refusing to take any compliments after I'd just failed to save my friend's life.

After that C-section, I went to find Ken, but, instead, found our friend, Anastasia. She was quietly rocking baby Abby in the corner of another labor room. "You are amazing, my friend. Thank you," she whispered.

"Thank you? How can you possibly say that?"

As I uttered my disbelief and defeat out loud, tears rolled down my face, and my body was overcome with grief. I just wrapped my arms around Anastasia and baby Abby, and I held them until the grief lifted.

"You just saved this baby's life. Cynthia thanks you. Ken thanks you. I thank you. Someday, Abby will thank you," Anastasia announced with joy in her voice and pain in her heart.

This mixture of emotions was something I had never felt before.

"But, every year on her birthday, this poor girl will be reminded of her mother's death. She will blame herself. How will Ken not blame her for losing his wife, and how will Ben not blame her for losing his mother?" I cried, barely able to get the words out.

Anastasia reassured me, saying, "They will never see it that way; Cynthia wouldn't want them to. She was so excited to have this baby. Abby is a miracle, and they will be forever grateful to have a piece of Cynthia still with them. If it wasn't for you, Cat, they would have lost mother *and* baby. You saved baby Abby's life. You need to understand that what you did was amazing and that things would have ended much differently if you hadn't been here—talking to your friend, being the compassionate, involved doctor that you are. God put you here today to bring Abby into this world."

"I did everything humanly possible that I could to save Cynthia. There was nothing more I could do!" I said as I wept even harder.

I then realized that I *had* done everything possible and that all the people helping me had done everything they could. It wasn't that we didn't start CPR fast enough or give blood soon enough or intubate quickly enough. I ran over the entire scenario in my head a hundred times, and I couldn't come up with anything that we could've done differently to change the outcome.

This gave me pause.

That realization gave me peace. As much as anything could, anyway.

That was a huge reminder of how great and complex life and death are. We can't possibly understand why wonderful, productive, young, healthy people are taken from us. What we *can* understand is how people react to these life-changing events and how we choose to let those experiences bring God into our heart and lives—or how we choose not to.

After a few hours of charting—doing all the paperwork that goes along with taking care of people—I went home. I walked through the snowy drifts back to my house. Behind me was the moon, shining so brightly that it reflected off the snow and lighted my way.

In my head, I heard Dierks Bentley singing:

I'm a Riser
I'm a get up off the ground, don't run and hider
Hey pushin' comes to shovin'
Baby I'm a fighter
When darkness comes to town, I'm a lighter
A get out aliver, of the fire, survivor

I felt God's presence guiding me home. I crawled into bed, and, luckily, my pager didn't go off for the rest of the night.

My mom was staying with me for the weekend because I was on call and couldn't find a babysitter to stay with the kids. When I woke up, I came down to the living room, and she was on the floor, playing with Fischer and Kensley, as if nothing bad had happened. My heart swelled with sadness for the fact that the world didn't stop when Cynthia died, and it also swelled with joy because I was so grateful to see my happy children and have my mom there to take care of me.

"Good morning, my loves! You playin' trains with Grandma?" I said, trying to sound okay.

"Kensley is Rosy, and I'm Thomas," Fischer said in his squeaky little toddler voice.

"Give Mommy some love!" I insisted as I tackled them with hugs, trying not to destroy their train set. Their giggles and hugs felt like duct tape around my heart.

My mom got up and gave me a big hug. She could tell something was wrong, but she didn't press me. After the kids ran off to play, I told her what happened. She comforted me and let me cry. Lord, did I need someone to take care of me; just for a bit, while I processed and grieved.

I called Anastasia a short while later to see how she was holding up, and she told me that her mom was in town for the weekend also.

227

"God obviously knew we would need our mommies this weekend," Anastasia surmised.

"Yeah, coming home and hugging my babies felt amazing, and, at the same time, completely unfair. Cynthia will never get to see or hug baby Abby, and never get to hug Ben again."

"Those kids will have people lined up, fighting to hug them and love on them; Nick and I already claimed first dibs. I will love them like they are my own. I finally have a little girl to love and spoil. We will make sure they are just fine," Anastasia reassured me.

"Yeah, but poor Ken. He just lost his wife and best friend, and, somehow, he has to carry on with life, for his children's sake, in spite of his broken heart. I can't even begin to imagine how difficult that would be. I think it would be impossible. I pray so hard that he finds peace and strength, somehow."

"I have no doubt that Cynthia is watching over him and will make sure of it!" Anastasia said confidently, with sadness cracking through her words.

We both knew we wouldn't get much sleep or rest for a very long time. We knew we had to be strong and continue on because, as we said in tandem, laughing, "That's what Cynthia would do!"

I thought, *What a beautiful soul she was! We were all blessed to have known her, and she taught us so much in the short time we had her in our lives. We need to keep her bright flame burning so that others can see her light and feel her warmth.*

I was more committed than ever to living my life with purpose, and I tried even harder to positively impact everyone I met, the way Cynthia had. I vowed to not let her death be in vain; I would celebrate her life, and her legacy of grace, fun, and compassion would continue on through everyone she loved, including Anastasia and me.

Thankfully, I had a marriage-counseling appointment scheduled the next day. I went alone because Kevin was still gone. I talked about losing my friend. Of course, the therapist had heard about it; it was all over the news. Amniotic-fluid embolisms only happen in about one of every forty thousand deliveries. People everywhere were trying to make sense of losing her. Sitting there without Kevin made my loneliness painfully obvious. I had more hard work ahead of me.

Cynthia, please help me through this, I prayed, believing she was watching over me.

Giving It Your All

Meanwhile, I was desperately trying to get my husband to love me. Of course, he said he felt awful for not being there when I went through all of that. Despite my sorrow, I took Kevin on his surprise trip for the New Year's celebration and the outdoor hockey game. I was going to save this marriage—or freeze to death trying.

On New Year's Eve, we had a great night of drinking and dancing. We enjoyed each other's company, and I felt like we were truly connecting.

I let my guard down and made a New Year's resolution to not hold any grudges, feel any resentment, or keep records against my husband. "I declare that 2012 will be the best year ever, and 2011 can fuck off and die!" I yelled as the ball dropped and everyone blew their noise makers.

Well, 2012 started off great, but it soon went into the shitter. In February, we went to the Bahamas. I really wanted us to spend some good time together and have fun. We needed to learn how to like each other again. We had fun snorkeling and just hanging out, like old times—or so I thought.

Only a few weeks later, while I was at work, another nurse's husband called and asked to talk to me. I sat at my desk, charting. I heard Carrie on the phone, saying, "I'm sorry. What did you say your name is, and what is this regarding?"

Just as Carrie said that, I received a text from Kevin: "CALL ME NOW!"

My stomach dropped. Then, my phone rang. It was Kevin, calling me.

Carrie put her caller on hold and tried to tell me that some man was asking to speak to me, but I answered my phone instead, feeling nauseated and scared.

"What's going on?" I said to Kevin.

"Just please listen. I need you to come downstairs and get in my truck," he said in a rushed, forceful tone.

"Why is some guy calling me at work? Is he the husband of the bitch you were texting?"

"Yes. Please come down here *now!* Don't talk to him. I need to talk to you! *Now!*"

I wanted to vomit. I hung up, stood up, and, trying not to hyperventilate, I said to Carrie, "Tell him I left and to never call me again. Reschedule my patients; I need to leave."

"Oh, honey, what's wrong?" Carrie wanted to know. "Are you okay? Where are you going? Please tell me what's wrong."

"I don't know. Kevin is coming to get me. I need to go." And I ran out.

I was so afraid of what was to come.

He came barreling into the parking lot, slammed on the brakes, and swung the front passenger door open from the inside. "Get in!" he shouted

I got in. "What is going on? You need to tell me right now!" I demanded as he drove away.

"That was Nancy's husband calling you. He caught us together."

"Caught you? Where? Doing what?"

"At their house."

"You were fucking her?"

"Well, not exactly. It didn't get that far. We were naked, but I was just going down on her."

I have never screamed so painfully loud in my entire life. My heart shattered into a million pieces at the thought of him doing something so intimate with someone else. "Let me out! Let me out *now!*"

He swung around the corner and pulled into our driveway. I ran into the house, hitting and destroying everything I could. He tried to talk to me, and I lost it even further. I threw everything at him that I could get my hands on. He kept trying to stop me and calm me down, but it wasn't possible.

All I could see was red.

It was almost an out-of-body experience. Every time I thought I could breathe again, the rage welled back up and drowned me. I calmed down long enough to call his mom, who was coming to town for the weekend to visit, and told her to come now to take care of her grandchildren because I needed to leave. "Your son has completely ruined our lives. I can't even think straight. I need to leave."

Kevin got on the phone and told his mom what happened, then he tried to get me to stay.

As soon as he got near me, I started hitting him and pushing him away. I couldn't stop myself. "Please get the fuck out of my way! I need to go!"

I screamed it in his face, over and over, until he gave up. I grabbed my purse and computer, and left. I drove for more than an hour, with no idea where to go. I was completely lost inside my mind. I finally checked into a hotel.

I ordered a bottle of wine from room service and lay in bed, bawling my eyes out. I kept wishing that someone was there with me: my mom, one of my sisters, Carrie, or Anastasia. But I was too devastated to even call anyone. The thought of explaining anything just made me start sobbing again.

I tried to always keep my marriage issues private, so no one really knew any details. I thought it was good for our marriage to not air our dirty laundry or get people involved; I didn't want anyone to not like Kevin or to treat him differently. Looking back, I'm not sure that was a very healthy way to deal with things. I was doing everything possible to keep our marriage together, including keeping up appearances, so, when we hit bottom, people were surprised and didn't understand why we couldn't just work it out.

That weekend, I tried to drink myself into oblivion, but, instead, I just felt sick. Kevin called me incessantly, until I caved and told him where I was. He came there and tried to apologize, but all I felt was rage and despair. I had no one to turn to. The one person I was supposed to always be able to turn to and rely on was the one person who was hurting me.

I started screaming through my tears, "I just want my husband to hold me and comfort me until it stops hurting, but you're the motherfucker who caused this pain! I hate you for doing this to me!"

I lunged and attacked him. He tried to hug and comfort me, but I physically beat on him until he finally gave up and left.

I hated him for having the power to destroy my life.

After three days of isolation and loneliness, I let him try again. He promised that it was over with Nancy. She was going to fix things with her husband, and Kevin was begging to fix things with me.

Know Your Worth

A few months earlier, we had started building our dream house. We were looking forward to starting our new life together in a new house. We had been planning and preparing for it for more than a year, and the building process was projected to take another year. I had dreams of a wonderful family life there—raising our children and making memories. We had promised to make every decision together regarding the house, so when he betrayed me again, it really threw a wrench in things. He ruined all that.

He tapped into all those thoughts and dreams I wanted us to create, and he promised he was still going to make it happen. He continued to go to counseling, and I forgave him and decided to trust in him. He promised he would be the man I had married a decade before, and he insisted that I deserved the fairy-tale ending. While going to counseling, he realized that he was behaving just like his mother had when he was young. Apparently, she cheated on Kevin's dad many times over the years, but his dad always ignored it or made excuses for her erratic, selfish behavior. They only got divorced because, eventually, his dad found someone else and left her.

Intellectually, Kevin knew that his mom's behavior was selfish and destructive to their family, but he refused to see that his actions and decisions were the same as hers had been. He had a different excuse for each of his affairs. He refused to acknowledge any issues that he might have to deal with. He was quick to say he was sorry, always wanting to just sweep it under the rug. It felt like my feelings didn't matter, and I shouldn't be allowed to dwell on what he did.

He would also make me feel guilty, acting like he didn't deserve me. He would say things like "You deserve the big, beautiful house and all the fancy trips, not me;" "You are the most loving mom I've ever known;" and "You are an amazing doctor who cares about your patients;" "You're honestly a good person, and you deserve to be loved and treated like the queen you are."

I wanted to believe him when he said those things, but then I thought, *If you think that, then why don't you respect me and stay committed to me? Why must you keep humiliating me? Why must you destroy every little bit of self-esteem that I somehow regain? Why can't I just be enough for you?*

And then I thought, *He's right; I do deserve this. I cheated on Luke and destroyed that relationship, so now karma is coming around, and I'm getting what I deserve from Kevin.*

I tried to accept that and take my punishment, so to speak, but I wasn't ready to give up again. I had learned from my past failures and promised myself to not make the same mistakes again. I was going to fight for my family and make different choices. Unfortunately, Kevin's thinking I was a great doctor and mother didn't stop him from acting on his desires, as I found out later.

Do the Impossible

In terms of making an effort to fix the relationship, I felt like I was doing everything I possibly could. I even started running. I had spent my entire life saying, "I can't run. I don't know how anyone can run a 5K, let alone a marathon."

Kevin had run three marathons by this point, so I asked him to teach me how. I needed to get into shape and gain some self-confidence, and we needed to spend time together. I knew it would be a tough challenge, but I needed to feel strong and in control of my life again. I made a promise to myself that I would be in the best shape of my life when I turn forty. That was only eight months away!

That gave me pause.

Forty years old? How can that be? I was just headbanging to Mötley Crüe with Brandy at the junior-high dances—I swear! Mentally, I still feel like a teenager. Physically, I feel like an old lady. This crap needs to change. My body needs to be able to keep up with my mind and spirit, I thought.

Once again, our nanny, Marilyn, was there for me. She would come over at 5:00 a.m., so Kevin and I could go running before work. At first, I ran for one to two minutes, then walked for one minute, then ran for two, then walked for one, and so on and so forth. I slowly increased the running time, and, after about a month, it felt better to keep running than it did to stop and walk.

Within a few months, I would find myself in my office during lunch, gazing out the window, feeling the desire to run. I used to fall asleep during lunch, if I was luckily enough to be done with patients before office hours started up again at 1:00 p.m. Now I was longing to run. It felt amazing. I enjoyed the way running made me feel—not necessarily during, but afterward. It often hurt to run. My knees would swell, my back ached, and my boobs felt like they were being ripped off me sometimes, but the adrenaline and elation that came with running made it worth it. While I ran, I would tell myself, *It's mind over matter. It's only thirty minutes. You can do this. You need to do this!*

I knew I wasn't damaging myself; I was out of shape, and that was why it hurt so much. I knew that If I kept running, someday, I would enjoy it.

So, I talked myself into ignoring the pain, and I focused on my husband and the beautiful surroundings of my town. We ran up the big hills, down to the beach, past the high school, and back to our house.

I started eating healthfully and purposefully, and, wouldn't you know it, my weight started dropping. I started to actually like the way my body looked. The next thing I knew, I was down to a size 4 and feeling comfortable in my own skin—for the first time in my entire life. I looked at my naked body and happily accepted what I saw. I didn't see stretch marks, big thighs, or a saggy butt. I saw glowing skin, tight muscles with definition, curves in all the right places, and a nice gap between my thighs.

It was encouraging, and I felt empowered by my results. It drove me to continue on. I signed up to run the 5K in May, and now that time was here. Kevin promised to stay with me the entire race and make sure I finished. Carrie insisted she wanted to run with me. I hadn't known her to be a runner, but she reassured me that she wanted to do it. I was impressed, because she didn't run on a regular basis. I had been running for six months and was nervous about it. I promised myself to run the entire way, without stopping or walking.

The race was painful and exhilarating at the same time. It was a gorgeous, sunny morning, and the course of the race was close to what Kevin and I had been running all along. When we got to the first huge hill, I had to break away from Carrie because she had stopped to walk. I felt bad, but I knew I had to do this for me, and she encouraged me to keep going. For some reason, the run felt a lot harder than it ever had before.

Kevin was pacing us with his watch.

"Are we going faster than usual?" I asked between breathes.

"Just a little bit. You're fine. You're doing great. Don't think about it," he replied and nudged me on the back to run harder.

The very end was a steep hill up to the high school. I saw it and wanted to give up. I felt like my body didn't have anything left to give. Just then, I saw Anastasia standing there, cheering me on. I realized Cynthia's spirit was there too. I felt her strength pull me up that hill to the finish line, the way she had pulled me up off the floor to finish coding her the night she died.

I crossed the finish line and tried to catch my breath. Once my body felt revived, I immediately felt the desire to run a 10K. I felt strong enough, physically and mentally, to do anything I set my mind to.

I saw Carrie come running up the hill, so I ran down halfway and ran back up with her as I cheered her all the way to the finish line. I was so proud of her for finishing and felt so humbled that she did that for me. I felt a strong sisterhood with my girlfriends. They empowered me and helped me accomplish my goals. That feeling of accomplishment was so powerful that I felt the need to pay it forward and do the same for others. That was my new focus with my patients: get them physically moving, help them set realistic goals, and empower them to make those goals their reality.

Listen to Your Heart

It felt like Kevin and I were reconnecting. He was very supportive of me, and I slowly let my guard down. I started to trust him again. For my own sanity, I had forgiven him, and now I was learning how to forget. I was focusing on us and our future. Unfortunately, it wasn't enough to repair our marriage. I thought the problem was that we were both consumed with our jobs, building our house, and taking care of our kids, but the reality was that Kevin had other interests and priorities.

I finally admitted that to myself. Everyone knows that a successful marriage takes work, active involvement, sacrifice, and putting your partner's needs before your own. It also requires both partners to be committed. One spouse can give 100 percent until they die, but that doesn't mean they will have a successful marriage. I'm not saying I was perfect; no one is. I failed Kevin, and he failed me. We failed each other and our children. The difference was that I was doing everything in my power to fix it, and he had mentally and emotionally given up.

The thought of getting divorced again made me sad. I knew I had failed, but I had promised myself long ago that I would never settle into complacency or live a lie. I acknowledged my failure, but I had to stay true to myself and my heart. I also needed to salvage my dignity. Everyone knew Kevin had other women on the side; it was humiliating.

In the meantime, our beautiful, huge, custom-built home was almost complete. It was almost impossible to focus on the few final decisions regarding the house because my personal life was in such disarray, but it soon became a nice distraction. During the last few weeks before our move-in date, there were many workers at the house. I kept finding myself talking to the electrician; at first, this was because I had to make some final decisions, but I soon realized I enjoyed his company. It was January, and he was there every day, working outside without any gloves on, wiring our hot tub and outdoor grills.

One day, Kevin said, "Hey, Cat, have you met Thomas, the electrician? He just got a kitten."

In his completely shy way, this adorable guy dressed in baggy carpenter jeans, an old sweatshirt, and steel-toed work boots, responded, "Yeah, do you like cats?"

His smile was a little crooked and sexy, like Elvis's. It made my heart flutter.

"I love cats! I knew you seemed like a good guy!" I replied with excitement.

"I knew you'd like Thomas; he's a good guy. He's one of those people that you just want to be around 'cuz they're good people," Kevin said to me.

Later, Kevin said, "We should invite Thomas to our housewarming party. He's a good guy and probably doesn't ever get a thank you or acknowledgment for his hard work."

"That would be a very nice thing to do," I agreed.

A few days later, I bought Thomas a really nice pair of gloves that had mitten flaps to keep his fingers warm while he was working. I brought them home and had Kevin help me cut off the fingertips so that Thomas would still be able to twist wires when he wore the gloves.

"I got him gloves because he's working outside without any," I explained.

"That was very thoughtful of you," Kevin said as he cut, without an inkling of jealousy.

I took the gloves out to Thomas. "I got these for you, so your hands won't freeze while you're working. You need to take care of them; they're your livelihood."

"You really didn't have to do that. Thank you. Why are you being so nice?" he asked.

"Because you deserve it." I smiled and walked back into the house.

When he came in a short time later, Kevin said, "Thomas, I think my wife has a crush on you. But can I blame her?"

"That happens to me all the time," Thomas said sarcastically.

His voice was sexy and smooth, but cracked with embarrassment. There was that crooked smile again.

We had many interactions like that over the next few weeks, and I found out that he had two children: a preteen boy and a younger girl. He hinted at his unhappy situation, living with an unsupportive girlfriend, having a bitter ex-wife, and not having joint custody of his kids because he had wronged his wife and was suffering the consequences.

One day, while making decisions on lighting fixtures for my beautiful walk-in closet, he opened up to me. I had to decide between flat, recessed lights or so-called boob-shaped lights. I picked the latter, and that broke the ice.

"You'd better make my boobs look good. They'd better be big and even!" I said, laughing at my own stupid joke.

"I'll take care of your boobs and make sure they look good. Don't worry," he responded in a typical construction-worker double entendre.

His shyness was endearing. You could tell he was uncomfortable playing that role; he wasn't really a smooth talker.

"So, tell me about your kids. I heard you have a boy about twelve and a girl the same age as my Kensley," I said, trying to get him to talk.

I was interested, but I also loved his voice. I found myself being distracted by the sound of his voice and realized I wasn't listening to what he was saying, so I asked more questions. Surprisingly, he kept on talking. I could tell he was really into his children. He told me how he never missed any sporting events or school functions, then he showed me pictures of his kids on vacation with him.

It made me realize how different Kevin was; he was content doing stuff without me or the kids. He was apprehensive about traveling with our kids, so they never came with us, and I often didn't even go. I had to admit to myself that Kevin didn't have a strong desire to have me or the kids around, and what was even more obvious was that he wasn't jealous of me giving someone else attention. It almost seemed like he was wishing someone on me, so I started to entertain the idea of liking Thomas.

The next time I saw Thomas, he was wiring the hot tub outside.

"I see you're wearing your new gloves; that's good. How have you been?" I said.

"Well, I moved into my sister's house."

What the hell am I supposed to do with that information? I wondered to myself, secretly excited that it must have meant he broke up with his girlfriend. "Oh, why? Is everything okay?"

"I just finally said something to my girlfriend about stuff that's been bothering me, and we ended up breaking up," he said, fumbling with his words.

He went on to tell me about their troubles and how she didn't understand his need to spend so much time with his kids, adding that she didn't respect him or give him the attention and time he needed. "I am always her last priority," he said.

"I completely understand," I responded, thinking of my own selfish partner.

Once the house was finished, I kept running into Thomas around town, especially because his son's baseball practice was next to the school where my kids had piano lessons. When I saw him, I would wonder what life would be like with a man who wanted a family life. This was a regularly occurring evening activity for me, while Kevin continued to work late and be secretive.

One night, I found myself sitting in the kitchen, at our twenty-foot Carrara marble island, eating my dinner alone as the kids took their baths, and I realized that our multimillion-dollar dream house was a joke. It represented the dream of the family I longed to have but that would never come to fruition. We would never have a regular schedule where we ate dinner all together as a family. Kevin wouldn't be around in the evenings to help with homework or bath time. He certainly wouldn't be there in the mornings when we were starting our day and getting off to school, because he would already be gone.

And this wasn't because we were both doctors. I've known many couples who were both physicians or crazy-busy professionals, and they had some semblance of a family life—because they both wanted it. They both made the effort and compromises to make it happen. I had a tough schedule, yet I made it a priority to be home; therefore, most of the time, I was. Kevin refused to set aside time for us. We just got whatever time he had left over, which was usually from midnight to 4:00 a.m., when the kids and I needed to sleep. And the weekends? Forget it. Those precious hours and days were filled in his calendar many months in advance, with work, running, skiing, or whatever else he had going on. Once, I even asked him in all seriousness to pencil us in, but it just got erased. *I guess I should've asked him to write it in ink; maybe that would have helped,* I sarcastically thought at the time.

That night, sitting alone and eating my dinner, I was acutely aware of my broken heart. I felt emptier than I ever had before, and being alone with my kids in that huge house made it all the worse. I looked around at the custom-made furniture, the three-story hand-carved mahogany staircase leading up to the five-foot hanging chandelier that Thomas had hung only a few months before. I remembered how Thomas spent many hours carefully assembling it and then hanging it twenty feet off the ground. He jury-rigged a platform from the staircase across to the upstairs bridge that connected the bedrooms from one end of the house to the other. He had to do a balancing act while he attempted to hang that chandelier. He risked his safety to make my dream house look amazing.

I kept thinking to myself, *Why can't I be married to a man like Thomas? He seems so caring, thoughtful, and selfless, and his only priorities are doing his best at work and making sure he is always there for his children. He must have learned from his hard lessons in life and now he cherishes every moment with them. Kevin was gone from his children for the majority of the last three years, and he still isn't putting them first.*

As I flicked the chandelier light on, I thought of St. Patrick's steeple all lit up in the dead of night. I remembered that I was not alone.

I whispered a prayer: "Dear Lord, please give me guidance. I feel so lost and alone. When will Kevin learn that our babies will only be young once? He needs to be in their lives now, helping me shape them into amazing people. That job is more important than anything else he could ever do; why can't he see that? Please help him see the truth."

Ideas and dreams of how life could be better started running through my mind, but I also realized that things couldn't get better if I was wishing for something else, so I tried to focus on Kevin and my upcoming birthday.

The thought of going away to celebrate was bittersweet. I was in the best shape of my life, and I felt content and fulfilled with my career and children—but I felt like a failure as a wife. I wanted to have fun, but I didn't want to pretend that Kevin and I were good. We got along great as friends hanging out, but, as soon as we had private moments as a couple, the damage was obvious. He was emotionally distant and outright interested in other women, which made me angry and insecure. It made me respond to him with bitchiness and sarcasm. We were spiraling downward, fast.

In his typical over-the-top way, Kevin set up an elaborate trip to New York City and had a private dinner prepared for us at a five-star restaurant to celebrate my birthday. He always wanted everything to be over the top. He enjoyed the best of the best, and he made that clear to everyone around him. He surprised me with diamond earrings, and even had the waitress bring me a designer chocolate cake with a candle on top.

"Make a wish!" the waitress cheered as she lit my candle.

I wish to find my person and my happiness, I wished inwardly as I blew out the candle.

Soon after, I found out that Kevin was on to a new woman: a fellow surgeon. As hurt as I was at the reality of my marriage being over, I was ready to find happiness again. I wanted to be married to a man who adored and respected me and who also wanted a family life.

I had stayed in my first marriage way too long, and I realized I was doing the same thing again. This time around, I was doing the hard work, but it wasn't making a difference. It takes two active participants to make a marriage work, and I was finally ready to admit defeat. I knew I had to make the hard decision and change my situation. It felt really scary—actually, terrifying—but, to me, the idea of *not* changing was even more terrifying. I couldn't bear the thought of continuing to waste my life by feeling unhappy, lonely, and unfulfilled in my relationship.

I told myself, *I only have one life, and I need to the most of it.*

One day, while fighting with Kevin about our pending divorce, he insisted that I must like someone else. "Why else would you leave me?" He wanted to know who it was. "Who are you going to date as soon as you are free? I deserve to know who gets to screw my wife after she leaves me."

His tone was jealous and controlling, which wasn't like him at all. "Are you finally realizing that you're losing me and I won't be yours anymore?" I asked.

"You'll always be my wife, in my mind. I will always love you."

I finally told him, "I want to see if Thomas is interested in me."

"That makes sense; he's a great guy. He can probably give you what you need. Apparently, a huge house, boats, trips, and a closet full of purses isn't enough. I'm sorry I failed you," he said as he cried.

"You're right, it's not enough—because it's not what I want at all! I want a husband, a father for my children, and a companion to do the day-to-day things in life with. I want someone who is committed to us and present in this life we've created."

"Why are you putting this all on me, like I am the only one with issues? We both made bad choices, and now you want to give up and go be with Thomas," he said.

"Here's the problem," I said. "It's not about me wanting Thomas; it's about you never being content and always wanting something new. You have it all, and you're still not fulfilled. You won't be until you deal with your mom's betrayals and how it tore your family apart. The fact that you and your dad have no relationship hurts you and makes it impossible to have any normal family situation. You don't understand what a normal, healthy family is. I'm trying to give that to you, but you thrive on chaos and dysfunction. It breaks my heart, because us getting a divorce just perpetuates the dysfunction. I've already caused Delilah to come from a broken home, and now we're going to ruin Fischer and Kensley. This whole thing breaks my heart."

"I'm sorry I've failed you. I will always love you. I want you to be happy, and, apparently, I can't make you happy," he responded in a defeated tone.

That response infuriated me. He wanted so badly to throw in the towel, but he wanted me to get the blame, like *I* was the quitter. He didn't want to do the hard, uncomfortable work to fix us. He was content with letting me look like the bad guy who was breaking up the family and leaving *him*.

After that, I was ready to admit defeat. I was ready to admit my failures and the inability to "fix" us. We wanted different things out of life, and I had suffered too much for too long.

I realize now that most adults don't have their shit together. They pretend they do because they need to, but they really don't. Everyone has demons, secrets, and messed-up thinking. Very few (at least in my world) have dealt with their childhood issues, which manifests as bad decision-making in adulthood. Their behavior is subconsciously self-destructive. They don't believe they deserve happiness and stability. They don't really know what those even are, much less how to obtain them. If they do manage to find happiness and stability, they subconsciously destroy them.

Let me emphasize that I *now* realize what I just described, but I didn't then. I called Anastasia, crying about the fact that my children were going to be scarred for life and continue the vicious cycle of dysfunction, because we had failed them and Kevin couldn't get his shit together.

She tried to console me, explaining, "My dad was a shit show most of my life, and my mom was in and out, but my grandparents were stable and rock solid. For me to understand a healthy relationship, I only needed that one clear example in my life that never wavered. If you can give that to your children, it won't matter as much what Kevin is doing. They will always love him and forgive him, but if you somehow show them a healthy relationship that endures, they will be okay."

I wanted to believe her. I came from strong families that stayed together, so I knew it was possible. I thought of all the Jansens and the Robbinses. I reminded myself that I came from survivors and that I was going to be fine. I wanted to try again for happiness, a healthy marriage, and a sound family. I wanted to get it right.

Third time's the charm! Right? I prayed inwardly.

I wanted Kevin to find happiness and stop being so self-centered and self-destructive. I prayed that us getting a divorce would finally make him get his priorities in order. I realized that we all deserve a happy life.

But how do we get it? There's only one answer: faith.

I went back to the church where Cynthia's funeral had been. It was filled with a lot of painful memories, because it was also the church where Kevin and I had gone a few times when we were going through counseling. But an amazing thing happened: in addition to all the pain I was experiencing, I felt a weight being lifted, and then a renewed sense of self and understanding. I found myself crying for the life I was losing but also feeling safe in the knowledge that I had God to rely on. I remembered that I always have Him, and I am never truly alone.

After church, I was standing in front of the nametag board, just to see who some of the church members were, when Thomas walked up and put his nametag there. "Hi, Catherine. What are you doing here?"

"I'm looking for answers." Then, redirecting the conversation, I asked, "What are you doing here?"

"This is my church," he said proudly. "I've been coming here almost every week since I got divorced. I drag my kids with me every other Sunday when I have them because I think it's really good for them."

"That's awesome! I'm so glad to see you here. I'm thinking of bringing my kids to see what they think. I just know we need God in our lives on a regular basis. I feel bad that they haven't really had that, so I want to get back into a church before it's too late, ya know?"

Just then, his daughter came running and jumped onto him. "Let's go get a cookie, Dad. Please!"

"You guys should definitely come next week. We'll look for ya," he said excitedly as she dragged him away.

"We will. Have a good week!" I said, smiling from ear to ear because his presence made me feel alive.

I felt strong when I left church that day. I felt ready to take control of my future. I had no desire to continue living in that house. I had no desire to fight Kevin for our stuff; he could keep the Jet Skis, boats, rental properties, and custom furniture we'd purchased. All I really wanted was a decent house with a swimming pool so that I could have quality time with my kids, like I dreamed. I was ready to walk away from all the other stuff. It was meaningless. I had found my truth. I wanted a new life with Thomas. I was going to make it work, come hell or high water.

Cat's Next Life

A few days later, I saw Thomas at the baseball field. "Hey, Thomas. It was good to see you the other day."

"Yeah, it was good to see you too."

"I was totally surprised that you go to that church; I have a lot of history there. Anyway, how are you doing? Are you still living at your sister's house?"

"Yeah. I've been looking for a little house to buy and fix up, but the only places on the market right now are huge houses. I don't need all that for me and my two kids."

"Oh really?" I asked, all excited. "How would you feel about helping me look for a house instead?"

"What are you talking about? You and Kevin just built an amazing house. Why would you guys possibly want something else?"

"I don't want to live there anymore. But Kevin ... is going to stay. We're getting divorced. Actually, that's why I went to church; I needed to feel God's love and strength to get me through this. I'm looking for a house for me and my kids," I said, adding jokingly, "So, if you want to just find me a house, then you can live with me. That would be cool." Despite my joking tone, I was trying to feel out his interest toward me.

The look of shock on his adorable face said it all, then the crooked smile came out, and I melted. In response to his gaping silence, I said, "I'm kinda serious. I really like you, and I really like the idea of being married to you."

"Well, can we go on a date first?" he asked.

"Only if it's house hunting." I smiled. "I'm kidding! We can have dinner together first."

From that afternoon forward, we talked and texted nonstop. We got together as often as we could. We couldn't get enough of each other. We fell madly in love. It felt like we knew each other inside and out; like we had been together our entire lives. All of a sudden, everything in the world made sense. Our future seemed crystal clear. Our children had already known each other from school and sports, so it was easy to explain who I was hanging out with. They seemed to take to Thomas, and they actually seemed okay with all the changes going on—as long as I gave them special time and attention.

Two months later, Thomas and I stumbled upon the perfect house for a big family, with a swimming pool. "I want it! There are enough rooms for your kids and mine to all have their own rooms," I said in all seriousness.

"You really want us to move in here with you?"

"Yes! I want this to be our home. I want us to be a family. You are an amazing man with a huge heart, and you deserve happiness just as much as I do. I know we can make this work, because we both want it. I trust you with my life and my children's lives. I've been hurt by people who claimed to love me, and I've hurt people, just as you have, but I believe in us. My little voice inside keeps telling me that you are my person. For the first time in my life, I am envisioning growing old with someone, and that someone is you."

"I think it's just my gray beard." He smirked.

"I'm serious, you goofball."

"I'm *your* goofball."

"Yes, you are! We are doing this! Okay?"

"Okay!"

I bought the house and took Fischer and Kensley to see it. I explained that I wanted Thomas and his children to move in with us. They were excited to have another person to play with. It was all new and exciting for them. Part of the reason that I pushed it so quickly was because I didn't like the idea of having them move in later, causing issues, which I knew would happen. I wanted all the children to feel equal in this new family I was creating. I didn't want my kids saying to his, "This is our house; you just live here," when a fight ensued or there were any issues.

Thomas was just as ready as I was to create a strong family and life together. I felt like I had found my person, and he felt the same way. We understood each other's frustrations and the reasons for our past failures and poor decisions. And, most importantly, he knew the importance of having a relationship with God.

We went to church together every Sunday and took our children as often as we could. We knew that we needed God at the forefront of our relationship for it to work. We needed to put God and our relationship first, with our children a short second on our priority list. We agreed that work should never be higher than third priority, which was a huge challenge for me to take on as a physician. I had spent fifteen years putting my patients above all else: my husband, my children, my health, and my sanity. Now I had to figure out how to be a fully committed doctor who still advocated for her patients, took the time for them that they needed, and never let them feel abandoned or alone—all while making time for myself and giving my family the time and attention they needed, so everyone in my life would feel loved, important, and fulfilled.

How did I do this, you ask? Well, first, I added two stepchildren to my priorities, which, you would think made it even more impossible, but it actually helped put things into focus.

Thomas was very committed to his children. He went to all

their sporting events, volunteered at school, went to their class-room parties, and so on, and he made me realize that I didn't want to miss those events. I realized how important little things like that were for our children's self-esteem and identity. Somehow, I started making time for my children's things and his children's as well. It wasn't as difficult as I thought it would be. It took a lot more planning and thinking ahead, but having a committed partner made all the difference. We kept each other in check when needed, but it rarely was needed because we had the same priorities and goals as a family.

He helped me figure out how to schedule my work life around my personal life, instead of the other way around. It felt amazing to be a good mom and a good soon-to-be wife to Thomas, while still being an awesome doctor whom patients respected and supported. It was amazing how supportive they were when they learned about my personal life and all the changes I was going through. My patients were giving me advice, lots of hugs, and endless support. They wanted me to be happy, and they reminded me that I was strong and capable and that I could get through anything. My patients truly cared about me, and that made me realize that I was doing something right.

I realized that my patients were just women coming to see another woman. We were helping each other out with life's struggles and trying to make sense of it all, trying to juggle it all, please everyone, right our wrongs, be successful, and not be judged by each other. I think it made some of my patients feel good to know I was human, with flaws and an imperfect life, just like theirs. No woman has it all. No woman is perfect or has a perfect life. No woman should even be striving for that—it's not possible or realistic.

We should all be striving for truth within ourselves, living the real life that we are supposed to live, supporting one another as women, and being graceful. By being graceful, I mean we need to understand when another woman is being catty or judgmental toward us, and then we need to let it go. Giving forgiveness without ever receiving an apology is golden. It will set you free!

Now, I may burp louder than a truck driver and swear more than a sailor, but I know how to be graceful. I don't talk about my friends behind their backs. I don't judge women for their looks. I admit my faults and try to be better. I don't blame others for my shortcomings. I don't blame my ex-husbands for our failed marriages. I don't blame my parents for my wild childhood. I don't blame my small town for my lack of opportunities as a child. I am not upset that I had to work hard, jump over a lot of hurdles, or go down a crazy, winding path to become successful.

I could place blame, focus on all my difficulties, and just bitch and complain about how miserable my life was, but, instead, I have chosen to see what I've gained from them. I celebrate my friends and lift them up. I judge women for their actions and help them make better choices next time. I live in my truth, without shame, and continually work to make better choices. I am thankful to my ex-husbands for my children, their understanding, and their ability to be cordial with me. I am thankful to them for supporting me during many rough years; I know that without them I wouldn't be where I am today. I am grateful for my parents' unconditional love and never-ending support and forgiveness. I am thankful for their spiritual guidance, for always living in love, and for showing me stability and perseverance. I am thankful for my humble beginnings. I love my town and the people who live there. I am proud to be from strong, honest, real people who struggle every day and own it.

I never want to live a lie, whether to pacify others or myself. Being real and vulnerable is an essential part of true happiness. The other part is not living in fear. When you live in fear, you think you have no choices about the situations in your life. Your fear doesn't let you make the tough choices, so you purposely do nothing, then say, "I didn't have a choice, so x, y, and z happened. My life sucks."

You may not get to decide what happens around you or what other people do, but you definitely have choices of how to react and respond to those situations. You always have a choice to take the high road, to do the right thing, to be selfless, to be thoughtful, to try again, and to forgive.

I'm Thomas's Wife

The summer after Thomas and I moved into our house with our kids, he surprised me. He had planned a weekend away for us, setting up child care and all of the arrangements. While I was in the bedroom, packing a suitcase, he came in with a large white box. It was wrapped with pink ribbon and a bow. Next to the bow was a tiny box attached to the ribbon.

I was confused and also very excited.

"Please open the small box first, my love," he said as he knelt down on one knee, holding out his hand.

I handed him the box, realizing what was in it.

He opened it and showed me a beautiful diamond wedding ring. "Catherine, you are my life. You accept me for who I am. You love me and my children unconditionally. You make me the man I knew I could be. You are my person. Will you please do me the honor of marrying me?"

With tears of joy rolling down my face I bent down, grabbed his face, and kissed him so passionately that he knew my answer. "Yes, baby, yes!" I tried to get out through my kisses.

I couldn't stop smiling. My heart was full.

"Can I open the big box now?" I asked excitedly, as I pulled him to his feet and hugged him.

"Yay!" I ripped off the ribbon and lid, trying to imagine what it could be. It was a gorgeous white beach dress, but it wasn't just a sundress; it was made from fine chiffon, with delicate lace appliqués along the neckline. "What is this?"

"Well, I had your mom make you a wedding dress. I hope you like it, because you will need it today," he said, trying to hold back his crooked half smile, knowing he had completely surprised me.

"I love it! But what the heck are you talking about? Are we really getting married today?"

"Yes, please." He smirked. "I organized a wedding on the beach at 4:00 p.m. today. All of our family and friends should be on their way here. We're not really going away for the weekend. The kids will be at the wedding. Your mom is getting them all dressed up. I even bought a ring for you to give to me, so you'd better say yes to all of this." He giggled.

"Of course I will marry you today! I will marry you every day of my life if you want!" I kissed his face over and over and over. "Thank you, thank you, thank you, Thomas, my person! You truly are amazing."

Our ceremony was picture perfect. Thomas had somehow found a way to get my childhood friend Charlie there, and she was our witness. He had even written his own vows. In typical Cat fashion, I winged it and just spoke from my heart. I was in shock that he pulled it off, because he was such a thinker and planner that he usually required a lot of nudging from me to actually "pull the trigger" on anything. He knew that I loved to be spontaneous and surprised, and he took that fact and ran with it. I was proud of him for getting out of his comfort zone. The fact that he actually went through with it and made it all happen showed me just how much he truly loved and cherished me. I felt like a princess who had found her prince.

Grandma Jansen came to the wedding, accompanied by two of my aunts. Mind you, she hadn't met Thomas yet, but she was excited for me. Apparently, my mom introduced him, and Grandma responded in her usual way—with an open heart and unconditional love and acceptance for anything I did. "If Cathy loves you, then I love you too!" she said to Thomas as she grabbed him and hugged him tightly.

"He was so surprised and embarrassed by the attention that you could tell he didn't know what to do," my mom explained. "So I saved him, saying he needed to come meet the rest of your family."

Hearing that made my heart swell. Having my grandma's acceptance was everything. I believed that she was the wisest, strongest woman I'd ever known, so if she was giving the okay, I knew what I was doing was right. She always told me to listen to my heart: "It will never steer you wrong, my dear."

That evening, at the reception, I thanked her for giving me that advice so many times when I was little, and for always supporting me and trusting my decisions. I told her about my little voice inside of me: "When I was little, I thought maybe it was your words repeating in my head, because they were always so loving and positive, but then, when I got older I worried that maybe I was becoming schizophrenic (because people said it wasn't normal to hear voices in your head), but, luckily, that wasn't true. Wherever that voice comes from, it seems like you, Grandma—loving me, encouraging me, and pushing me to be my best. So, thank you. Thank you for never giving up on me when I was a bad kid or Crabby Cathy or a pregnant teenager or even now, when I'm on my third marriage."

"I think I know who that little voice is, Cathy." she whispered as she leaned in, holding my hands.

"Who?"

"God."

And she said it in the warmest, most loving tone that felt like it hugged my heart. That blew me away. I didn't know my Grandma Jansen was religious or really believed in God. She never went to a church or talked about her faith. Her acknowledgment of God solidified in my heart everything I had believed. *She is completely right. How did I never realize that? Yes, it is God talking to me! Who else would love me unconditionally and never forsake me?*

All this time I'd been praying to God, and He was actually responding and guiding me. What a revelation. My strength and perseverance came from God. My self-worth and love for others came from God. At that moment, I knew how to explain to people how I became successful. So many times, people had asked, "How did you rise above and succeed?"

For so long, I would just answer, "I guess I wanted it badly enough" or "I don't really know; I just knew I had to do it." But, at that moment I realized, *I am just a child of God, one who listens.*

I listened to that little voice telling me I was better than my actions, I was good enough, I wasn't the bad names that people called me, and, most importantly, I wasn't alone in this life.

> "For I know the plans I have for you," declares
> the Lord, "plans to prosper you and not harm you,
> plans to give you hope and a future."
>
> Jeremiah 29:11

Somehow, at an early age, I had learned to listen to and trust that little voice inside me. I did not always know how to make good or right decisions, but I kept listening because that little voice never gave up on me. Eventually, I followed His guidance because it seemed to lead me down a better path in life: one of selflessness and serving others. My purpose was laid out before me; I just needed to listen and follow my heart.

Dr. Tabatha's Ten Keys for Success

1. Believe in yourself—even when no one else does.
2. Listen to your inner voice. Know that there is a higher power who loves you unconditionally and is guiding you toward your purpose. Know that you are special and worthy of an amazing life, simply because you are you. You are a child of God; therefore, you are enough.
3. Put yourself in places and situations you want to be in, with people you strive to be like. Surround yourself with supportive, positive people who are living selfless lives and trying to make our world a better place.
4. Embrace your fear. Embrace your discomfort. Embrace the unknown. Be brave.
5. Verbalize your plans. Be proud of your ideas, and show people that you believe in your abilities. Focus on your strengths. Stay positive and motivated in your thoughts.
6. Use your weaknesses to your advantage; those struggles have made you the strong, unique person you are. See your struggles as life lessons that taught you something someone else has yet to learn, and share that wisdom with others.
7. Do the unexpected. Forgive others before you receive an apology. Forgive yourself, and try again. Admit your failures and faults, and change your behavior the next time.

8. Delay your gratification, and put in the hard work. If you're following your path and purpose in life, the road will not be too long or too difficult. Nothing is impossible.
9. Dream it, see it, do it, live it. No dream is too big!
10. Pay it forward. Use your life to effect change. Strive for equality, justice, freedom, and love.

Now go out there and make the most of your life! *No fear!*

Printed in the United States
By Bookmasters